Sillu Mitu
(Night Shadow)

D.L. Roley

Copyright © 2021 D.L. Roley
www.jdrpublishers.com
All rights reserved

Map Illustration by Veronika Wunderer/www.veronika-wunderer.com

Cover Illustration by Novans V. Adikresna/www.behance.net/Novanshocker

> Misha and Mira,
> Please enjoy reading about Darius and his continuing adventures

DEDICATION

To my wife Jenny. Your continued support allows me to pursue this dream of mine.

ACKNOWLEDGMENTS

Thank you to John, Dan, Sarah, and Stephanie for all of your help and support on this project. Your feedback was invaluable.

Contents

PART I 0
1. Nasu Rabi 1
2. Mustar Atmu 12
3. Old Friends 24
4. Point of the Spear 33
5. Sillu Mitu 41
6. Eridu 53
7. Anna 67
8. Stones 82
9. Assault 92
10. Lieutenant Kabir 96
11. Wrath 111
12. Duty 120
13. Patel's Rest 139
14. The Alchemist 152
15. Spies 164
16. Invaders 177
17. Traitors 191
18. Manhunt 201
19. Backtrack 219

PART II 222
20. Ullani 223
21. The Pike and the Rose 234
22. Magora 252
23. Life at the Palace 263
24. Playing with Fire 276
25. Captain Zima 295
26. Reunited 301

27. Dragons and Lions 309
28. The Siege Begins 320
29. Fly by Night 330
30. Sibling Rivalry..336
31. Betrayal 342
32. Prisoner Exchange 347
33. Sands of Saridon..354
34. Epilogue 358

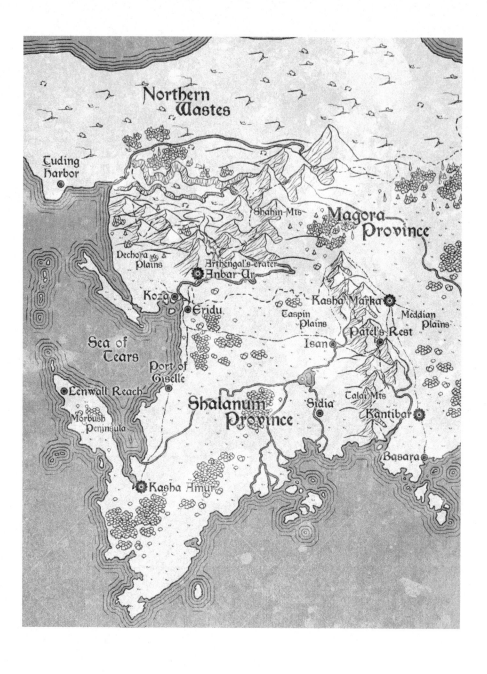

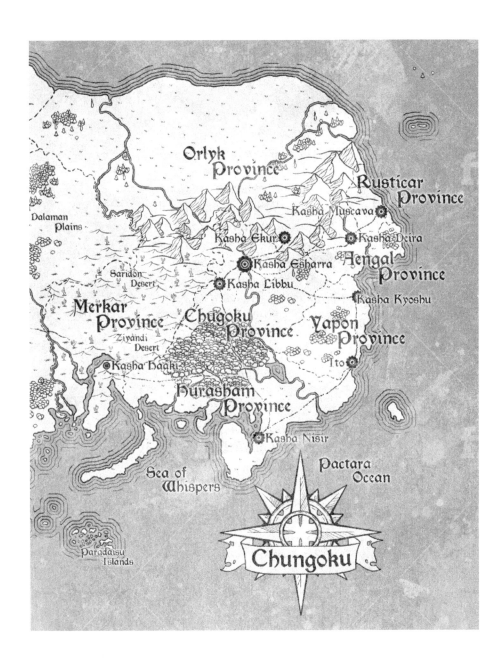

PART I

Weeping silver tears
My brother has betrayed me
Even the clouds sob

Remember past years
Fields overflow with laughter
Children chase the wind

Rejoice days gone by
Galas, feasts and maiden's song
Young men sow wild oats

Coronation day
Honor my brother's glory
Nobel king ascends

Celebrate love's joy
A prince finds his maiden's heart
Beguiling flower

Jealousy betrays
Love and power know no bounds
A king's leering gaze

Fresh flower stained
Mourn my brother's avarice
Vengeance comes alive

Lilies decorate
Still graves fill the countryside
The mighty oak falls

-Unknown author
Fifth/Sixth Dynasty – The Schism

Spring - 34 A.E.

Chapter One
Nasu Rabi

The night was dark and moonless. A gentle summer wind played off the mountains and rustled Micah's hair. He knelt at the entrance to the canyon letting his eyes adjust to the darkness. Captain Vasiliev crouched a few paces ahead doing the same. The captain had split their forces, leaving forty behind in the abandoned city of Anbar Ur to make sure none escaped from the mountain valley. The captain had been imprecise regarding what forces they may face. Captain Vasiliev had told them that the infamous Nasu Rabi had led an armed assault against the emperor's compound and had escaped with important intelligence and thirty or more workers from the nearby farm. Their mission was to eliminate the hostile forces.

Captain Vasiliev turned to face the men.

"Remember." His whispered voice carried to the back of the group. "Nasu Rabi is mine. Your job is to take care of the rest."

Micah and the other soldiers nodded their understanding.

"You." Vasiliev pointed to the closest soldier. "Take point."

The soldier, a veteran Night Bird, glided silently into the darkness. Micah tracked the shadow a dozen paces before it dropped suddenly from sight. The night was broken by a muffled cry, and the group surged forward. Micah could feel the tension in the air. *Are we being attacked already?* he thought.

"Damn it." Micah heard Lieutenant Popov curse. "He has the entrance trapped."

Micah stood and watched as they pulled the soldier out of the pit and inspected his leg. The smell of blood floated on the breeze and a few of the recruits shuffled nervously. Micah remained calm and surveyed the ravine walls for threats. This may have been his first real mission, but he wasn't about to embarrass himself in front of Vasiliev and Popov by acting like a child faced with the task of cleaning his first fish.

"There's a pit with spikes." Whispered messages rose from the crowded men. It was impossible to distinguish the speakers. "It looks bad. He'll probably lose the leg."

A pair of medics carried the soldier past Micah, bound for the entrance where they could treat the leg.

Captain Vasiliev motioned them onward. They inched forward more slowly, testing the ground with spears as they advanced. They exposed five more traps of the same design but managed to avoid further injuries.

The next surprise came when the new point man disappeared suddenly. He was snatched into the air as if the claws of a giant bird had reached down and plucked him from the canyon. His cries could be heard from the darkness above. He was trapped in a net far overhead.

Lieutenant Popov tried to organize men to lower the soldier back to the ground but there was something wrong with the way the ropes were tied and the man plunged from the heights and landed with a sickening crunch on top of two of his rescuers. All three men had to be evacuated.

Micah sighed, anger rising. They had lost four men already and they hadn't even glimpsed the enemy yet.

The darkness opened up before them. Micah could sense the vastness even though he couldn't see into the pit of the volcano. A winding path led downward into the valley below. Micah heard a collective sigh as reports circulated back. The hardened trail wouldn't allow pits and the single cliff wall wouldn't provide the leverage needed for the mantraps.

The column moved forward more quickly. The first time the steel bar swept away from the cliff wall it took ten men with it. Popov cursed and once again they inched forward at a snail's pace, inspecting every step. Even with their caution, more than a dozen more soldiers fell victim to General Alamay's vicious snares. Each time it happened Micah's anxiety grew, and he could sense the nervousness of the men on either side of him.

Captain Vasiliev was furious by the time they reached the stream that flowed out of the mountains into the lake.

"Kill them all!" the captain shouted over the roar of the waterfall that thundered somewhere to their left.

Micah clutched his spear and followed the dark shapes of his companions as they ran forward. He ran more cautiously than the others and soon fell behind.

The darkness was broken by a scream ahead.

Stupid, Micah thought. *Now the enemy will be alerted.*

Then a man's shout echoed through the woods and pandemonium ensued.

Micah entered the camp to see black leather-clad figures chasing frightened men and women through the trees. A tall man armed with a spear stepped in front of him. The man was untrained but fought with a passion born out of fear. He never managed to strike Micah directly, but the ferocity of his blows damaged the shaft of Micah's spear. After he killed the man, Micah broke the spear shaft at the weak point and hefted it like a sword. He liked the feel of it. It was more comfortable. He similarly broke the man's spear and tested the feel of the weapons in each hand.

Cries and shouts surrounded Micah. His training had prepared him for some level of chaos in battle, but this was ridiculous. There was no order, no discipline. Their commanders had abandoned the men to anarchy. He saw a flash of brown charge through the trees chasing one of the Night Birds.

Was that a bear?

Micah saw Captain Vasiliev through the trees. He was fighting an older man with dark skin, long salt-and-pepper hair, and a well-trimmed gray beard. Their battle was illuminated by torches that had been planted in the ground near a small cabin.

That must be Nasu Rabi.

The man was impressive, despite his obvious age. He moved like water, flowing around each strike, to deliver precise counter attacks. Micah had seen Captain Vasiliev spar. The man had an aggressive style that leveraged his strength and relative youth. Still not yet forty, the captain was in his physical prime. But this old man had him on his heels. The captain spent more time on defense than offense, which was unusual for him.

Another woman ran past clutching a torn dress as she tried to escape the Night Bird who ran after her.

Where are the other soldiers? I thought an army invaded the emperor's compound. All I see are farmers.

Micah saw Lieutenant Popov glide through the darkness to his right. Micah followed the lieutenant hoping he would lead Micah to the enemy. Popov scrambled up a nearby fir tree and then leapt from the branches to make a surprise attack on a young blond man carrying a sword.

Well that was unnecessary, Micah appraised.

The attack was ultimately ineffective as the man just stepped back and countered the blow. The lieutenant's opponent settled into a strong defensive stance as Lieutenant Popov prepared for another assault. The young man looked familiar somehow. He was tall and had long blond hair. He wore a loose linen shirt with short sleeves. In the flickering torchlight Micah could see the rippling muscles on the stranger's arms. Despite his size the blond man moved with a grace much like General Alamay. This must be the general's apprentice.

A deafening roar broke the darkness and distracted Micah. He turned to see the largest bear he had ever seen battling six Night Birds in a nearby clearing. The bear batted away spears and swords as if they were gnats. A massive paw swept at one of the soldiers and slashed his chest open like paper.

Micah turned back to the lieutenant's fight just as the blond man turned into the torchlight, providing Micah a clear view of his face.

Darius? No, it couldn't be. Micah was stunned, unable to move. He had not seen Darius since the night of the raid. Micah remembered little from that night or the weeks that followed. Micah had been shot in the chest while leading Darius to safety. Only fever dreams had followed that night until he woke up weeks later in a hospital cot far to the north. Micah rubbed the wound absently through his shirt while he watched his brother fight his commander. He was happy to see that Darius was alive but couldn't understand what he was doing here.

Blood trickled down his brother's arms, and his shirt was stained red from more than a dozen lesser wounds. Darius stumbled and Lieutenant Popov took advantage of the opening and moved into Striking Adder. Darius turned the stumble into a graceful move that Micah had never seen before. As Popov advanced Darius dodged and delivered a delayed thrust that pierced the lieutenant's heart.

As the lieutenant fell, Micah stepped into the torchlight clutching his two spears. Darius turned to face him and then his mouth gaped, and his face turned pale.

"Micah?" Darius whispered.

Micah winced. The tone of Darius's voice sounded awed and hurt at the same time, as if he had just caught his older brother stealing one of Mother Shala's pies.

Micah didn't know what to say so he pointed at the body of his fallen commander.

"You're good," he said lamely.

"What?" Darius sounded incredulous. Micah mentally kicked himself. It had been the wrong thing to say.

Darius looked so serious. Micah had to lighten the mood.

"You may even be better than me," Micah said in a joking tone.

This just seemed to anger Darius more.

"Micah, what are you doing here? With these murderers."

Micah held back another wince and tried to project an air of strength.

"Serving His Holy Emperor Lao Jun Qiu," he said with a confidence that he didn't feel under his brother's accusing gaze.

"Serving…these men that kidnapped your mother, enslaved your neighbors, and slaughtered our friends." Darius spat the words. His voice continued to rise until he was almost shouting. "Your *emperor* is a vile criminal who wants to put the world back under his thumb of tyranny."

No. That's not right, Micah thought. *The emperor wants to reunite the world. A world that is suffering due to the neglect and malfeasance of the rebel barons who wrested power away and are using it to fuel their own selfish ends. Darius must recognize this. What have the barons ever done to improve our lives?*

"The emperor saved us, Darius," Micah tried to explain. "He saved me."

Darius has to understand. I finally have a purpose. Something to fight for other than fish and deer. I can provide a life for him and Mother that is better than one of mere subsistence in good years and near starvation in bad.

Darius raised his sword as if he were going to attack Micah. Micah stared at the blade but refused to engage. He would not fight his brother. He had to save him.

"Saved you?" Venom practically dripped from Darius's tongue as he said the words. "He kidnapped you. After his men shot you in the chest. I thought you were dead."

Micah's heart ached for his little brother. What must that have been like for Darius? To think that Micah was dead and that their mother was gone. He met his brother's angry gaze, trying to think of something to say. Micah's recovery had been long and difficult, and he admitted, at first, he was angry. However, he had learned so much since he had joined the emperor's army. The emperor was a good man, and he wanted to improve the lives of all the people, not just the rich merchants or the nobility in the cities.

"He saved me from a meaningless life." He decided to try to explain things to Darius. "I have a purpose now beyond the mundane existence of subsistence farming and hunting. I've learned skills that I never imagined."

"Purpose? Is your *purpose* slaughtering innocents?" Darius waved a hand at the battle around them.

Ouch! Darius threw Micah's own assessment of the situation back in his face. The chaos and reckless slaughter were definitely not something Micah approved of. The Night Birds were supposed to pride themselves on subterfuge and infiltration, but this mission was going poorly due to Captain Vasiliev's hubris and bad execution. They could have easily captured the escaped farmers as well as General Alamay and his men without any bloodshed.

"No," Micah was forced to admit. "We were sent to apprehend a criminal and his followers who invaded the emperor's compound and murdered a dozen of the imperial guard. This was unfortunate."

"Those *criminals*," Darius lowered his voice and took on a dangerous tone, "were my friend and me, Micah."

Micah felt his hands twitch involuntarily at the challenge in Darius's voice.

What? No. Where are the soldiers?

"We were there to rescue *our* mother and others that the emperor had kidnapped."

Mother? She's alive? He felt a mixture of emotions, hope, guilt, anger at being lied to, but under it all a sense of duty that had driven him this past three years.

"Mother?" Micah started to voice his question when he was cut off by a bugle sounding in the woods. It was the signal for retreat.

"Fall back!" Corporal Kaya's voice called from the darkness. "The captain and the lieutenant are dead, and the assignment has been completed."

Micah glanced in the direction of the captain's battle that he had been watching earlier. Captain Vasiliev's body lay on earth torn from the violence of the battle, his throat cut. His opponent, General Alamay, stumbled away from the battle clutching his side. Micah could see the shimmer of blood on Alamay's hand as he leaned against a tree. It was a lot of blood. He wasn't dead yet but soon would be without immediate care and a miracle from the gods.

Micah turned back to Darius. "Come with us, Darius. I saw you fight Lieutenant Popov. The emperor would have a place for a warrior of your skills. Maybe even in the Night Birds, and then we could fight together."

The look in Darius's eyes was one of pure defiance.

"I will not help you enslave others," Darius growled.

No, not enslave…liberate. How had Darius become so brainwashed to the selfish goals of the barons? It must have been General Alamay. He had been one of the leaders of the rebellion. It only made sense that he would corrupt Darius with the party propaganda.

"You don't understand." Micah didn't have much time. He had to convince Darius to return with him. "The emperor wants to liberate the nations. To free the people from the rule of the barons. To return the empire to its pinnacle of progress and raise it up to be a shining example for the rest of the world to follow."

Darius shook his head angrily. "No, Micah," Darius yelled back. "They've tricked you somehow. These are evil men that you follow. They don't want to help the people, they want to oppress them. Stay with us. Mother is here."

Mother? Micah's thoughts drifted to childhood momentarily. The desire to see his mother, to hug her again, pulled at him, nearly breaking his resolve. He wished with all his heart that he could stay, but he had a duty to the empire. He had to fight for its liberation. He had to serve the holy emperor.

"You will see, Darius." Once the emperor raises a shining empire. "I'm right. When we meet again, you will see. I just hope it's not too late by then."

Micah turned and raced through the darkness after his men.

Summer - 34 A.E.

Chapter Two
Mustar Atmu

Emperor Lao Jun Qiu traced a finger along the curved carvings of his chair while his eyes scanned a wrinkled parchment held loosely by his other hand. A gentle breeze flowed through the pavilion through the open flaps opposite him. The clamor of the camp outside soothed him. His concentration was broken by the faint sound of wool brushing against the canvas tent flap.

Without looking he could tell that the commander general had entered. Jun finished the sentence he was reading before glancing up. General Sharav was every inch the career soldier. He was lean and muscular with a severe countenance. His graying beard was perfectly trimmed as was his shortly cropped hair.

Sharav held the deep bow, that was customary when entering the presence of the emperor without flinching. He would hold that pose until he collapsed with exhaustion if Jun didn't acknowledge him. Jun had been tempted more than once to discover how long that would take.

"What's your report, General?" Jun finally asked.

The general straightened and addressed his emperor.

"The Night Birds returned last night - what's left of them anyway." The disappointment was clear in the general's tone. "And one of our operatives just arrived from Eridu."

Jun raised a curious eyebrow.

"They report success?" Jun asked.

"Of a sort," the general replied. "Captain Vasiliev took Lieutenant Popov and forty Night Birds along with sixty of the new recruits. Less than half of them returned."

"Interesting," Jun mused. "Not the outcome I would have expected against an aged general, his apprentice archer, and a couple dozen farmhands. I would very much like to hear the report directly. Please fetch the captain and lieutenant to present their report."

Sharav cleared his throat.

"Is there a problem?" Jun asked.

General Sharav looked uncomfortable. "Neither Captain Vasiliev nor Lieutenant Popov survived the assault."

"Very interesting." Jun suppressed a scowl. "Who commands the remnants?"

"Sergeant Demir," Sharav responded.

A sergeant? It had been a long time indeed since someone who wasn't an officer had reported to him. *This should be interesting.* "Very well. Show the sergeant in."

General Sharav gave a crisp bow and backed out of the tent. He returned a few minutes later trailed by a battle-scarred veteran flanked by two younger men. All four men bowed deeply as they entered the tent.

"You may rise," Jun addressed the soldiers. They rose more awkwardly than General Sharav. "Sergeant Demir, the general's report is somewhat troubling. I would like to hear your version of events."

The older soldier spoke in a deep, gravelly voice, "With respect, Your Majesty, I was not involved in the assault. I was commanding the men guarding the roads out of Anbar Ur to prevent any from escaping the valley. Corporal Kaya here is the ranking survivor from the Night Birds that infiltrated the valley."

Jun gave the man a wry smile. "A corporal? That is who you wish to deliver your report? A bold choice. Very well, *Corporal* Kaya, please continue."

The sergeant took an uncomfortable step back and blushed under a sharp glance from General Sharav. The man to the sergeant's left stepped forward tentatively. His voice squeaked slightly as he spoke.

"Your Majesty," Kaya started. "Captain Vasiliev commanded one hundred men. He left forty in the city to guard against any retreat and led sixty of us into the valley. General Alamay had set many snares and traps to guard the entrance to the valley."

"Not surprising," General Sharav interrupted. "Vasiliev should have been prepared for that."

"As you say, General," the corporal continued, clearly embarrassed. "He did have us searching for traps, but they were well hidden, and it was very dark. We took heavy losses entering the valley, almost half of our men."

Very effective traps indeed, Jun thought to himself.

"The valley residents were all sleeping when we arrived at their camp, and we got the jump on them, but then they mounted a resistance that was surprisingly effective. We lost another twenty men before I gave the signal to retreat."

"There were no survivors among the enemy, I presume?" General Sharav asked.

The corporal looked confused. "No, I mean yes, there were," he said, flustered. "The captain and the lieutenant were dead, and we had accomplished our mission and there were only a few of us left and…"

"It doesn't sound like you accomplished your mission," Jun interjected as the corporal's voice faded. "Tell me, what were your orders?"

The corporal's posture stiffened, and he answered confidently. "Captain Vasiliev ordered us to capture or kill the criminal known as Nasu Rabi."

"Interesting." Jun shot General Sharav a glance. "I seem to remember issuing slightly different orders."

The general remained stone faced.

"And General Alamay is dead? You are sure?" Jun asked.

Corporal Kaya nodded. "Before he died, Captain Vasiliev struck a mortal blow, piercing General Alamay's chest. You don't survive a wound like that."

"I did," the third man muttered under his breath. Then, as if realizing he had spoken out loud, he lowered his eyes to the floor.

"Did you now?" Jun turned his attention to the young man. He was tall and had a thick head of strawberry blond hair, an unusual color for a soldier. "What is your name?"

"Micah, Your Majesty," the man muttered.

"Just Micah?" Jun asked bemused. "No rank?"

"Sorry, Your Majesty. Cadet Kabir, Your Majesty." Micah raised his eyes as he spoke. Jun saw a confidence there that belied his demure response.

The corners of Jun's mouth raised ever so slightly at the irony. "A corporal and a cadet. Certainly not the traditional imperial report."

"No, Your Majesty." Cadet Kabir spoke again oblivious to the fact that the statement had been rhetorical.

This young cadet was piquing Jun's curiosity. "So, you don't believe that General Alamay died from his wounds?"

"He might have, Majesty. But our orders were to make sure. With respect, I believe we retreated prematurely," the cadet answered. "We were also told there would be more soldiers with General Alamay, but—"

"Insolent…" General Sharav cut the cadet off and started to step forward. He stopped when Jun raised a hand.

"And General Alamay's archer? Was he killed as well?" Jun asked.

It was Cadet Kabir's turn to smile. It almost looked like he was grinning with pride. "Not an archer, Your Majesty. Well, I guess he can shoot too, but he was a master swordsman."

General Sharav scoffed.

"He killed Lieutenant Popov in single combat," Kabir said defensively.

"Impossible," Sharav exclaimed indignantly. "Popov was one of the best swordsmen I ever recruited, nearly as good as Vasiliev."

"And Darius killed him in a fair fight." The pride was clear in Cadet Kabir's voice this time.

General Sharav started to advance again. He clutched at a leather riding crop that dangled from his belt.

"Darius?" Jun interrupted again and Sharav stopped. Jun recognized the fire in General Sharav's eyes. The boy didn't know how close he was to being strapped for insubordination. "You know him then?"

"Yes, Your Majesty. He is my brother," Kabir responded.

"This report just keeps getting better and better." Jun's grin widened. "And do you know why your brother and General Alamay invaded the imperial compound?"

"Yes, Your Majesty. Darius said they were there to rescue our mother."

Jun could not help but laugh.

"So, General Sharav," he said with amusement. "Not an assassination attempt, as we thought, after all.

"Did your mother survive the assault?" Jun asked the cadet.

"I think so, Your Majesty."

"And you didn't stay with your brother and your mother?"

"No!" The man straightened. "I serve the empire and Your Majesty. I tried to convince Darius to come back with me. I know we could use a swordsman of his skill against the rebels."

"I see," Jun said. "And he declined?"

"Yes, Your Majesty." A note of frustration edged his voice. "He doesn't understand how things should be. I think he lived too long with that rebel general and was corrupted. Now that General Alamay is dead I'm sure I could convince Darius to see the right way."

"What is your assessment of the assault?" Jun asked the cadet.

"I think it was bloody mess," Kabir blurted. "Pardon, Your Majesty. Meaning no disrespect, but I think Captain Vasiliev wanted nothing other than to prove himself better than Nasu Rabi."

General Sharav growled at the use of the moniker.

"We should have entered the valley with more caution, taking more care to search for traps," Cadet Kabir continued. "The Night Birds pride themselves on infiltration and subterfuge. We should have ended it quickly and quietly. There should not have been a battle."

"That would have meant the death of your brother and mother," Jun countered.

"True," Kabir considered. "But I didn't know that at the time. You asked for my assessment of the mission. I don't regret that they survived but the assault was handled poorly."

Sharav was fuming and Jun couldn't entirely blame him. Even though Jun found Cadet Kabir's lack of protocol amusing, he knew the general would not see it that way. Jun studied the cadet. He demonstrated a confidence and strength that his corporal did not. Jun steepled his fingers and pressed them to his mouth, considering.

"*Mustar Atmu*," Jun said.

"Pardon, Your Majesty." The cadet looked confused.

"It means pretentious little bird."

The cadet looked shocked and offended.

"Don't take offense. A little arrogance is a good quality in a leader if groomed correctly."

"Sergeant Demir." Jun turned his attention to the veteran before the cadet could respond.

The older man jumped. "Yes, Your Majesty."

"What is the remaining command structure of the Night Birds?"

"Gone, sir. I'm the only one left"

"I want you to take command, Lieutenant Demir," Jun said. "Reform four squads and place Sergeant Kabir in charge of one of them."

General Sharav looked aghast and Jun found it difficult not to smile. Jun would deal with the general later but at least for now Sergeant Kabir would be safe. Sharav would not dare punish someone Jun had personally promoted. The boy interested him. Jun saw potential there, if rough. This was a stone that could be polished.

"General," Jun spoke again.

"Yes, Your Majesty."

"Once the Night Birds are reformed select another five platoons from the Daku Mitu. I have a special mission for them."

"Yes, Your Majesty."

"Thank you for your time, gentlemen. You are dismissed," Jun commanded. "General, I would like to speak to the operative from Eridu."

"Yes, Your Majesty."

"Alone."

"Of course, Your Majesty." Sharav snapped a quick bow before spinning on his heels to stride from the tent.

*****

"You're sure he's dead?" Emperor Lao Jun Qiu asked the cloaked man who sat across the table. The hood of the man's cloak was pulled back to reveal a rugged face and a crown of silver hair. The man's otherwise well-groomed beard was broken by a deep scar that ran across his left cheek from chin to temple.

Jun studied the Weiqi board and placed a white stone.

"Yes. They burned funeral pyres for their fallen and buried our men in an unmarked grave in disrespect." The man looked disgusted as he placed a black stone.

"Good to have confirmation, at least." Another white stone was placed in the chain, extending diagonally to the left.

"What about the boy?" Jun Qiu asked while his opponent considered his move.

The man refused to be drawn into the emperor's trap and placed another stone flanking the top of the white chain.

"In Eridu, they sold the horses and gear that was stolen from our men as well as a sizeable load of rope and nets. Then they headed west. He met with the garrison commander, Colonel Da Rosa, before he left so it is a safe bet Kasha Amur will fall to order soon to confront the threat we pose."

Jun placed another white stone on the opposite side of the board claiming the open territory. "I wouldn't worry too much about Kasha Amur. I already have plans at work there."

"He has a box," the man spoke as he countered the new move.

"What kind of box?" Jun's eyes narrowed.

"I only got a fleeting look. Dark oak and bound in iron, and it had a double lock. It looked very much like the reliquary of Chung Oku Mai."

Jun felt a momentary jolt of excitement at the mention of the artifact. He suppressed the emotion and placed another stone, on the strong side of the black stone. "But you aren't sure?"

"As I said, I only got a brief glance." He strengthened his position. "It would make sense that the reliquary would be in the care of General Alamay."

"Where is the boy headed now? You said west, not south?" Jun extended his line from the new territory.

"Isan first, then on to Kasha Marka," the man answered, and played strengthening his southern position further.

Jun's eyebrows rose. "That seems an odd place for a farm boy to go. It adds credence to your assumption. General Alamay would trust the box with no others."

"Farm boy no longer. From what we were told he is every bit the swordsman that Arthengal was."

Jun smiled. "You are the second person to tell me that today. You think he travels to meet Bedria Kess, or to someone else."

"We don't know. He hasn't betrayed that trust yet. We only know that on his death bed Arthengal asked the boy to take the box of *keepsakes* to a friend in Kasha Marka. The baroness would make sense, but General Alamay had other allies in the city."

"We need to get that box. We must confirm what is inside," Jun said.

"It could be nothing."

"Or it could be everything." Jun placed a final white stone and then studied the board. The two men were at an impasse. They could keep playing but it was clear that the game would end in a draw. Jun sat back in his chair, satisfied with the outcome.

The man studied the board for a moment and reached the same conclusion. "You played well, Majesty."

"Thank you. It is always a pleasure." This was the closest he had ever come to beating the man. "I think I will have General Hamazi send a company of lancers to investigate this box. He is the closest to Isan, I think."

"As you say." The man nodded. "Placing a bounty on the boy and the box may also be helpful."

"Do it," Jun agreed.

"I must be getting back, to prepare things in Eridu." The man stood and raised his hood. "You're sending the men I requested?"

"Yes, they will be there by midsummer," Jun considered. "I'm sending a young sergeant with them. Sergeant Kabir. I would like you to evaluate him. If the potential I see exists…well, you will know what to do. I can think of no better instructor."

"It will be done. Fare well, Jun. We will speak again when you arrive." With that, he swept out of the tent and disappeared into the night.

Chapter Three
Old Friends

Darius moved slowly. He placed his feet deliberately and controlled the motion of his arms. After years of training with a single blade, the second sword still felt awkward in his left hand. He was determined to honor Arthengal by learning how to use both blades, but he would have to relearn every form from scratch.

Never sacrifice form for speed. Arthengal's words echoed in his mind.

It would take time, but then, that's all he had now. Time and his weapons. And his mother. And Antu.

Four years he had trained, focused on learning all he could from Arthengal so the two of them could rescue Cordelia. Now, he had gotten his mother back. So why did it feel like his whole world was empty? He should be rejoicing, but he still found that he had to fight back tears each night as he tried in vain to fall asleep. Darius barely remembered his own father. Arthengal had filled a void Darius hadn't known was there, and now he was gone, murdered by the same men who had kidnapped his mother and brother.

Slow and steady. Pick up speed as the movements grow more comfortable.

He trained now even harder than before. It was the only time when he could empty his mind. The only time when he felt peace in his heart. He had taken back his mother from the emperor and had lost everything else in the process.

Darius closed his eyes and Arthengal was beside him. They were outside of the cabin near the lake. The two of them moved in perfect time gliding smoothly through the sword forms. Arthengal smiled and Darius felt the warm sense of pride rush through him.

"How long are you going to do that?" His mother's voice snapped Darius out of the reverie.

"Why?" he barked.

Cordelia raised her eyebrows in a way only a mother can. "Don't take that tone with me. You're not too old that I won't turn you over my knee."

"Sorry," he said more gently as his cheeks flushed.

His mother looked better. All of the refugees did. The last month had been good for them. They had bought nearly twice the supplies they would normally use on the journey to Isan, but the others had needed it. They had all put on weight and looked healthier for it.

"Well?" Cordelia crossed her arms. "How much longer? The rest of us have been packed up and waiting for you for half the morning. Antu gave up on you an hour ago and wandered off."

"He's probably hunting rabbits." The bear liked to do that when he was bored.

"You're wasting time," she accused. "You know we're going to reach the farm today and you're afraid to face them, aren't you?"

Darius sheathed the blades.

"I'm done, we can go."

She was right, of course. What would he say? What could he say? Arthengal had known Hanish since he had been born. He was a favorite uncle to Kal, Nash, and Anna. Poor Anna would be crushed. Arthengal had been the light of her world when she was a little girl. If Arthengal's loss had been hard on him, what would it do to them?

Before they could return to the others a shout came from the camp.

"Riders coming."

"What now?" Darius grumbled.

Darius stomped back to camp. Marku was at the western edge of the camp with his hands on his hips. He was watching a cloud of dust quickly approaching from that direction.

"They're riding fast," Marku said once Darius was at his shoulder.

Nicolai and Gunnar came from behind. They had retrieved their quarterstaffs from the wagons as a precaution. Cordelia and Lianna waited with the horses. Cordelia had loosened the straps that held her bow to her saddle.

Darius's group had been attacked three times already since leaving Eridu. Brigands couldn't resist a heavy wagon and a lightly armed party. Each time they had driven the thieves away. If Darius was honest, it had mostly been Antu that had driven them away, but in either case the group had learned to be cautious of strangers.

Where is Antu? Darius wondered. Ever since the bear had "adopted" Darius he was never far away.

Darius motioned to Nicolai and Gunnar. The twins slipped their quarterstaffs from the back of the wagon and took up positions on either side of the horses. Marku took Lianna behind the wagon and watched over the girl while she hid underneath, belt knife in hand. Cordelia retrieved her bow from the seat of the wagon and quickly set the string. She leaned against the wagon, obscuring the quiver of arrows that hung from the side.

The riders slowed as they neared the party. There were five of them. They were better equipped than the typical brigand. Their clothes were neither torn nor shabby. The saddles looked to be made of quality leather, and despite being dusty from the road, were in good repair. Darius noted that each of the men carried a sword at his hip.

Darius casually unhooked the strap that secured his sword in the sheath. He took a confident step forward. "Good morning," he said. "How fares your day?" While the men looked suspicious there was no cause yet for poor manners.

The riders ignored the question. The foremost, a heavyset man with a thick brown beard and a rough look about him, retrieved a parchment from his saddlebag. He unrolled the scroll and held it out at arm's length. He looked at Darius and then back at the paper.

"It's him." The man's low, gravely voice acted as a signal for the other men.

As one, the four riders dismounted.

"The writ's only for him. Take him," the leader instructed. "If they resist, you know what to do."

What in the sands of Saridon is going on? Writ?

"Be careful," the leader said with a sneer. "They say he's a sword master."

The other four men laughed and then drew their blades. They spread out as they advanced, forming a semi-circle around Darius.

Darius took a step back in surprise and drew his own blade, preparing to defend himself. He left Arthengal's sword sheathed. This was not the time to practice new skills.

The men charged the short distance between them. The brigand on the left jerked backward falling to the ground with one of Cordelia's arrows jutting from his chest. Darius ducked low into Scooping the Moon to avoid the first attack, his sweeping blade barely missing the man's feet. He countered immediately, springing upward into Wild Horse Leaps. With a high, downward thrust he pierced his attacker's throat.

The remaining two men circled Darius, trying to divide his attention. He didn't wait for them. He charged the first with the aggressive block and jab movements of Lion Shakes his Mane and then transitioned into Fox Dances with Dandelions to slip nimbly between his attackers. The initial attack sent his foe stumbling backward, and Darius ducked under the swinging blade of the second, slashing him across the middle. He completed the form with a strike across the man's back and he joined his companions on the ground.

Darius turned to face the remaining man with fire in his eyes.

"Run," he growled.

The man dropped his sword and started to sprint across the grassy plain. Antu appeared over a nearby rise and saw the fleeing brigand. The bear chased the man with long loping strides. With a final leap Antu tackled the assassin and the two of them rolled from view over the hill.

Darius shrugged. "Well, I tried."

The twang of Cordelia's bowstring broke the momentary silence. Darius turned to see the leader clutching his chest as he slumped and fell from his saddle. The hand crossbow that he held hit the ground first and fired. The bolt grazed the flank of the man's horse. The horse reared and with a panicked whinny fled in the opposite direction. The leader's foot was trapped in the stirrup and Darius saw the limp form bounce several times before it dislodged and tumbled to the ground.

"What in the name of the gods was that about?" Darius shouted.

"I think it had something to do with this." Marku stooped to pick up the parchment from the ground.

Marku studied the scroll for a moment. "It's a pretty good likeness," he said, handing it to Darius. "I guess the emperor didn't take kindly to you disturbing the peace of his slave camp and killing a bunch of his men,"

Darius took the paper and unrolled it. It bore a sketched image of a square jawed man with long, light-colored hair. A jagged scar ran vertically across the man's left eye. It wasn't a perfect depiction but close enough to mark Darius as the target. Beneath the picture was a message that read, "Five hundred drachs."

*****

The farm was large. They passed a wooden fence and a carved sign signaling its presence half a league before they saw the first buildings. Cows grazed in the fields as they rode past, paying them no mind. There were more cows than Darius had ever seen in his life. Hundreds of them.

Finally, he saw the house, or houses. They were a collection of squat, single-story log cabins with thatch roofs. There were at least a dozen buildings built in a semicircle around a spacious central courtyard. Several cooking fires decorated the yard. Kettles hung over some and Elsie Cherian worked a spit on one. She was turning what looked to be the entire hind quarters of a steer roasting over the fire.

A large barn had been erected to the west of the compound and was surrounded on three sides by corrals. That is where the activity was. Twenty or thirty men worked together to separate calves into pens. Some of the men drove the calves into different corrals while others carried sacks of grain and bushels of hay to long feeding troughs.

Elsie turned when she heard the horses approaching. Darius dismounted and led Micah by the halter. The others reined in and waited while Darius approached his friend. Elsie wiped her hands on her apron and scanned the group.

Darius let go of the horse's halter and continued the final few steps alone. Elsie must have seen something on his face or noticed Arthengal's absence in the group.

"Oh, Darius," was all she said, and she spread her arms wide.

Darius collapsed into her embrace and buried his face against her shoulder. And the dam burst.

Men came to take the horses and show the others to lodging and food. Darius noticed none of it. His body shook as he sobbed, and the world sped around him as he took refuge in Elsie's strong, comforting arms.

Hours later, Darius sat on the rails of one of the corrals watching the sun set over the western horizon. He heard footsteps approach from behind, but he didn't turn.

"Did he die well?" Hanish asked as he leaned an arm against the fence.

"He was wounded defending my mother and the others from the emperor's soldiers." Darius's voice choked.

Hanish nodded. "A warrior's death. He would have liked that."

Darius turned to look at the man. "How can you say that?"

"Oh, come on, Darius. You know as well as I do that Arthengal was never more alive than when he had a sword in his hand. He was like my da' that way. To die defending the weak and fighting for justice. That's the way both of 'em would have wanted to go. It tore me up inside to watch my pa waste away in a bed at the end. The helplessness of it killed him as much as the wasting disease did. If'n my da could have gone out in a blaze of glory instead of in his sleep there wouldn't have been no question."

Darius turned back to the sunset. Crimson, violet, and amber washed together beyond his tear-filled eyes. "I guess so."

"Here." Hanish thrust a tin plate toward Darius. It held a large slab of beef and some sort of clumpy, yellow porridge. "Elsie says if'n you don't eat she's going to make Kal and Nash hold you down and spoon feed you."

Darius smiled weakly and drew his sleeve across his eyes. He took the plate, holding it loosely.

"Come in when you're ready," Hanish said as he turned to go. "Elsie made a bunk up for you with the boys. I told them not to bother you none with any questions about Arthengal so you needn't worry about that. They'd all like to see you is all."

"Thanks," Darius whispered.

"I'm glad you saved your ma," Hanish called over his shoulder. "She seems like a real nice lady."

Chapter Four
Point of the Spear

Micah knelt on the canvas floor of the tent. His head was bowed, and the palms of his hands were pressed tightly to the tops of his thighs. He was one of thirty men arrayed in ranks before the emperor. Micah ventured a glance up at the man, the god, seated in the high-backed chair. His robes were a deep green, the color of jade, and were decorated with two intertwined dragons sewn with golden thread. Atop his head the emperor wore a tall, yellow silk hat. Ancient symbols in the old tongue were painted in black on the hat to indicate his family and station.

Micah's palms were beginning to sweat, and the backs of his legs were starting to cramp. They had been sitting like this for nearly half an hour while Emperor Lao conversed in a hushed tone to Commander General Sharav. At last, the general rose and moved a few paces from the imperial throne to stand at attention.

"You all have been handpicked to take part in a very important mission," Emperor Lao began. "The city of Eridu stands as the entryway to the province of Shalanum. It is the first major seaport on the Sea of Tears. It has a deep harbor which can accommodate large ships for war and trade, and it guards the crossroads to the center of the province.

"Eridu will be our first step to recovering the kingdom. You thirty and the men you command will be the tip of the spear. While General Sharav and I march our central army south, you will prepare Eridu for our arrival. Colonel Vincent Da Rosa, of the baron's first corps, commands a legion defending the city and its wall. You will be outnumbered twenty to one.

"Captain Sobol will have the command. I expect you to secure the city and the palisades with minimal loss of life to the common people. I also expect you to secure any ships that remain at port. Do you have any questions?"

"No, Your Majesty," the other men exclaimed almost as one. Micah remained silent. He glanced around at the other men and then back to the emperor.

When he realized that no one else was going to ask any questions Micah raised his voice. He spoke with the same confidence that he had when delivering his report of the raid. "Your Majesty, may I ask a question?"

"Please, Sergeant Kabir." The emperor waved a hand inviting him to continue.

Several of the other men gave him sidelong glances.

"Will we have any help from those inside the city?"

"An excellent question. The answer is yes," the emperor replied. "We have several operatives inside Eridu that have rallied support amongst the merchants. When you arrive at Eridu you should seek out their commander."

"We aren't a large enough party to lay siege to the city and I expect they aren't going to just let us march in with weapons and armor, Your Majesty." Micah paused to consider a moment. "Will your operatives have weapons for us? And should we sneak into the city? Maybe disguised as travelers from the country or something?"

"That would be wise," Emperor Lao said patiently. "And yes, weapons will be available once you enter the town. The Daku Mitu are experts at subterfuge and infiltration. I realize you are new to their ranks, Sergeant Kabir, but you should work with Captain Sobol and your lieutenants to devise an appropriate plan to enter the city and work with our men in Eridu to develop a strategy to take the city."

"Forgive my ignorance, Your Majesty." Micah swallowed. He knew he was pressing his luck, but he had one question left. "If I may, one more thing."

The emperor nodded. He looked amused.

"Is it possible that we might also request the support of a small contingent of horse archers? Large enough to pose a threat to the defenses of the city but small enough to make an attractive target for the legions in Eridu. Once we have made our preparations in the city they could approach and draw some of the army out. We may be able to secure the gates and the rest of the city trapping them outside and maybe attack them from both sides."

The emperor considered. "Why horse archers?"

"They would be more mobile. They could attack the walls from a distance but could still lead the enemy troops away from the shelter of the walls. It's just a thought, Your Majesty. I just thought that attacking from inside and outside at the same time might have a greater chance of success."

"We will take it under consideration," the emperor replied. "We will send word to our agents in the city one way or the other. Now, if there are no more questions, you have a long journey in front of you."

*****

"That boy is going to be trouble, Your Majesty," Sharav said after the men had left.

"Maybe," Jun responded. "There is no harm in a few questions, especially for one who is inexperienced. I would rather our leaders ask questions if they are uncertain than make critical mistakes due to ignorance."

"Of course, but he should be addressing his questions to his commanders, not the emperor."

"Yes," Jun mused. "He does need to be educated in protocol. But I think he has potential. His idea about support outside the walls was not a bad one."

"No," Sharav admitted reluctantly. "It's similar to a plan we had discussed with Guo Wen. We hadn't considered light cavalry but otherwise it is similar."

"Why was the plan rejected?" Jun asked.

"We could get a small company close enough to lend aid without alerting the Shalanum forces. But they must think the army is still months away once we enter the Dechora Plains. We don't want them to mobilize the navy before we are in a position to defend Eridu harbor. The problem is that Da Rosa would never fall for it. He's a forty-year veteran and would see right through the feint. His counterattack would likely tear our forces apart, even something mobile like light cavalry."

"What if Da Rosa wasn't around?" Jun asked.

"I don't know," Sharav hesitated. "I know his command staff. Every one of them is a veteran of the rebellion and they are fiercely loyal. They've been with him for years and know his strategies as well as he does. There is a reason Kasha Amur sent Da Rosa's legion to protect the gateway to the south."

"If he and his men are so experienced why haven't they advanced? Da Rosa should be a general. Why is he still only a colonel?" Jun asked.

"Politics for one, Your Majesty. He doesn't play well with the ministers, and the baron hated him," Sharav explained. "There was also an incident during the rebellion. He was in charge of guarding the port at Basara. Things got a bit dark. Let's just say he isn't above torturing prisoners of war to get information if he's desperate enough. His behavior would not have been unusual under Emperor Chen, but the barons didn't care for it. They're soft that way. Ultimately, he was forgiven for what they called 'war crimes,' but his career advancement ended there."

"I see," Jun said. He fell silent, considering the problem.

"Maybe Rouen," Sharav said almost to himself.

"Excuse me?" Jun asked.

"Sorry, Majesty," Sharav apologized. "Captain Marcel Rouen. He's from Aengal Province originally. He's a bit of a hothead and was dismissed from service there after he struck his commanding officer. He joined up with Da Rosa after Basara. The two get on like brothers. Rouen is a fierce fighter but doesn't have a head for tactics. And, as I said, he has a temper. He could be goaded into a fight."

"So, if we could make sure Rouen was placed in charge of the forces at Eridu the plan might have merit?" Jun asked.

"Maybe," Sharav said. "There would be some details to work out."

"Do you think five hundred horse archers could travel under cover and make it within striking distance of the city without being noticed?" Jun asked.

"Possibly, if we sent them by way of the old mining road to Anbar Ur. That area is less heavily patrolled, and they could wait in the forested hills for a signal from Guo Wen. As I said, with Rouen in charge, an attack of that size might draw out Eridu's cavalry and pikemen."

Jun nodded. "Think about it. See if you can make something of Sergeant Kabir's plan. Let me know once you have a more calculated strategy. In the meantime, I'll discuss with Guo Wen, and see if we can deal with the leadership problem. There would need to be a series of unfortunate accidents to avoid raising an alarm."

"Of course, Your Majesty. May I be excused to attend to my duties?" Sharav asked.

The emperor waved a hand. "You may."

The general bowed deeply and strode from the tent.

*****

"Boy!" Lieutenant Demir's gruff voice gave Micah a start. "You have got to learn to mind your tongue."

"I'm sorry, sir. I didn't mean to embarrass you," Micah said earnestly.

"Bah," Demir waved a hand. "You didn't embarrass me. I'm just worried you're going to end up mucking stables again if you don't learn when to keep your mouth shut."

"But the emperor asked if we had any questions," Micah stated, confused.

"A little tip for you, son. When the commander general or the emperor asks you if you have any questions, the answer is always no. Save your questions for me, and I'll save mine for the captain. Beyond that, consider everything else above your pay grade."

"But I want us to succeed. Shouldn't we present the best plan to help make that happen? If we had asked more questions last time maybe half of us wouldn't have died."

Demir shook his head and rolled his eyes.

"Yes," Demir said simply and then continued in a patient, if condescending, tone. "Bring your ideas to me. If I think they are worth the captain's time I'll pass them along. When you have a few more years and a few more battles under your belt I may even let you plan a few missions on your own. Small ones, mind you. Until then, keep your eyes and ears open and your mouth closed."

Micah's chest tightened. He felt like he had let Lieutenant Demir down. He nodded curtly, determined to do better next time. "Yes, sir."

"It was a good idea, though," Demir admitted. "Just not the right time or place to voice it."

"Thank you, sir."

"Good. Now get your gear. We head for the gap within the hour."

Chapter Five
Sillu Mitu

Darius wrestled the calf into position. He held the animal's body tightly between his legs and used his strong hands to hold the head steady. The ranch hand, Ander, flipped the knife expertly and carved a triangular notch out of the calf's ear. Darius released the calf and stepped away quickly to avoid the animal's flailing hooves as it ran away. The calf rushed forward where it was ushered into another pen by Nash.

"You're getting better," Ander joked with a smile. "You didn't get kicked this time."

Darius grinned and reached for the next calf that Kal had let into the corral via the opposite gate.

"Darius." He turned at the call and saw Anna approaching with a clay pitcher. "I brought you some water."

Wow, she has gotten pretty, Darius thought.

Anna was not as tall as her brothers or Darius, she only came to their shoulders, but she had the same sturdy frame that Darius imagined Elsie had when she was young. Her hands looked strong but gentle. She wore a blue dress today, and her luxurious brown hair shown in the sun and fell across the embroidered yellow flowers on her shoulders. The hair framed her perfect, oval face and her eyes twinkled as she realized he was staring at her. Her full lips quirked in a smile.

"You gonna hold that thing all day?" Ander asked.

Darius realized that Ander had marked the ear and was waiting for him to set the animal loose. Absently Darius released the calf and stepped toward the fence, not quickly enough. The calf lashed out as it ran away and one of the hooves grazed Darius's right thigh.

"Rat spit," he cursed and clutched his thigh.

Anna giggled. It sounded like a mountain stream bubbling over rounded rocks.

"Why don't we take a break?" Ander suggested.

Nash burst out laughing.

Darius limped to the fence and accepted the outstretched mug.

"Thank you," he said breathlessly after draining the cup. "I hadn't realized how thirsty I was."

"You seem to be settling in okay," Anna noted.

Darius nodded. "I like the work. I'm sore and tired at the end of the day, but in a good way. The way that you know you've accomplished something. It also helps me keep my mind off of…things."

Her smile grew sad for an instant, then brightened. "Your mother is going to tell a story after dinner tonight. You should join us."

"Maybe I will. That sounds nice. I haven't heard one of my mother's stories in what seems a lifetime."

She took back the cup.

"Don't forget to take a bath before dinner," she said. "You stink." She wrinkled her nose. Then she winked with another heart-stopping smile and trotted back to the bunkhouses.

"Hey," Kal shouted. "Don't we get some water?"

"Go get your own," Anna called back without slowing. "You know where the well is. I'm not your servant."

This produced a bewildered look from Kal and more peals of laughter from Nash.

Darius blushed. He had forgotten all about the other men. He cleared his throat. "Uh, shouldn't we be getting back to work?"

*****

"The war was in its fourth year." Darius heard his mother's voice as he approached the cook fire, munching on a crust of bread.

Several logs had been arranged around the fire for seating. Cordelia leaned forward as she spoke, and the dancing light from the fire gave her face a mystical look. Lianna shared the log with her. Elsie and Kal sat together. Elsie's five nieces and nephews, all younger than Anna, took up two logs. Several of the children belonging to the ranch hands rounded out the group, sprawling on the ground between the logs and the fire. Nash sat on a stump several paces away sharpening a knife and doing his best to appear disinterested. Anna sat alone.

When Anna saw Darius approach, she smiled and patted the log next to her. Darius brushed the crumbs off his hands and sat down a respectful distance from her. She immediately scooted over on the log until their hips touched. He could feel her heat through his calf-hide pants.

"You missed the first one," she whispered. "About Nasu Rabi and the Pirate King, Cheung Po."

"I've heard it," he whispered back. "Remind me someday and I'll tell you his version."

She looked confused for a second and then laughed. "I always forget when I listen to the stories that they are about Uncle Arthengal. It doesn't seem real that the campfire legend is the funny old man who used to muss my hair and bring me honeycombs."

It didn't seem possible, but Anna inched a little bit closer until her shoulder pressed into his arm. He could feel her along the entire length of his body. He was glad for the dark as he felt heat explode in his cheeks. He was sure his face would rival the morning sun for its shade of crimson.

"Nasu Rabi was laying siege to the imperial forces in the capital." Cordelia's voice finally penetrated the buzzing in his ears. "But Emperor Chen's forces were rallying in the south. Baroness Magora feared an attack on Kasha Haaki, which would create a fatal disruption to their supply lines.

"The imperial forces in Hurasham were commanded by General Hamazi, the youngest of Emperor Chen's generals. Despite his youth, he had a reputation of brutal effectiveness in his campaigns. This was partly due to the meticulous care he took in planning each operation. He seemed to have the capacity to anticipate and adapt to any situation. Baroness Magora had to know what he was planning, but penetrating his camp seemed an impossible task because of how diligently he trained and positioned his sentries.

"Baroness Magora had recently promoted a promising young soldier from the ranks of their spies to serve on her war council. The soldier had joined the cause at the outset of the war at the impossible age of seventeen. She had proven herself adept at subterfuge and at coming up with battle plans that the enemy least expected. The young soldier had earned the nickname Sillu Mitu, or Night Shadow. This seemed the perfect task for Sillu Mitu.

"Magora summoned the young woman and explained the situation. Sillu Mitu asked for thirty soldiers and as many night stars as the baroness could spare. She promised that she would return with the general's plans or die trying.

"The jungles of Hurasham were dense and fraught with danger." Cordelia's voice took on a more ominous tone. "Panthers patrolled the trees at night. Snakes big enough to swallow a man whole slithered through the underbrush. Spiders with poison as deadly as nightshade lurked behind every branch."

Anna shuddered and clutched at one of Darius's hands. She entwined her fingers with his and pulled it closer, holding his hand with both of hers. His arm pressed tightly against the side of her body the bare skin of his upper arm tickled by flower stitching on her bodice. His heart began to beat faster and not just from his mother's story.

"Sillu Mitu's journey through the jungle was perilous. One dark night the stillness of the camp was broken by the spine-tingling growl of a panther and the terrified scream of a man. Then there was silence. Another morning the soldiers awoke to find two of their number missing. The sentries swore they hadn't seen a thing, but the soldiers were just gone from their blankets. Their packs and weapons lay untouched beside their beds. A tiger raged through their camp one day, killing two more.

"It seemed Sillu Mitu's mission was doomed to fail before they even reached the general's camp. But her determination was unbroken. She rallied her men and soldiered on. Finally, they did arrive, minus a third of their number. They had beaten the jungle, but the true objective still lay ahead.

"Sillu Mitu spotted the first of the sentries nearly half a league from the center of Hamazi's camp. The first perimeter was spread thin and it had been easy to sneak by. Once inside, she ordered most of her soldiers to spread out and encircle the camp. They were to wait until just before dawn, when the jungle would still be dark, to execute her plan.

"She hurried on with only two of her comrades in tow. The second group of sentries had been harder to pass. The three of them had been forced to crawl at an agonizingly slow pace through the underbrush to sneak past. When she could finally see the final perimeter guard her heart sank. Hamazi had arranged a tight circle around his camp. Each soldier was only a few paces apart and could easily see his fellows. The underbrush inside the camp had been cleared and the only cover would be the tents."

Anna's thumb began to twitch nervously against the back of Darius's hand. It produced a light stroking sensation that made the hairs on the back of his hand tingle. He felt a shiver run up his spine.

"I know," Anna whispered. "Your mother is such a good storyteller."

"Uh huh," Darius gulped.

His mind was a jumble. He was having a hard time concentrating on the story. This was Anna; she had been like a sister to him for the past four years. He glanced at her out of the corner of his eye. She watched Cordelia with rapt attention. She had grown up so much in the past year. She was such a beautiful young woman now, and she was holding his hand. What did it all mean? Emotions stirred in him that he didn't fully understand.

"Sillu Mitu circled back to the second line of sentries. They searched for a gap which would suit her needs. When she found what she was looking for they sprung like cheetahs on a calf. They slew three of the guards, stashed their bodies in the underbrush, and stole their armor and weapons. Then, returning to the inner perimeter, they waited.

"The night erupted all around the camp as night stars shot into the air and exploded. The showers of silvery sparks lit the trees in an eerie glow. The guards were suddenly alert, and the camp began to stir. Sillu Mitu waited for the second barrage and then led her companions at a sprint toward the line.

"'They're inside the perimeter,' the taller of her two companions shouted.

"'Hold,'" the sentry captain shouted. 'Where do you think you are going?'

"'The rebels are inside the perimeter,' Sillu Mitu's soldier responded. 'Lieutenant Wang sent us to warn General Hamazi.'"

"Why was her soldier speaking for her?" Nash interrupted. His knife lay across his lap, forgotten. "Wasn't she in command?"

Darius hadn't realized that Anna had been squeezing his fingers tighter and tighter until she loosened the grip when Nash spoke. Blood rushed back into his fingers and made the tips tingle.

"That's a good question, Nash," Cordelia said. "Emperor Chen believed that women were inferior warriors and had no place in the military. Women were banned from serving in the imperial army. Sillu Mitu had to hide behind her two men during the confrontation with the sentries and hope she wouldn't be noticed."

"So, why go in at all and take the risk?" Nash asked. "Why not just send in her men to steal the plans?"

"Because she wasn't inferior," Cordelia said mildly. "She was the best at what she did. Infiltration, subterfuge, and distraction tactics were her forte. She insisted on infiltrating the camp to make sure it was done right. She also had a better head for tactics than almost any officer in Baroness Magora's army. They didn't actually intend to *steal* the plans but rather analyze them. If they stole them, Hamazi would just change them. If they could sneak in and study them, they would have insight into his strategy without his knowing and could adapt their defenses. At a glance Sillu Mitu could analyze and assess the strategy and make recommendations to Magora for the best way to counter them. She had to be there, or the mission was for naught."

"Oh," Nash said, somewhat awed.

Anna was rubbing the back of Darius's hand now as if she were trying to warm it. The hand did grow warm as did Darius's face again.

"Why did her soldier say Lieutenant Wang?" Nash asked. "Did they have spies inside the camp?" The last was said with a note of intrigue.

"It was a calculated risk," Cordelia explained. "Wang was just about the most common surname in the imperial army. He was hoping the guard captain would know someone by that name and let them pass."

"Sneaky," Nash said appreciatively.

Anna's fingers were tickling the back of Darius's knuckles. A shudder ran up his spine again, and she giggled.

"And it worked," Cordelia continued. "The guard captain passed them through and began ordering his men to prepare defenses along the line."

Anna's hand came to rest on the back of Darius's as Cordelia resumed the story.

"The night stars were exploding at regular intervals from all around the camp. Sillu Mitu's troops would fire a volley and then move to a new position in an attempt to keep the imperial forces disoriented. The camp was in chaos as soldiers were roused from sleep and tried to prepare for an invasion for which they had had no warning. General Hamazi was moving from one battalion commander to the other, efficiently organizing his forces.

"Sillu Mitu knew they wouldn't have much time. They hurried through the chaos to the command tent. Circling around to the back to avoid the soldiers guarding the front they made a small incision along the seam just big enough for her to slip in. Her men stood guard outside acting every bit the imperial soldier.

"The tent was empty. She studied the maps on the war table and scanned reports as quickly as she could. She could hear voices approaching outside."

Anna disentwined her fingers from Darius's and began slowly dragging her nails from the tips of his fingers to the base of his palm. The effect was intoxicating, and Darius's head began to swim. His breath and heart rate quickened.

"Sillu Mitu finished her evaluation quickly and then dove for the torn seam as she heard the soldiers outside the tent flap snap their heels together and one of them shout in greeting, 'General'.

"She wormed her way outside and disappeared just as Hamazi entered the tent. She and her men used the activity in the camp to their advantage and made their way past the front line. They melted into the jungle and found one of her *lighting bringers*. At Sillu Mitu's instruction the woman launched a final night star. It burst over the camp in a shower of red sparks. With that the assault stopped, and she and her soldiers disappeared.

"General Hamazi waited for the attack that never came. We don't know how long he waited. Sillu Mitu and her night guard, as they came to be called, made it back to Kasha Haaki and the intelligence that she secured allowed Baroness Magora to turn Hamazi's troops back at Asha'ha Woods near the boarder of Merkar and Hurasham.

"It became the turning point of the war. Margora was able to follow Hamazi's retreat into Chungoku. Before the year's end she suppressed any further imperial resistance outside the capital."

"Wow." Anna released Darius's hand and stood. "What an amazing story." She stretched and gave an exaggerated yawn. "Thank you, Cordelia. You should be a bard. Your stories are so wonderful. I'm tired though, and I think I'll head to bed."

"You're welcome, Anna." Cordelia smiled. "It is late, it's probably time we were all off."

"Good night, Darius," Anna said with a smile and turned to walk toward her cabin.

"G-good night," Darius stammered.

Darius sat there for several minutes more while, one by one, the others left to their sleeping quarters. His fingers still tingled from Anna's touch, he could almost hear the hammering of his heart, and his thoughts were a torrent. Images of Anna flashed through his mind, her face, her smile, her bodice. He blushed without knowing why.

"You coming?" Nash asked after stowing his knife and sharpening stone.

"Huh?" Darius was broken from his trance. "Yeah, I'll be right there."

Chapter Six
Eridu

"What are we *doing*?" Micah whispered, concern and doubt in his voice.

He knelt next to Lieutenant Demir behind a large patch of blackberries. His bow and quiver rested on the ground beside him. Demir looked at him like he had gone mental.

"What are you talking about?" Demir hissed. "This was your idea."

"No," Micah insisted. "My idea was to *trade* for clothing, mules, and merchandise so we could pose as traders and sneak into Eridu more easily."

Demir sighed and shook his head. "Let me ask you something, Kabir. What happens if we follow your plan? The trader happily takes our money and then maybe he goes home. Or maybe he continues on to Eridu to spend his well-earned coin. Then maybe he decides to have a pint or two. He brags to his fellow traders that he didn't even have to haggle with the merchants in town. He sold all of his goods, his wagon, his mules and made a pretty penny.

"'How did you get so lucky?' they will ask.

"'Well, I just sold everything to a bunch of soldiers up north. Queerest thing, I don't know why a bunch of soldiers would want to buy all my extra clothes and my mules too. Anyway, another round on me.' And that might be it for him. He might not ask too many questions. But what about his friends, and their friends? Pretty soon, before you know it, there are half a dozen rumors running around Eridu about soldiers buying up merchants' clothes and gear. What do you think the garrison is going to think when they hear the rumors?"

"I guess I hadn't thought about that," Micah said glumly.

"It's still a good idea but this is the best way to get the supplies we need," Demir said.

A runner came up behind them.

"The captain has seen a good one coming down the road. Get ready."

Micah raised his bow and nocked an arrow. He watched the roadway to the north. He could hear the jangle of bridles and the squeak of a wagon's wheels. The group cleared the rise in the road and Micah could see them more clearly. A short, balding man in farmer's clothes led a pair of mules pulling a wagon loaded with barrels. A second wagon came up behind the first led by a younger man in simple linen shirt and pants. Three guards flanked the wagons on either side. At least they appeared to be guards. They were dressed in leathers and carried quarterstaffs and bows. Micah suspected they were hunters for whatever village this merchant hailed from.

Micah felt a pang of guilt. Remembering his life in Koza he thought it likely that these two wagons represented all of the trade goods for the merchant's entire village. He wondered briefly what would happen to the village when the merchant didn't return with any supplies and six of their best hunters went missing.

Lieutenant Demir raised his hand. As one, the soldiers hidden in the bushes and trees along the road raised their weapons. Micah raised his as well and drew the string back. Micah focused his attention on the chest of one of the guards. He cleared his mind, just as he had taught Darius to do when they were younger. There was only the arrow, the string, and the target. The rest of the world faded away as he became one with the weapon.

"Fire!" Demir shouted.

The merchant and guards only had a second to react before the flurry of arrows rained down on them. It was over before it started.

"Okay, clear the road and reset for the next group," Captain Sobol shouted.

Men hurried from cover and began moving the horses and supplies to the makeshift camp they had assembled several hundred paces back in the trees.

*****

Micah guided his mule a few more steps forward. The line of people waiting to get into Eridu was longer than he had expected. They had met several travelers on the road to the north and had learned that in addition to the normal traders there were a fair number immigrating to Eridu from the north for fear of the barbarian raids that had been happening more frequently in recent summers.

The line moved ahead again, and Micah turned to the two men that were travelling with him. "When we get up here let me do the talking."

They both nodded. Lieutenant Demir had mostly populated Micah's squad with men he had trained with as cadets. They accepted his leadership and respected his judgment. These two, Joral and Moab, had been Micah's closest friends during training.

Moab was shorter than the other two. He had a thick neck and a barrel chest. His pudgy cheeks made him look younger than he was. Moab's jet-black hair always looked greasy. The man was loathe to bathe unless forced to. In their current circumstances that served to their advantage. Micah sniffed. It was definitely time for Moab's weekly bath.

Joral, by contrast, was tall and lanky. He prided himself on his appearance and made sure his uniforms were clean and free of wrinkles. He made up for Moab's lost baths, sometimes bathing twice a day if the opportunity presented. Where Moab's dark eyes always held the glint of danger, Joral's blue eyes shone with mirth. The three of them had been like brothers during training. When Micah had been promoted Moab and Joral became his self-appointed personal guards.

Both were solid bowmen and were mediocre with the sword. Micah didn't know what sort of weapons they would be provided once they arrived to Eridu. In all honesty, he would be content with the three hunting bows that were strapped to the bundles on the mule's back.

The final group in front of Micah passed through the gate and a guard approached Micah's group.

"Good evening," Micah said before the guard could speak. "Pretty busy today. Is it always like this?"

"Not usually," the guard admitted. "Is this your first time in Eridu?"

"Yeah, my pa would usually make the trade runs, but he got gored by a boar this spring and his leg isn't up to the trip. He sent me instead."

"What are you here to trade?" the guard asked.

"Mostly salt and a few seal skins," Micah said. He leaned in and lowered his voice. "And a couple of pearls." He patted the belt at his waist.

"Where are you arriving from?"

"Up Whiting Bay way," Micah answered. "A little fishing village. I'm not even sure it has a name. Just sort of sprung up a few years ago. My pa and a few of his friends got tired of chasing cattle on the plains and decided to try their hand at fishing instead. I gotta tell you, it's not as lucrative as you might think. We was…"

The guard looked bored and then eyed the long line behind Micah and the fading light. "Okay, you're good. Move on through."

"Thank you kindly. Have a nice evening." Micah yanked on the lead rope of the mule and led it and his men through the gates.

"It's just that easy, huh?" Joral whispered once they were clear of the gate.

"Same dead-eyed stare all of you lot used to give me when I'd try to tell you stories about growing up in Koza." Micah smiled. "For some reason life in a simple fishing village doesn't seem to hold anyone's interest for long."

"They didn't even inspect our load. And didn't even ask about the bows," Moab noted.

Micah shrugged. "I don't think hunting bows get much notice. Half the people we passed were carrying them. As for our goods, I wasn't lying. That's what we got off that merchant up the road."

Micah glanced around at the tall buildings. The city was as large as it had been described but seeing it up close was impressive. The streets were crowded, and they had to jostle the mule through the throng.

"Did you notice that they only had a couple dozen archers on the walls?" Joral asked as they passed a group of soldiers moving toward one of the public houses.

"Yeah, but don't let that fool you," Micah said. "The captain said that the commander here is experienced. I bet there would be ten times that in a heartbeat if any sort of threat approached the city. And that's just the north wall. I was more impressed by the fortifications. The palisades are solid all the way through and the walkway up top could fit two men abreast. The gates were solid oak and banded in iron. The crossbar was two spans thick. I bet it takes at least a dozen men to lift it into place. If we take the city it will be a trick for them to take it back. By land at least."

"Where are we going again?" Moab asked.

"Some ale house down by the waterfront called the Busty Barmaid," Micah said.

"Interesting," Joral smiled. "I wonder if it lives up to its name."

"We'll soon see." Micah made the turn onto the wharf road and could see the provocatively decorated sign up ahead.

He led the mule around the back of the inn and handed the lead rope to a stable boy. The boy eyed the three suspiciously.

"Nice night for a game of dice, huh?" Micah repeated the phrase that he had been instructed to give.

The boy seemed satisfied. "Just go on in through the kitchen there."

Micah entered the back of the building followed by Joral and Moab. They passed through a small room in the back where firewood was stacked along either wall and entered a large kitchen. Two cast-iron cooking stoves and a wide brick oven dominated the back half of the room. In the center of the room was a long wooden counter.

A portly woman with her gray hair done up in a bun was issuing orders to a pair of cooks and a half dozen bustling serving girls. One of the girls had a row of tin plates arrayed on the counter and was scooping portions of roast pork and corn mash onto each before handing them to the rest who would then disappear through a doorway at the back of the kitchen only to return a few minutes later.

"Move on through," the gray-haired woman shouted. "It's busy enough in here without you three gawking."

Micah led the other two into the dining area. Six long wooden tables took up most of the center of the room. Smaller, square tables formed a ring around the outside. The room was packed to capacity and the clamor of activity was deafening. It looked like more than half of their men had already arrived. Through the throng Micah could see a small stage at the back of the room. A minstrel sat on a tall stool playing the lute, but Micah couldn't hear a note over the noise from the soldiers.

Micah spotted Lieutenant Demir near the stage and shouldered his way through the crowd.

"Ah, you made it," Demir shouted. "You're one of the last."

Micah glanced around the room. "Surely not."

"Everyone is meeting here but after a bite and a pint we're sending them off to separate inns for lodging," Demir explained. "The city is pretty full as it is with all the refugees coming in from the country, so it's been a trick to find rooms. We've had to get creative. Only the officers and sergeants will be staying here. We'll get you details about where your men are staying once the dust settles. Find a seat and one of the girls will be along."

Micah gazed around the room, baffled. "Find a seat?" he muttered.

To his amazement, he saw Joral waving at him from a table near the stage. He and Moab had somehow managed to secure three wooden stools.

The music could be heard more clearly from the table. It was a lively song, if a bit out of tune. As he settled onto a stool, tension that he didn't realize he was feeling began to melt away. They had made it safely inside the city. The first step was done.

"Check out the serving girl over there." Joral nodded toward a raven-haired girl handing out pints of mead at one of the long tables in the center of the room.

"Aye, she's healthy." Moab smiled and elbowed Micah in the ribs. "She can serve me anytime."

Joral laughed.

Micah grinned. He still wasn't sure, in his new position, where to draw the line between friend and commander. He had been trying to observe the interactions of some of the other sergeants during the march south, but the routine of march, eat, march, eat, sleep, march, hadn't provided much opportunity for real study. Maybe he could ask Demir once the inn had cleared out a bit. He hadn't known Demir long, having only joined the Night Birds as a cadet for the Nasu Rabi mission, but he seemed ready to teach Micah the ropes. And he had nearly twenty years as a sergeant in the army, so if anyone would know, he would.

Micah played it safe. "I don't think you'll have much time for flirting tonight," he said.

"Flirting!" Moab laughed. "Who's talking about flirting, country boy? I've been on the road for more than a month. I'm hoping for a little more than flirting."

Moab, it seemed, had decided that Micah's promotion meant no change in their relationship. His voice was getting louder as he spoke, and he drew looks from a couple of the girls.

"Anyway," Micah continued, "Lieutenant Demir is moving everyone through pretty quick. You'll have time for a quick meal and then you'll get your sleeping assignments. They're spreading us all out across the city."

Moab looked disappointed.

"That's smart," Joral said. "A force our size would surely be noticed by the garrison here. Even if we are all dressed like farmers and merchants. Spreading us out into smaller groups will be less conspicuous."

Micah noticed one of the girls whispering to the gray-haired woman near the kitchen.

A stout, blonde woman in a gray frock and yellowed apron approached their table.

"Evening, boys." She spoke to Micah with a cordial smile. "I'm Elsbet, I'll bring 'round a couple mugs of ale and some dinner. If you're needing anything else, you make sure to let me know."

Elsbet was older than the other serving girls. She had a blockish face and wide hips. A large brown mole decorated her right cheek and she appeared to be missing a couple teeth behind her smile.

If it was possible, Moab looked even more disappointed. He recovered quickly and with a hawkish grin said, "How about the name of that black-haired beauty over there?"

Elsbet's smile never changed. She leaned in and spoke quietly. "You're not going to be any trouble, are you, boys? It would be a shame to have to chase you out of here with a broom in front of all of your friends."

Moab looked shocked, then his eyes narrowed. He started to say something else.

"No, ma'am." Micah recognized the look on Moab's face and interjected quickly before the soldier could say anything that would make the situation worse. "The pork and the pints will be fine. Thank you."

Joral suppressed a grin as Elsbet walked away. Moab's face had colored slightly and there was a dangerous glint in his eyes.

"The black-haired girl would be too much for you anyway." Micah decided he needed to break the tension. "You can't just jump from wooing sheep to the prettiest girl in the bar. You've got to work yourself up to it. Maybe Elsbet would give you a roll in the hay. That'd be a good start for you."

Joral covered his mouth with a hand and looked down at the table.

Micah leaned in toward Moab and took a long, dramatic sniff.

"On second thought, maybe you better stick with the sheep. Until you've had a bath at least."

Joral burst out laughing.

Moab looked hurt but then grinned.

"Yeah, well at least where I grew up, we had girls to talk to. The way I hear it, Joral there comes from Larissa where all they got is cows."

Joral shrugged. "At least the cows don't talk too much and don't expect you to take them for a moonlit walk after."

All three laughed and Moab's good spirits seemed to have returned.

Elsbet returned and placed three mugs of ale and three plates on the table.

"Drink your ale," Micah said. "It's been a long march. Appreciate the fact that we're not eating oat cakes and drinking brown water."

The other two dug into their dinners, but Micah could swear he saw Moab assessing Elsbet's hips as she walked away.

*****

It was well past first bell by the time the inn had cleared out. Only the officers and a couple dozen sergeants remained. When the last of the troopers left, Lieutenant Demir bolted the front door. The servers distributed a final round of ale and then disappeared into the kitchens.

Micah had moved to one of the long tables and was talking to the other Night Bird sergeants when a hush fell over the room.

A lean, gray-haired man had emerged from the kitchen. His back was rail straight and he walked with the presence of someone used to issuing commands. The man wore a tight, silver beard. The most shocking feature of the man's face was a deep scar that ran the whole left side of his face, from chin to temple.

The man's calculating, almond-shaped eyes scanned the men arrayed at the tables. Captain Sobol joined the stranger at the front of the room.

"This is Guo Wen," Captain Sobol announced.

A series of hushed whispers rippled through the room. Micah turned his head, trying to catch what was being said, but it evaded him.

"He commands the loyalist forces here in Eridu," Captain Sobol continued. "He has coordinated plans with the emperor and commander general. Tonight, he will fill you in on the role we will play."

"Thank you, captain." Guo Wen stepped forward. His voice was strong and confident. "Our strategy will have multiple phases and each of you will play your part. However, as I'm sure you can understand, it is important to keep the overall strategy secret. The first phase will begin tonight. I will only need a few of you to carry it out. If I call your name, you stay. The rest of you can retire for the evening."

"Lieutenant Alexov and your *blood knives*," Guo Wen called out.

"The *amanu'dami* are here to serve." Alexov snapped a salute.

"Lieutenant Utkin and the Mortikai with you," Guo Wen continued.

Utkin gave a slight bow.

"Lieutenant Demir. I will only need Mustar Atmu and his unit of Night Birds."

"Yes, sir," Demir responded.

Micah jumped at the mention of the nickname the emperor had given him.

"That is all," Guo Wen concluded. "The rest of you can turn in. You will be called upon for future assignments. Have a good night and long live the emperor."

"Long live the emperor." The shout resounded through dining hall and men began filing up the stairs or out the back of the inn.

"The rest of you." Guo Wen turned to the dozen men remaining. "Let's get to work."

Chapter Seven
Anna

    Darius completed Lazy Viper, ending in the starting position, and began again. The forms that were made to work with a shield were easier to adapt to two swords. He had begun focusing exclusively on those. Once he had mastered the techniques with both blades he would work in other forms.

    The sun was nearing its zenith and the yard was getting hot. He had shed his shirt hours ago and sweat glistened on his chest and arms. Again and again he ran through the technique. He was determined to master it.

    Out of the corner of his eye he spotted Anna sitting on the porch of one of the cabins watching him practice. A wicker basket sat at her feet and she held a wool blanket on her lap. Her hair was tied back with a pink ribbon and she wore a yellow dress with a white sash tied in a bow at her waist. He completed the series and then stopped.

    "I'm sorry." Darius addressed her while he searched for his shirt. "I didn't see you waiting there."

    "Oh, don't worry about it," Anna said with a smile. "I could watch you practice all day."

He blushed and stammered, "Y-y-your uncle gave us the day off since we finished marking the calves and I figured I would get caught up on practice."

"I know," Anna said, still smiling.

"How long have you been sitting there?" Darius asked.

"A while," she said dreamily.

"Did you need something? Were you waiting for me?" he asked.

"I thought you might like to take a break for lunch." She pointed to the basket. "I know a little stream just south of here. It would be the perfect place for a picnic."

"That sounds nice," Darius said, and started to pull his shirt over his head.

Anna wrinkled her nose. "Aren't you going to wash up first?"

"Oh." Darius pulled the shirt off and held it limply. "Yeah, I guess I should."

He glanced around looking for a place to wash and settled on the well. He dropped the bucket and pulled it back up, sloshing water. He scooped his hands into the bucket and splashed some water on his face.

"Eww!" Anna exclaimed. "We drink out of that. Stay there, I'll be right back."

She dashed into the cabin. Darius stood dumbly, water dripping from his face. He swept his hands through his long blond hair showering the dusty ground with water and sweat.

Anna returned a few minutes later carrying a basin. A linen cloth was draped over her shoulder. She set the basin on the ground at Darius's feet and dipped the cloth in the water. She startled Darius when she stood and started to gently wipe his chest.

"Hold still," she scolded.

She rinsed the towel and wiped his chest again, scrubbing at his chest where the sweat had mixed with dust in a grimy smear. The water was warm, and her touch was soft. Darius's mind was abuzz. He wasn't sure how to react and was too embarrassed to look her in the eye, so he stood rigidly and let her do her work while he studied the shape of the white fluffy clouds on the horizon. Anna rinsed the rag several more times before turning him around to wash his back and under his arms. She finished by wiping the dirt from his face, pausing briefly to lightly touch his scar.

"There," she said, dropping the cloth in the basin with a satisfied plop. "Now I won't have to smell you while I eat. Put your shirt on and I'll take this back inside."

Darius stood in a daze while Anna carried the basin into the house.

"That's a pretty girl you've got there."

Darius jumped, startled by the sound. He turned to see a middle-aged, olive-skinned man leaning against the fence of one of the corrals. The man wore black leather knee-high boots. Bright red pantaloons flared to a stop just above the boots. His purple brocade shirt shimmered in the sun and the yellow laces were undone at the chest showing a tanned chest denude of hair. The outfit, which in

Darius's mind made the man look every bit a clown, was completed by a broad brimmed hat decorated with three peacock feathers. At the man's waist was a patterned leather belt from which hung a long, thin sword that looked more like an exaggerated knitting needle than a weapon.

"Can I help you?" Darius questioned.

"I am Juan Carlos Estaban De La Vega of the Kasha Deira De La Vegas. Son of the last prince of Segeda, of late in asylum in Kasha Amur." The man gave a deep, flourishing bow sweeping his hat from his head in a graceful motion.

Darius was as confounded by De La Vega's introduction as he was by the man's attire.

"You are Darius Kabir of the Koza Kabirs, I presume."

Darius almost laughed at the ridiculousness of the audacious honorific. "Yes. How can I help you?"

"I have come to reclaim my family's legacy and to win the favor of his Imperial Highness Emperor Lao Jun Qiu with your capture and return. If you would prepare your belongings for travel and bid your family farewell I would much appreciate it."

This time Darius did laugh. He couldn't be serious.

"I don't think so," Darius said.

De La Vega's polite smile turned to a frown, but his voice retained the polite tone. "I would prefer very much not to have this scene turn ugly." He tapped the rapier at his belt. "But I am prepared to enforce my claim if it becomes necessary."

Darius heard a gasp from the porch of the house and turned to see that Anna had returned.

"I think you should leave," Darius said.

De La Vega sighed. "If it must be, it must be. I offer my apology to the young lady that I must do her lover harm."

"Lover?" Darius's protest was cut short by the ring of steel.

"Daddy," Anna called inside the house, but Darius barely heard her.

Darius drew his longsword and turned to face De La Vega.

The nobleman paused, momentary hesitation in his eyes. "If you want to draw your other blade, I will allow it. I would not ask a man to fight me at a disadvantage."

He must have been watching me practice. He thinks I normally fight with two swords.

Darius grinned at De La Vega's misunderstanding. "I'll be fine, thanks."

De La Vega advanced. His form was unusual, like a dance. Darius stood in a defensive stance contemplating how best to respond. De La Vega lunged suddenly and then danced away again. Darius felt a sharp pain in his rib and touched his chest with his free hand. He felt blood. The attack had been so fast.

Now Darius moved. He couldn't just stand there and let the man keep poking him. He pursued De La Vega with Striking Adder, but the man danced away. At the end of the form, before Darius could transition to the next, De La Vega darted in again. Darius moved his heavier blade to block but wasn't fast enough. The deflected foil scored a long scratch along his right bicep.

He needed to assess De La Vega's style. Darius moved through a series of defensive stances while he studied his opponent. Wary Badger blocked the next thrust. Willows in the Wind deflected a series of darting jabs and slashes.

"Ah-ha, there we go," De La Vega complimented. "You are doing better."

Darius grinned but his muscles were already starting to ache. He was wishing now that he hadn't practiced so long this morning. Dancing with Lights failed to defend against the spryness of De La Vega's next series of attacks and three more minor wounds were opened on Darius's chest and arms.

A crowd was starting to form now. Hanish was there as well as Anna's uncle. Ranch hands had emerged from buildings surrounding the yard. Some were cheering Darius on while others watched in amazement. Darius saw Nicolai and Gunnar run back into their bunkhouse and return with their quarterstaffs.

De La Vega's fighting style reminded Darius of all the times Arthengal had mentioned the imperial court. Arthengal had repeatedly jested about Eridu's small-town festival dances being nothing compared to an imperial ball.

"You will understand if you ever go to court," Arthengal had teased Darius when he taught Darius a form of his own invention.

Darius moved into the elegant steps, looking similar to De La Vega's movements. The nobleman retreated a step analyzing the form. When Darius appeared to stumble momentarily De La Vega pounced at the opening. The delayed thrust of Fashionably Late met the man as he charged, and Darius's blade sank through his ribs up to the hilt.

Shock filled De La Vega's eyes.

"You have slain me," the strange knight gasped.

It was only then that Darius noticed that De La Vega's rapier had similarly pierced Darius's shoulder. Had it not been for a momentary twist at the end of his maneuver Darius was sure the foil would have struck his heart.

Both men fell backward, the blades tearing free as they parted. Darius gave a grunt as he struck the dirt farmyard and a cloud of dust engulfed him. He heard a woman scream, or multiple women, he couldn't tell. He felt dizzy and wanted to close his eyes. His chest felt warm. He forced himself to sit up. De La Vega would be counter attacking soon. He scrambled to his knees and saw the swordsman lying on the ground. The man's eyes were blank, the spark having left them.

"Sit down." Anna shoved Darius back to the ground. He landed awkwardly on his rump. He tried to focus on her face, but it swam before him.

"Water! Bandages!" Anna shouted. The barnyard came alive with activity. Darius closed his eyes and felt himself starting to drift to sleep. He was so tired.

His eyes shot open again when Anna slapped him. Hard.

"Stay awake, damn you," she admonished.

A drink of water and Anna's ministrations kept Darius from blacking out. Slowly alertness returned as she worked. Anna cleaned the wound then packed a poultice around it. She delicately positioned a patch of folded, white linen over the wound before wrapping the shoulder in strips of cloth. The shoulder dealt with, Anna moved on to the other cuts and scrapes that decorated Darius's chest and arms.

"Put your shirt on," Anna demanded as she secured the bandage atop the last of Darius's wounds.

Darius climbed to his feet gingerly and pulled the shirt on. His head had cleared. His mother had brought him water and Elsie had plied him with bread and meat. He munched half-heartedly on both while Anna tended his wounds.

"Here, you carry the blanket," she said, thrusting it at him.

"What? We're not still going, are we?" Darius said weakly.

"I won't have that ruffian ruin my plans," Anna said with a huff. She seemed more annoyed by the delayed picnic than she did the fight.

Darius glanced around the farmyard. The ground was disturbed from the fight but there was no sign of De La Vega. Several ranch hands had carried the body away.

"Where is the stream?" His voice squeaked when he spoke.

"Just over the hill there. Less than a league. Come on, the walk will do you good." She started walking east and he had to hurry to catch up.

"But," Darius sighed. With the exception of the shoulder, most of the wounds had been minor. He had collapsed from exhaustion and heat more than from blood loss. He admitted that he was feeling better, if still tired. He plodded after her.

"When do you guys have to leave for Kasha Marka?" Anna asked as they walked. Her tone had improved but still held a hint of annoyance.

"I don't know. Your uncle Eban says it's almost a month by horse from here. I told him I wanted to be back before the snows fall."

"So, you're coming back then?" Anna asked.

"Well, yeah. What else am I going to do?" he said. "I wouldn't have a clue what to do in a city that size. Here, I know I can be of help. Your uncle has offered to hire me on permanently and he says my mother and Lianna can stay too."

"What about the others?"

Darius shrugged, "I don't know. I guess I haven't asked them. Nicolai, Gunnar, and Marku said they would travel with me to Kasha Marka. I guess I assumed they would find work once they got there."

Anna nodded thoughtfully. "Why do you have to go?"

"I told you," Darius explained. "Arthengal gave me some of his things that I'm supposed to take to an old friend of his, Saria. Once I do that I can come back."

"What if I came with you?"

"Oh, I don't think your father would like that very much."

"Why not?" she huffed. "I would love to see Kasha Marka. It would be an adventure." Her eyes twinkled. "I've never had an adventure."

"I just don't think he would be too keen on you marching off for two months with four men."

"Isn't Cordelia going?"

"I thought she and Lianna would stay here. There will be a lot to do to get ready for winter. Eban says now that the calves are marked, we'll start separating out last year's steers. We'll drive them up to Isan to sell, maybe in a month or so. After that they'll need to buy and preserve produce to get us through the winter. Mom and Lianna can help Elsie and your aunt Delila with drying fruit and pickling vegetables."

"Oh," Anna seemed disappointed.

They walked in silence for a time. The sun was warm, but not uncomfortable. The smell of ryegrass and clover smelled fresh and clean unlike anything Darius had been used to. In Koza, it had always smelled like salt, and vaguely of fish. In Arthengal's valley he had grown used to the smell of evergreens with an underlying scent of sulfur from the volcanic lake. He inhaled deeply, enjoying the pureness of the air.

I could get used to this, he thought.

The stream flowed through a wide meadow. A handful of apricot trees grew near the edge of the stream. Both of them visibly relaxed at the sight. Darius admitted he did feel better after the walk and Anna's tension had eased while they talked.

Anna angled toward the closest of the trees. They spread the blanket out in the shade of its branches and sat down. Anna started unpacking the basket. She had brought a loaf of bread, apples, cheese, and a large jug of water. She tore off a hunk of bread and handed it to him.

"Thank you," Darius said. He helped himself to the water.

After they had eaten Anna untied the pink ribbon and let her hair spill across her shoulders. She lay back on the blanket and watched the leaves dance in the breeze.

"So, you know," she said, drawing the words out, "I turn sixteen this fall."

"Really?" Darius said, surprised. "I thought you were younger than that."

She sat up suddenly.

"You've known me for almost four years, and you didn't know how old I was?"

"Well, no…it's just that…I always thought. No, I guess not." Darius stumbled over his words. "It's just that you were always so gangly and awkward I just thought you were younger."

She punched him in the right arm, hitting one of the recent injuries. It hurt but didn't start bleeding again.

"Ow," he exclaimed, rubbing the arm.

"Oh, sorry." Momentary concern filled her eyes. Then her tone changed. "Gangly, awkward. You are quite the charmer, Darius Kabir."

"No, what I meant was -- well, like last summer you were still playing with us at your house. Kicking the sheep's bladder around the yard. You know, you weren't that good and..."

Anna's face darkened and her eyes narrowed.

"...not that you were that bad either," he said quickly. "But you know, last summer you were shorter, and skinny, and now—"

"Now what?" She huffed and crossed her arms under her breasts.

"Well, now you're beautiful."

A smile played across her lips. She leaned forward and kissed him softly on the cheek. Her lips lingered for a second, barely brushing his skin before she sat back.

"I only thought you were a year younger," Darius whispered.

"Shut up, you'll ruin it."

He fell silent.

She watched him for another minute, still smiling. Then she leaned casually on her elbows. "So, anyway. I'll be sixteen this fall." She glanced at him out of the corner of her eye, expecting him to say something. When he didn't, she continued. "Most girls back in Eridu would have suitors lined up down the lane by now."

"Suitors?" Darius was confused by the direction of the conversation.

"Of course, if you aren't married by the time you're seventeen you might as well buy a cow and become a milk maid."

"Sixteen!" Darius exclaimed. "Girls get married at sixteen in Eridu? I can't imagine getting married at sixteen. That sounds so young."

"That's because sixteen-year-old boys are idiots," she said with a note of condescension. "And apparently so are eighteen-year-old boys," she added under her breath.

"What was that?" he asked, not sure he'd heard her correctly.

"Nothing," she smirked.

Darius scratched his head. "So, what are you saying? Are you sad because you're not at home and don't have suitors lined up?"

Anna rolled her eyes. "No. That's not what I'm saying. Besides, Caleb Schall, Adin and Libby's boy, from down the lane, came this spring and asked my dad if he could court me."

"So, you're going to marry Caleb Schall?" Darius felt a knot tighten in his stomach.

"No, you idiot," Anna was starting to get flustered. "I don't want to marry Caleb Schall. I want to marry you."

The knot turned into butterflies.

"You want to…wait. What?" Darius could hear his heart pounding. "Since when?"

"Since forever, you dummy. Well, maybe not forever. At first I thought you were pretty gross. I mean, the first time we met you were covered in dirt and your clothes had more holes than hems. But you grew on me." She smiled.

Darius was dumbfounded. Anna was beautiful, of course. But he hadn't ever thought about marriage. He hadn't thought of much in the recent years beyond getting his mother back from the emperor's enslavement. He had always thought he, his mother, Antu, and Arthengal would just stay in the valley and live happily for the rest of their lives.

I mean, a wife would be nice, I guess, he thought. *Someday. But now?*

"So?" Anna asked.

"So, what?" Darius replied.

"Are you going to ask him?"

"Ask who?" Confusion was setting in again. It seemed like they were having different conversations.

"My dad," she said with a sigh. "Are you going to ask him if you can court me?"

Fear suddenly gripped him, which made no sense, because Hanish was one of the nicest men Darius had ever met.

"How would I do that?" Darius said. "I wouldn't know what to say."

"It's easy," she said. Then in a deeper tone that Darius guessed was supposed to be his voice: "Mister Cherian, sir. May I have your permission to court your daughter?"

Darius's eyes bulged.

"I couldn't say that."

"You can and you will," Anna said firmly. Her eyebrows knitted in a determined expression and her arms folded across her chest again.

His arms enveloped her. He did not yet know how he would do it, and he cringed at the thought of Hanish's reaction, but he somehow knew he would be unable to deny Anna her demands.

Chapter Eight
Stones

Micah slammed the door to his room behind him and leaned against it to catch his breath. After a minute he crossed the room and poured water into the ceramic basin that sat on the table. He splashed it on his face and watched as the water turned from clear to gray. Dark rivulets ran down his hands. He scrubbed at his face and his hands until they were clean.

He sniffed. He lifted his shirt to his nose and sniffed again.

That will never do, he thought.

Micah stripped off his clothes and stuffed them into the bottom of his pack. He'd either have to burn them or find a place to clean them himself. The girl that tended his room could never find them.

He smoothed the new shirt out, trying to look more presentable. His hair probably smelled the same as his clothes but there wasn't anything he could do about that without a bath and there wasn't time.

The bells outside were ringing louder. Micah pulled on his boots and hurried out of the room. He entered the common area of the inn and looked around with an exaggerated yawn.

"What's that racket?" he asked one of kitchen hands as he rushed by, carrying a pair of buckets.

"There's a fire, down by the courthouse," the boy replied in a rush. His eyes were wild with fear.

"A fire!" Micah exclaimed. "Do they need help?"

"Yes." The boy looked at him like he was dense. He lifted the buckets in his hands. "That's what the bells are for. They need people for the bucket line. Come on, I'm on my way there."

Micah followed the boy as he rushed out the front of the building and hurried in the direction of the docks. Two lines of people were already forming. One line passed full buckets from the harbor. The second passed the empty buckets back to the water's edge. Half a dozen men scooped water as quickly as they could to keep the cycle moving. The lines twisted around the corner out of view.

Micah found a gap in one of the lines and filled in. He grabbed a bucket and passed it to his neighbor then repeated. He saw Moab hurry up from the left and join the line closer to the turn in the road. Joral and Sasha joined soon after. Micah watched one by one as his men joined the ranks.

Where is Marco? He thought.

Micah continued to watch but Marco never appeared.

Damn it all. Micah stewed.

The water line worked for more than an hour before someone finally called back down the line to halt. Soot-covered men and women began walking from the front.

"What happened?" Micah grabbed the arm of a man as he passed. The man's face was stained black and his eyes were still watering from the smoke.

The man coughed before he could answer. "Well, we stopped the fire from spreading but we couldn't save the command barracks."

"By the gods," Micah exclaimed. "Was anyone hurt?"

"A couple of the senior officers got out, but most didn't. I don't know who made it and who didn't. Do you mind if I go get cleaned up?"

"Of course, of course, sorry," Micah said and released the man's arm.

Micah walked up the street in the direction of the fire. He caught bits and pieces of conversation as he walked.

"Damn shame."

"It's their own fault, threw that barracks up so fast it was a tinderbox."

"It was a lantern."

"It was a spark from the fire."

"The hay caught out back."

"No, someone's blankets caught inside."

"No, the roof caught."

Micah came within view of the command barracks, or what was left of it. The untreated logs and thatch roof had burned fast and hot. Scorch marks scarred some of the surrounding buildings. He scanned the crowd looking for rebel officers. He saw one or two but didn't see Colonel Da Rosa among them.

Then he saw Marco. He slumped against the side of one of the other barracks. His hands were bound behind him and his feet were tied. A thin trail of blood trickled down his forehead and right cheek. His chin rested on his chest. Micah wasn't sure at first if Marco was unconscious or dead. Then the man stirred and let out a groan.

Six soldiers stood guard around Marco. They held long spears, and each wore a cutlass at his waist. Micah was sure Marco had been right behind them when they ran. He had no idea how Marco had been nabbed.

Damn the luck, he thought. There wasn't anything else he could do tonight. They arranged to meet and debrief in the morning.

*****

"We've got to deal with Marco before he can tell them anything of use," Sobol said.

"Marco's a good man," Micah argued. "He won't tell them anything."

"Son," Demir said. "Everyone talks eventually. Especially if Da Rosa's men are doing the asking."

"And with the loss of Da Rosa, they won't be holding back," Captain Sobol added.

Micah nodded his understanding.

"I'll do it. He's my man, it should be me."

Demir cocked his head. "Are you sure?"

"Yeah," Micah sighed. "I'll take care of it. Tonight."

"Okay," Sobol agreed. "But get it done. Marco won't hold out for long. In the meantime, keep the rest of your men out of sight. There are more than a few descriptions floating around and some are more accurate than I would like."

"Do we know who they put in charge?" Demir asked.

"Rouen," Sobol answered. "So, at least that part went according to plan."

"What about the ships and the harbor?" Demir asked.

"Alexov is still working on it," Sobol answered. "They should have something in a day or two."

*****

Micah braced himself against the chimney. He could see the tent where they were interrogating Marco from here. There were surprisingly few positions where he could see into the tent when someone entered or exited, at least not without being in the center of the rebel camp.

The roof sloped more sharply than the neighboring buildings and the wooden shingles were slick under Micah's feet. He ventured a quick glance at the cobblestones in the alley below. It was ten paces at least. If he fell from here, he doubted he would survive.

Micah pressed his foot more tightly against the chimney and scooted back up the roof a bit. He raised his bow carefully. He had only brought one arrow. He wouldn't have time for a second shot. He judged the distance. It was about two hundred paces to the tent. The wind was light from the west. He drew the arrow and waited.

He had seen Marco the last time a soldier had left to relieve himself. They had him strapped to a chair in the center of the tent. His head and body had been slumped forward against his restraints.

Micah's breath was shallow. His fingers were starting to ache. Finally, a sliver of light betrayed someone by the flap of the tent. Two soldiers walked out, holding the flaps aside.

Micah released.

The arrow soared between the shoulders of the two men. Both jumped in surprise.

The flaps of the tent brushed the fletching as they dropped, and the arrow wobbled. Micah couldn't see the result, but from the shouts of alarm inside he knew that he had hit his target. A momentary twinge of guilt was all he could afford. He had to move quickly. Eyes had already turned in his direction.

He scrambled over the peak of the roof and slid down the shingles. He dropped off the edge of the roof and landed lightly on a balcony outside a third-story bedroom. He bounced to the railing and flung himself across the alley to the next building. Micah rolled as he landed, holding his bow out of the way.

Micah stilled his breath momentarily and listened. He heard shouts over the sound of his hammering heart and heard boots slapping the cobblestones. He hung from the railings of the second porch and dropped onto a similar one the level below. From there he jumped to the roof of a small shop at the end of the alley.

"There he is!" Micah heard the call from the end of the alleyway.

He sprinted across the roof and leapt to the next building. Shouts came from the right so he veered left. The buildings were close together here and he could move easily from rooftop to rooftop. More shouts rang out and he turned again. They were driving him toward a more prosperous section of town. The buildings would be farther apart there. He had to lose them.

Micah ducked under a clothesline stretched across a rooftop garden. The stone parapet crumbled as his foot pushed off. He managed to grab the roof edge on the neighboring building, but his breath was knocked out of him as he slammed into the wall. He almost lost his grip. Scrambling quickly, he continued his flight.

He spied a small stable yard to his left, his original escape plan, and angled in its direction. Micah sprinted the distance and without looking leapt off the opposite side. His stomach jolted at the sensation of falling, then he tucked and landed in the wagon full of hay.

Micah scrambled out the back of the wagon and dove into a covered sheep pen as torches passed on the bordering street. He waited with bated breath as the sound of the soldiers turned down another alley and faded.

He exited the pen quickly, sticking to the shadows. He crept along the sides of buildings and down darkened back streets, making his way back to the inn. Only after he was safe in his room and had collapsed on his bed did Micah allow himself the luxury of emotion. He sighed deeply, knowing that what he had done was necessary for the security of their mission. Marco had been a good man and it pained Micah to have lost him. He whispered a quick prayer that to the gods and the Holy Emperor to ask that they watch over Marco's soul.

*****

Micah watched the harbor from the window of his room. He hadn't been outside in two days. The search continued in the city for the assassin who had killed Rouen's prisoner.

"It's your turn," the ancient man said.

Micah turned back to the board. Guo Wen had placed a black stone alongside one of his white stones in the center of the board. The old man had been keeping Micah company during his sequestration and had decided to pass the time by teaching Micah to play wei-chi. Guo Wen had destroyed him during the first few games, but Micah was starting to get the hang of it.

He could extend his position and block Guo Wen's attempt to surround his stones but eventually he would run into a wall that the old man had already established in the south. He could try to turn Guo Wen's assault and claim a small amount of territory, but Guo

Wen would claim a larger section of the board as a result. Finally, Micah decided to sacrifice the stone and placed a white piece in the west to block Guo Wen's incursion there.

Guo Wen nodded appreciatively at the move.

"It is not many who are willing to sacrifice one soldier for the sake of the larger battle," Guo Wen said.

"You call the stones soldiers. Why?" Micah asked.

"Wei-chi is like war. It is a battle for territory and control. There is never a way to control all of your opponent's men. You will lose territory if you try. Control your opponent's most dangerous assaults, sacrifice those of limited value. In the end, if you control the flow of the battle you will find that you win the war instead."

Micah turned back to the window as Guo Wen considered his next move. He saw a ship leaving the pier. It was one of the larger merchantmen. The sails were drawn on two of the three masts.

The ship turned north, unusual since the entry to the port was directly west. Micah's eyes lifted to the four towers guarding the entrance of the harbor. In the distance he could see a large red flag being flapped wildly by someone in the tower.

The ship turned. It started to go west but then drifted south. It looked as if the captain of the ship had started his morning with a few pints at the Dusty Sailor.

Or maybe he's still going from last night, Micah thought as the ship made another sharp turn.

The ship was drifting north again and was going to miss the mouth of the harbor if the captain didn't correct. Micah heard a horn echo across the broad expanse of water. The ship made another dangerous turn that left it angling toward the closest tower.

The horn blasted repeatedly now but the ship didn't slow. It looked, for a moment, like the captain was going to correct and make the channel between the rock jetties and the stone towers but at the last minute it veered again. Micah watched in horror as the sails suddenly billowed as they caught a breeze coming off the Sea of Tears. The bow crashed into the base of the closest tower. Stone and wood shattered. The ship slipped off the rocks and settled into the water. Micah watched as the vessel sank, like a great whale submerging after a breach. Soon only the tallest mast remained above water adorned with a single flag flapping a golden lion on a field of blue.

The groan and snap of stone could be heard across the bay. Micah's eyes shifted to the tower. It was like watching an old fir tree fall. First it leaned precariously toward the channel. Then the top of the beacon picked up speed. Stones showered the shore and water as the tower collapsed. The top of the structure collided with the mainmast of the ship and then even the last vestiges of the craft were gone. Waves rolled toward the shore rocking the boats that remained moored at the port.

Guo Wen placed a stone. "And they are blocked in the west."

Micah turned in shock. The man's face was calm. There was even the hint of a smile. Understanding dawned.

"Alexov?" Micah asked.

Guo Wen nodded. "A sacrifice worth every stone."

Chapter Nine
Assault

Micah hid in the shadows of the alley, watching the gate. Even in the city he could smell the mist and dew that came with predawn. He glanced up at a series of rhythmic thumps. Another volley of arrows had struck the wooden planks on the second story of the buildings to either side of his hiding place. Another soldier fell off the wall, landing a dozen paces away.

The rebel pikemen were forming up inside the gate. A bugle blasted down the road a ways and a dozen soldiers moved into position to lift the massive crossbeam. Once it was out of the way a pair of men to either side of the gate began working the counterweights. The hinges squealed as doors as thick as a man's arm was long slowly parted and swung outward.

Before the opening reached half its full width another bugle cry sounded. The pikemen began marching. Micah couldn't see them once they passed the bulk of the wall but he guessed they were forming up on the field outside. Micah tried to count them as they passed but failed.

The pikemen were followed by archers who would form up to the rear. The attackers were already stretching the range of the soldiers on the wall. Having bowmen in the field would allow the rebels to press the attack.

The ground shook as the cavalry approached. Micah was impressed by the horsemen, dressed in full armor, holding lances high, as they thundered past. It would be truly terrifying to meet them on the field. He wished he could watch the melee outside, but he had his own concerns.

The last of the horses exited and the iron-banded doors began to swing closed again. Micah heard the thump as they settled into their final position. He eased out of the alley. When he was sure none of the soldiers at the gate were looking his direction, he sprinted the distance to the wall and knelt behind a barrel of water.

The rain of arrows from outside had stopped. Micah scanned the rooftops and saw shadows moving across them. He heard the call of a falcon in the darkness above and he got ready to run.

A barrage of wood and steel crossed the short distance overhead as the Daku Mitu began firing on the wall from above. Cries of alarm rose, but Micah paid them no mind. He was already moving. He drew his sword as he ran. Two squads of Night Birds and at least that many Mortikai emerged from the darkness and descended on the gate.

The first soldier that Micah encountered was so shocked he didn't even have time to raise his weapon. Micah cut him down as he ran past. He had his sights set on the captain of the gate guard. He was a wiry man in his forties and looked like he could handle himself in a fight. Micah was determined to find out.

Micah danced past the captain's first attack using Rose at Sunset. The captain quickly adjusted and attacked with Lion Shakes his Mane. Their swords clashed as Micah refused to yield the attack. Micah was pressed into the man using his greater weight to drive the smaller man back. The captain spun out of the melee and reengaged Micah from the right. The captain used more precise, lighter strikes, recognizing that he couldn't overpower Micah.

Micah settled into a series of defensive forms waiting for an opening. When he saw it he sprang. Dancing Mongoose scored matching strikes on both of the captain's shoulders. The officer staggered back. Micah pressed the attack and hamstrung the man with Scooping the Moon. Micah finished it with a final thrust and then looked around for another opponent.

Ropes fell from the roofs above and men dressed in black began rappelling down the buildings. They stormed the ladders leading up to the walkway atop the wall. The few remnants of the wall guard fought valiantly but were no match for the Daku Mitu.

A soldier rushed Micah from the side, but he fell to a Mortikai saber before reaching Micah. The gate was theirs. Micah began shouting orders to the Night Birds to form up and prepare to defend the gate from anyone that attacked from inside the city.

The fighting above them on the walkway died out and he could hear the commander on the wall assembling imperial archers.

Micah and his men waited but no attack came. It appeared that Captain Rouen had fully committed to routing the attackers. With no reserves remaining inside the city, Captain Rouen would have no way to retake the gates once they were closed without laying siege to the city.

Stupid, Micah thought. *And arrogant.*

Micah reminded himself to always leave men in reserve. With that in mind, he searched the darkness for Moab, lurking in the shadows with twenty more men, prepared to surprise any counterattack from behind. A brief glint of steel in the torchlight gave away his friend's position, if one knew where to look.

Above him the imperial archers began firing on Rouen's back lines. The archers would be the first target to prevent any counterattack. With nowhere to retreat, a highly mobile force to his front, and fortified archery units to his rear, Rouen would be finished by midday.

Chapter Ten
Lieutenant Kabir

The First Order filed through the open gates of Eridu at a slow trot. Jun's covered carriage was in the middle of the precession. He could hear the shouts and cheering as he approached the wall. He pulled back the silk curtains to watch the crowds as he passed. Hundreds lined the streets. Even if half of them were his soldiers it was still heartening. He felt pride at the successful liberation of Eridu. It would be the first of many.

Jun waved at a pretty girl in the front of the onlookers. She was waving a silk, yellow handkerchief and was shouting.

"Long live the emperor. May the gods bless Emperor Lao."

When she caught his eye and saw him wave, she fainted. A burly soldier keeping the crowds out of the street caught her before she hit the stones on the road. Jun smiled faintly. Yes, it felt good to be loved by his people. There would be dissenters, of course, there always were. But for now, he contented himself to bask in the joy of the liberated.

The procession wound through the streets and stopped in front of the magistrate's court. Guo Wen's first act after the liberation had been to convert the hall into imperial quarters, of a sort. It was still not a palace, but it would be more appropriate than the small house he had lived in during his exile.

A dozen imperial guards surrounded Jun as he stepped out of the carriage. Guo Wen and Captain Sobol waited for him on the steps of the hall. Both took a knee and lowered their heads as he approached.

"Your Majesty," Guo Wen spoke. "Welcome to Eridu."

"Thank you, uncle." Jun nodded his head slightly. "Shall we tour my new quarters?"

"Of course." Guo Wen rose.

Captain Sobol glanced up, uncertain how to proceed since he hadn't been addressed.

"You may join us, captain," Jun said graciously.

"Thank you, Majesty."

Guo Wen led Jun up the marble steps of the three-story stone building. The building had a main entrance hall and matching wings angled slightly toward the center of town. If his memory was correct, the western wing had been the home and offices of the mayor of Eridu. The eastern wing had been the court and held offices for the more prominent magistrates.

A broad expanse of grass surrounded the building. The lawn was still in poor condition due to the tents and men that had occupied it less than a month earlier. Captain Sobol's men had removed all the tents but it would take the groundskeepers the rest of the summer to repair the damage.

"Has the transition been peaceful?" Jun asked.

"There were a few incidents early on, but they were dealt with quickly," Guo Wen responded. "When it became clear that we meant the residents and refugees no harm, order was restored. We've set up temporary camps outside of town for the refugees. Many also returned to their homes in the north once we assured them that the barbarian threat had been dealt with and there would be no more summer raids."

Guo Wen led Jun into the eastern wing first.

"This is where the imperial guard will be quartered, Majesty."

Jun inspected the quarters. The offices had been cleared and rooms had been set up for the officers. The rest of the guard would sleep on cots in the two spacious court rooms.

"General Nowak will be taking over here once the Commander General leads our forces south. Have arrangements been made for him and his men?" Jun said as he casually examined the rooms.

"Yes, Majesty." Captain Sobol replied this time. "We've cleared several fields past the eastern gate for the general to set up a command post and camp. They will have easy access to provide for the defense of the city without creating a burden on the town directly. As ordered, sir."

"Good." Jun was pleased. He wanted the people to be assured that their lives would be improved by the liberation, especially the merchants, and quartering troops in the city would not lend itself well to that goal.

Guo Wen returned to the spacious entry hall where twin marble staircases led to the upper floors. Starting on the ground floor, Jun followed Wen into the western wing.

"What's the condition of the harbor?" Jun asked as he entered the former mayor's audience room.

A high-backed leather chair had been placed at the southern end of the room. Wooden benches were aligned along the northern wall. A red carpet, two paces wide, decorated with entwined golden dragons, led from the petitioners' benches to the imperial seat.

"We cleared the debris. Twenty ships were in port during the liberation. We have reimbursed the captains appropriately and sent the ships north to meet Admiral Kusami at Tuding Harbor," Guo Wen explained. "Kasha Amur is still in disarray. News of Eridu has reached them, of course, but they can't seem to decide on a response. From what we hear, they can't decide on a plan of attack."

Jun smiled. "That was the plan. Please send word to ministers Cray and Aydin that it is time to send their armies north. We don't want General Sharav to have to march the entire length of the province to meet them."

"As you say, Majesty." Guo Wen nodded.

"You look confused, Captain," Jun noted, seeing the emotion plainly on Sobol's face.

"No, Majesty. Well, yes, Majesty. I was just unaware we had support in the ministry."

"A little secret of ours, Captain. Minister Cray and Minister Aydin lead opposite factions in the ministry. It took decades to position them. Their supposed opposite views have allowed us to keep Shalanum province from meeting its full potential over the years. It has also been helpful to dampen their response during this latest crisis."

"I see, Majesty. Do we have similar operatives in the other provinces?" Captain Sobol asked.

Jun gave the captain a condescending smile. "Let's just focus on Shalanum province for now, shall we?"

"Of course, Your Majesty," Sobol said quickly. "Apologies."

Jun followed as Guo Wen exited the audience chamber and walked up the two flights of stairs to the imperial apartments. The rooms were lavishly decorated with hand-carved furniture, silk draperies, and woven tapestries depicting peaceful scenes of nature and wild animals.

Jun stopped before one tapestry. It was an expertly woven piece showing a black panther resting in the branches of a kapok tree. The lush rainforest spread out behind the creature. The panther's eyes seemed alive and appeared to follow him as Jun proceeded down the hallway.

"Tell me about the battle, Captain. How did it go?"

"As well as we could have hoped, Majesty. Once our light cavalry began bombarding the city, Captain Rouen led the majority of his men onto the field. He meant to crush our forces decisively. He only left a few hundred defending the walls and gates and we dispatched them with minimal losses. After that we had him trapped between both our forces. Once he realized his mistake, he led his horsemen in a retreat to the south. His pikemen and archers tried to follow but we harried them through the entire retreat. Rouen escaped with less than half his men and at last report our scouts indicated he leads a forced march to Port of Giselle."

"Our losses?" Jun asked.

"Five hundred casualties in all, Majesty. Mostly from the Eridu partisans, but Rouen did lead a spirited retreat and we lost a third of our light cavalry."

When they arrived at Jun's private parlor he stopped outside the door.

"Captain Sobol," he said. "Thank you for the excellent work by you and your men. You are to be commended on a successful campaign. If you will excuse us now, I would like to have a private word with Minister Guo."

"Of course, Your Majesty." Sobol snapped a quick bow and then retreated down the hallway.

"A good man," Guo Wen noted. "If somewhat unimaginative."

"Yes," Jun considered as he watched the officer retreat. "Speaking of imaginative, how is my little pet project, Mustar Atmu?"

"He's got a good head for strategy, that one," Guo Wen said, dropping the formality now that Sobol was gone. "He played me within fifty points on more than one occasion, and unlike our esteemed Commander General, the boy seems to actually understand the relationship between wei-chi and battle tactics. With proper training he could become a good officer."

Jun nodded. "His training may have to be in the field. I have a few ideas. Send him up when we are through. I would like to see how he plays. But first, tell me of our search for the reliquary."

*****

When Guo Wen exited the emperor's chamber, he found Captain Sobol waiting for him in the hallway.

"Can I help you with something, Captain?" Guo Wen asked.

The captain seemed uncertain at first then he cleared his throat. "Master Guo, may I ask you a question?"

Guo waved his hand indicating to proceed.

"Our approach to managing the populace here in Eridu. Should we not take a heavier hand to restore order?"

"You question your emperor's orders, Captain?" Guo Wen asked.

"No! Of course not," Sobol responded quickly. He seemed to consider for a moment. "I only wish to understand better what we do here."

The captain grows bold. Could this be the influence of our young Lieutenant?

"Captain, let me ask you something. Where do you get the supplies to feed your men?"

"We purchase meat and grain from the local farms," Captain Sobol responded.

"And clothing, shoes, repairs for your weapons, gear for your horses? Where does that all come from?"

"The merchants and shopkeepers here in Eridu."

"Do you suggest we procure those supplies elsewhere?" Guo Wen asked.

"No, but do we have to pay market prices for things? It seems like a waste of resources when we could just take what we need."

"Ah, I see," Guo Wen replied. "How motivated would the farmers and the merchants be to continue to produce what our men need if they were not paid a fair amount for their goods and services?"

"But we had no need to pay such exorbitant prices in the north. The workers were housed and fed and clothed. That and the devotion of the emperor was motivation enough."

Guo Wen laughed. "Possibly. It could be that the presence of several thousand soldiers motivated them as well. Dear Captain, this is not the Northern Wastes. There the workers had nowhere to run, nowhere to hide. They did not have the support of foreign armies. If we try to employ the same tactics here as we did there, we will soon find abandoned farms and shops as people flee in the night to Kasha Amur or Kasha Marka. A wise leader knows when to employ force and when to employ guile. If we have to give a few marks back to the merchants and farmers to keep the economy going and the people calm and happy, isn't it worth it? Or would you rather deal with rebellion and desertion?"

Captain Sobol considered his words for a long moment. "I think I understand, sir. Thank you for explaining it to me." The captain bowed quickly and left.

*****

"Enter," Jun responded at the knock at his parlor door. He marked his place in the book that he had been reading and closed it on his lap.

An imperial servant entered and knelt on the mat just inside the door. The man wore blue robes to mark his station as a senior attendant. His head was shaven, as was tradition. The servant waited patiently to be addressed.

"What is it?" Jun asked.

"There is a soldier here to see you, Majesty. Sergeant Micah Kabir."

"Thank you, please show him in."

The servant retreated. Sergeant Kabir entered and stood awkwardly by the door. The attendant cleared his throat. Belatedly, the sergeant remembered to bow at the waist with his eyes at the floor. Jun grinned. Protocol was definitely not his strength.

"You may rise, Mustar Atmu," Jun said.

The soldier blushed at the nickname and seemed uncertain what to say. He settled on a mumbled, "Thank you, Majesty."

"My uncle tells me that you have been learning wei-chi." Jun waved a hand to the wooden board set on a table between his padded chair and a more utilitarian wooden chair on the opposite side. Jun placed his book on a table beside his chair.

Sergeant Kabir seemed confused. "Master Guo is your uncle?"

Jun nodded. "He is my mother's brother. He is a trusted advisor. He has been teaching you the game?" Jun repeated the question.

"Yes, Your Majesty," Micah answered. "I don't think I'm that good, though. He beats me every time."

"Let me be the judge of how good you are," Jun said mildly. "Guo Wen is a renowned master at the game. I rarely beat him myself. I would be surprised if you had beaten him. Would you join me for a game?" He gestured to the wooden chair.

"Of course, Your Majesty," Micah said after a moment's pause.

The young soldier seated himself, somewhat uncomfortably, and stared at the board. A bowl of white stones had been placed on the north side of the board and a bowl of black stones rested to the south. He glanced up at Jun, obviously not sure how to proceed.

"It would be tradition to allow your emperor to place first," Jun quipped.

"Of course," Micah said, relaxing only a little. "Your move, sir. I mean, Your Majesty."

Jun selected a white stone from the bowl and placed it on the shaded circle in the northeast corner at the intersection between the third lines.

"Captain Sobol said that you performed well during the liberation of the city," Jun commented while he waited for Kabir's move.

The sergeant placed a black stone in the northwest corner at the intersection of the third column and second row. It was a more conservative opening move and demonstrated caution.

"Thank you, Majesty. I helped take the gate. Our work wasn't as difficult as the men who had to capture the wall or the soldiers outside facing the rebel forces. We played our part, but those were the true heroes of the liberation."

Jun placed in the southeast, claiming that corner and strengthening his position on the eastern wall. Kabir followed suit and claimed the southwest.

"I've also heard word that you had to deal with an uncomfortable situation with one of your men. He was captured, I understand?"

"Yes sir," Micah said sadly, forgetting the honorific again. "Marco was a good man. It was a shame."

"Sacrifices must be made in any war, but it is always a shame when they occur," Jun consoled.

Jun played in the southeast again, locking his position there. "I have word that your brother passed through here before we liberated the city."

Micah stiffened at the change in subject and glanced at Jun. "I had not heard that." The sergeant recovered and then placed a black stone along the eastern wall at the intersection of the midline and second row. It was an aggressive move that split Jun's eastern forces. Apparently, he had touched a nerve with the young man.

Jun counterattacked by placing a white stone close and just inside Micah's western position in the south. What followed was a quick sequence of placements which ended with Jun controlling most of the south. Micah had lost his hold on the southwest corner but had formed a defensive line of eyes to guard his northwestern position. This put the sergeant in a good place to control most of the west. Play slowed after that as the two men considered their next moves.

"Our operatives have been tracking your brother, with limited success, toward Isan." Jun picked up the prior conversation.

"What's in Isan?" Micah asked.

Jun strengthened his position in the north extending his position along the wall. Kabir answered by moving diagonally from his northern position trying to join with his line to the south.

"Friends of your brother and the traitor Nasu Rabi, from what I've been told," Jun answered as he continued his effort in the north.

Micah shrugged and moved toward the center.

"Your mother is there, too." This earned another suspicious glance. "Do you really think you can bring your brother to our cause?"

"I'm sure I can," Micah insisted. "He just needs to see reason."

"I don't know," Jun drawled. "He hasn't been very *reasonable* with our agents so far."

"You've been chasing him?" There was just the hint of an edge to his voice.

"We've been following him," Jun corrected. "We suspect he has something that may belong to the imperial throne. An artifact of sorts that my cousin, Emperor Chen, is said to have lost after his defeat at the battle for Kasha Esharra. General Alamay commanded the insurgency there so it is reasonable to assume he may have stolen it."

"Why would Darius have it?" Micah asked.

"We're not sure he does," Jun admitted. "However, he carries a very expensive looking box, the type you might store an artifact of such importance in. It is rumored that he is taking this box to Kasha Marka. It would make sense that if General Alamay was guarding this relic, then he would want it sent into the protection of Baroness Magora upon his death."

"Hmm." Micah nodded, seeming to accept the explanation.

Jun took a moment to study the board while he waited for the sergeant's next play. Kabir had secured most of the west and a third of the north. Jun owned the south and the rest of the north. The center of the board remained contested.

At this point, Micah did something that surprised Jun. He placed a black stone in the east, two spaces diagonally from the stone he had placed on his third move. Jun realized that he could race to secure more territory, but he could not stop Micah from linking this group of stones to the series of eyes he had built during the battle for the southwest. A sequence of placements played out in Jun's mind. If Micah placed just right, he would secure the center of the board and most of the west. The game would be close to a draw. So close that Jun felt his heart race at the prospect. He forgot the conversation and focused on the board.

Jun sat back in his chair with a sigh once it was done. He steepled his fingers and rested his chin on his thumbs and counted the points again. He had won, but only by five points. It was exhilarating. He had been playing Sengiin Sharav for decades and the commander general had not come this close to beating him since Jun had been a boy. He studied the young man, who was also counting the stones. He seemed genuinely disappointed.

"Good game, Your Majesty," Micah said, finally looking up.

"Indeed," Jun smiled.

"I thought I had you for a moment, but I couldn't outpace your soldiers in the north." Micah smiled as well.

"Tell me, sergeant," Jun started. "Would you like the chance to bring your brother into the imperial fold?"

"Yes, sir...I mean, Majesty."

"I would like you to take the Night Birds to Isan and see if you can convince him."

"Me?" Micah said, surprised. "Surely, you mean Lieutenant Demir."

"I have decided that Lieutenant Demir will take over command of the rest of the blood knives. Lieutenant Alexov's sacrifice was supreme and it is only fair to those men that they be placed under the command of another veteran from the liberation. You will take over command of the Night Birds, Lieutenant Kabir."

The soldier was dumbfounded. His mouth hung open slightly and he seemed to be trying to absorb the news.

"General Hamazi has already sent a detachment of lancers toward Isan," Jun continued. "You will meet them there."

Micah nodded dumbly.

"I do not know who commands the lancers." Jun reached inside the folds of his robes and produced a parchment sealed with wax, stamped with the imperial seal. "Show the commander this. It gives you authority over both units. It will eliminate any confusion in command since I'm sure the officer there will be your senior, by years of service, if not rank."

Micah accepted the letter, holding it lightly in his hand. He ran his thumb over the wax seal reverently.

"It has been a pleasure playing with you, Lieutenant. We must play again when you return."

Micah took this for the dismissal that it was and stood.

"And Lieutenant." Micah turned from his walk to the door. "Even if your brother is not ready to join us, please see that you retrieve my property and return it. If he has it, of course."

"Of course, Your Majesty."

Jun grinned to himself as the door closed.

Chapter Eleven
Wrath

Darius watched the wind play with the yellow and orange leaves over his head. Even in the warm afternoon sun the wind brought a chill. The mountains to the east were already starting to show white caps along the jagged peaks. It would be time to go soon if he was going to make it back to the ranch before winter.

"Another, please."

He glanced down to his lap where Anna's smiling face beamed back. Her head rested on his thigh and her body stretched out across the blanket. He reached into the small tin box on the blanket next to him and pulled out one of the wrinkled brown objects. He placed one gingerly inside Anna's open mouth.

"Mmm," she moaned in delight. "So sweet."

The dates had cost him nearly a month's wages when the trader had come through last week, making the overland trek from Kantibar to Eridu. Such merchants were rare, but when they did travel through, they always brought strange and wonderful delicacies. The dates had been worth every penny to see Anna's delight with each bite.

Of course, Darius didn't really need the wages that Anna's uncle paid him. He had over two hundred marks stashed in his belongings that Arthengal and he had saved over the years. His mother also managed the money they had made from selling the emperor's horses which she used to cover their expenses. He was happy to spend his earnings from the ranch on things for Anna.

"Another, please."

He smiled as he placed another delicacy between her plump red lips. A groan drew his attention to the left. Antu yawned as he stretched in the autumn sun. Lianna grunted again as the bear disturbed her. When Antu had finished repositioning himself Lianna sank back against his bulk and opened her book to the place marked by her finger.

Lianna satisfied one of Hanish's courtship requirements. If Darius and Anna were going to spend time together, he insisted on a chaperone. He had muttered something about "knowing what young men were like" and had stomped off in mock indignation. The truth was Darius couldn't remember ever seeing Hanish so happy.

"She doesn't talk much, does she?" Anna whispered, nodding in Lianna's direction.

Darius thought about it. "I can't say that I've ever heard her talk. Maybe to my mother but she's never said a word to me."

"So, if she doesn't talk, how is she going to tell Daddy if we sneak a kiss or two?" There was a mischievous glint in Anna's eyes.

Darius laughed. "I'm sure your father would find a way. I made him a promise to be a proper gentleman and I intend to honor that promise. Besides, spending time with you is reward enough."

Anna rolled her eyes. "Another, please."

Anna wiped the edge of her mouth with her sleeve after she finished swallowing the date. "Antu seems to like Lianna."

Darius nodded. "I think he knows she is special. He is always gentle with her. He keeps almost as close an eye on her as he does me. I think we are his adopted cubs." Darius laughed at the thought.

Anna smiled and watched the pair a moment longer.

"Why don't you ever talk about Micah anymore?" Anna asked.

The abrupt change in subject caught Darius by surprise and his mood immediately darkened.

"You used to talk about him all the time when you would visit." Anna continued. "I haven't heard you mention his name once since you arrived."

"He betrayed us," Darius growled. "He is dead to me."

"Wait, what?" Anna sat up suddenly. "What are you talking about?"

"He was there, with *them*. The night that Arthengal was killed. He was *helping* them."

"He's alive?" she exclaimed. "Well, that's wonderful. I thought he had died in the raid all those years ago."

"No." Darius heard his voice beginning to rise. "He survived. And then, after we rescued our mother he was there, killing the rest of those poor people we had rescued. *Slaughtering* them."

"You saw him slaughtering people?" Shock filled her eyes and she stifled a gasp with a hand to her mouth.

"No," Darius admitted. "But he was there and that's what the emperor's men were doing. He didn't try to stop it. He was armed. He said they were there for Arthengal and me."

"You talked to him?" Anna furrowed her brow. "How come Cordelia never said anything? Wait! Does your mother even know he's alive?"

"No. I couldn't bring myself to tell her that he had betrayed us."

"He's her son." Darius was taken aback by Anna's sudden anger. "She has a right to know that he's alive."

"He betrayed us," Darius repeated, but with less force than before.

"Darius Kabir," Anna said firmly. "Micah is your brother. He was a slave to the empire for four years, just like your mother. You have no idea what they did to him. How they may have manipulated him to get him to fight for them. You see how Marku is. How his hands shake every time he has to touch an axe to chop wood."

"What about Marku?"

"Your mother said they beat him until he couldn't even look at a weapon let alone raise one in anger."

"She never told me that." Darius was mystified. "That explains --"

"Don't change the subject." Anna's voice rose. "You have to tell your mother that Micah is alive. I can't believe you kept that from her. I am so mad at you right now. It's shameful."

Darius was rescued from further tongue lashing by the approach of a rider.

What now? Darius thought. He had been assaulted twice more since the fight in early summer. Now, anytime he saw someone he didn't recognize approaching it put him on edge. He stood and picked up the scabbard from next to the blanket.

Both horse and man were sweating, and Darius could tell they had been riding hard. Darius didn't recognize the man, but he was dressed like a ranch hand, so Darius relaxed.

"Sorry to interrupt." The rider was out of breath. He removed his brimmed hat to wipe his arm across his brow and then replaced it before continuing. "Nicolai said I should ride here as fast as I can. He's off to get Gunnar and warn the others."

Nicolai had been helping out on the Abrams ranch on the other side of the valley the past few weeks. That explained why Darius didn't recognize the ranch hand.

"Warn them about what?" Darius asked.

"A couple hundred lancers just rode into Isan. They fly the flag of the black dragon. They've been asking around in town about a group that sounds just like you and your friends. They described you right down to the scar on your eye."

"Imperials," Darius spat the word.

He belted on his sword and without another word he untethered his horse and mounted.

"Darius, wait!" He heard Anna call from behind, but he was already riding in the direction of the houses.

*****

Anna galloped into the yard as Darius was coming out of the bunk house strapping his second sword belt around his waist. Lianna clung to Anna's waist as Anna reined in the horse.

"What are you doing?" she panted.

Darius saw Hanish sprinting in their direction. A cloud of dust rose behind him as he ran.

"They're looking for me," Darius barked. His hands were practically shaking with rage. "I'm gonna make them wish they weren't."

Hanish skidded to a stop in front of him and placed a hand on his chest.

"Whoa, boy. Nicolai and Gunnar just told us. You best not be thinking about doing something crazy."

"They killed Arthengal, Hanish. They deserve to die." Darius spoke through clenched teeth. He could feel the muscles of his face twitch with each word.

Hanish took a step back at the ferocity in Darius's voice, but he kept the hand on Darius's chest.

"And what happens when you go off and get yourself killed?" Hanish spoke so softly Darius could barely hear him. "What happens to your mother? What happens to Anna and the rest of us? I know you are hurting, and you are angry, but this isn't the way."

A crowd was gathering around them. Cordelia and Elsie watched from the porch of one of the cabins. Nicolai and Gunnar stood by one of the corrals; both held quarterstaffs. Kal leaned casually against the stone well, bow in hand. Several other men had wandered in from the barn and cattle pens.

"Look around you, Darius." Hanish continued to speak so quietly that the sound didn't carry beyond Darius's ears. "If'n you go off and do this crazy thing some of those men will follow you. You won't just be forfeiting your life but theirs as well. There are two hundred lancers up in Isan. Trained soldiers. Do you think any of these men would stand a chance?"

Darius glanced around at the assembly. Doubt filled his eyes followed by tears. Darius's shoulders slumped and he hung his head. "What would you have me do then? They deserve to be punished. If they aren't Arthengal died for nothing."

"No," Hanish corrected, firmly. "Arthengal died protecting you and your mother. As for punishing, that ain't your job. Your job is to protect your kin and your friends. Going off on a fool's errand like this would just be dying."

"Tell me what to do," Darius whispered. The rage that had filled him only moments before had left him and he felt exhausted.

"You run, boy," Hanish said. "All of you. They ain't looking for none of us. The descriptions they're passing around are just you and those that come with you."

Anna's uncle Eban had joined them and stood a few paces off.

"Run where?" Darius asked. "The road to Kasha Marka is north, toward Isan. That's where you're telling me not to go."

"There might be another way," Eban said.

Both Hanish and Darius looked at the man.

"There's a pass south of here. It heads up into the mountains where there is an enclave of sorts. I wouldn't call it a city, more like a mountain fort. A crazy old man owns the place. It's not a very good road and the traders don't go that way much. It takes twice as long to get to Kasha Marka as the north road. The pass will be snowed shut in the winter, but it should still be open now."

Darius considered and then nodded.

Hanish patted his chest. "Good boy. Now let's get you some gear for the trip."

"I'm going too," Anna piped up.

"Damned if you are, girl," Hanish snapped back. "You are staying right here with your family."

"But --" Tears started to well in her eyes.

"None of that," Hanish narrowed his eyes. "That might work when you're trying to buy you a pony, but it ain't gonna work for going off on some hairbrained adventure with some boy you ain't even married to yet. No offense, Darius."

Darius grinned despite himself.

"Now go help your ma to get together some food and supplies. And saddle their horses. It's best they set off as soon as they can. It won't be long before someone points those soldiers in this direction."

Anna hurried off, wiping her eyes. Once she was gone, Kal strode up and stood tall in front of his father.

"I would like to go, sir."

Hanish considered his son for a moment.

"Fine," he sighed. "But you listen to Darius and the other men. And keep yourself out of trouble. If'n there's fighting to be done, you let the other men handle it."

"Thank you," Kal said, and raced to the barn.

Darius felt numb. It barely registered when Kal insisted on coming but as a few other men approached him and asked if they could go as well, his heart lightened. He had made friends here, and they were determined to see him to safety.

Autumn 34 A.E.

Chapter Twelve
Duty

Micah rode into the camp astounded at the lack of order. The tents were organized haphazardly. The horse pickets were unmanned. There were lances lying in the mud, and worse, bows, still strung, leaning against tents with their string nocks stuck in the dirt. He had heard stories lauding General Hamazi for his tactical skill. He had not expected the camp of one of his officers to demonstrate such disorder.

"Is that screaming?" Joral whispered. He and Moab rode close behind Micah having appointed themselves his personal guard.

Another cry echoed through the camp.

"Yep, definitely screaming," Moab commented with less subtlety.

Micah shuddered. This camp did not represent what he had become used to serving with the imperial army. If disgrace wasn't the right word it was close. Micah wanted to limit the exposure to his men until he could investigate the cause of such atrocious discipline. He turned to one of his sergeants, Frederick. "Sergeant Garin. Take the rest of the men and set up camp on that rise over there. I want a good view of the surrounding area."

"Yes, sir," the soldier replied and began shouting orders to the men. Two files of horsemen peeled off to the east leaving Micah with Joral and Moab as escorts.

Screams echoed through the camp again. Micah did not approve of torture. There was always a better way to get information. He observed the resident soldiers as they steered their horses between the tents. A few flinched each time a scream rang out, but most seemed oblivious to the noise. That was bad. Either these men were monsters or the practice was commonplace and it no longer bothered them.

Micah made for what he assumed was the command tent. It was larger than the rest and two soldiers stood casually outside posting what Micah assumed was meant for a guard. Micah dismounted and was followed by the other two. He handed his reins to Joral and approached the entrance of the tent.

"Is your commander inside?" Micah asked the soldiers in front of the tent.

The guard studied Micah for a moment, maybe mistaking him for a messenger. Then he seemed to notice the patch of rank on Micah's black coat. "Yes, sir."

"I would like to speak to him, if you please." Micah's voice was calm but firm.

"He's busy," the second soldier replied.

"I'm here on business from the emperor. Make him unbusy," Micah's tone changed to one of command.

The first guard smirked. "Okay, but he's not going to like it."

Micah chose to ignore the impudence, for the time being.

The soldier ducked his head inside the tent and shouted. "Lieutenant Zhukov. There's a soldier out here to see you. Says he brings a message from the emperor."

There was a rustling inside the tent. A few moments later a man in his mid-thirties emerged, his person reflecting the state of his camp. His coat was unbuttoned to the waist and he was buckling his belt as he emerged. It looked like he hadn't shaved in at least a week and his dark brown hair was tussled.

"Give her a few minutes and then show her back to town," Zhukov addressed the two soldiers.

Moab started to grin before Micah gave him a withering glare and then he dropped his eyes to the ground.

"What is it? Lieutenant." Zhukov seemed surprised to see Micah's rank.

"Do you have somewhere we can speak more privately?" Micah asked.

"Uh," the other lieutenant considered. "My tent is…occupied. Walk with me. We can check the sentries." He said the last as if it were a novel idea.

Micah motioned for his companions to stay put and he followed Lieutenant Zhukov on a meandering route toward the edge of the camp.

"I have orders from the emperor." Micah reached inside his coat and retrieved the sealed letter.

Zhukov broke the seal carelessly. He spread out the folded paper, reading as he walked. His lips moved as he read. He gave a startled glance at Micah at one point, looking him up and down, before returning to the letter.

"It says here," Zhukov thumped the letter, "that you are to take over command. It says that I am to report to you, and that you will organize the search for the escaped prisoners."

Micah nodded.

Lieutenant Zhukov spat on the ground.

Micah narrowed his eyes, his blue eyes meeting Zhukov's steely gray. "Are we going to have a problem, Lieutenant?"

"No, sir," Zhukov said, sounding just like Abel Rennert had when Micah was ten and accused him of stealing the cookie Micah's mother had made him, even though Micah could still see the crumbs around Abel's mouth.

Micah had broken Abel Rennert's nose.

I could break his nose, Micah thought. *But I don't think it would do any good. Something else, then.*

"Good." Micah smiled, ignoring the sarcasm. "How long have you been with General Hamazi?"

Zhukov seemed surprised by the change of subject, but then he puffed up with pride. "Ten years now. He hand-picked me for this mission."

I doubt that very much.

Micah nodded. "Because your methods get results?"

"Yeah, they do."

"Do you love your emperor, Lieutenant Zhukov?" Micah kept his tone mild. Curious.

Confusion played on his face again. "Of course I do. Long live the emperor."

Micah nodded again as if understanding there were no other answer.

"Do you think the emperor loves his people, Lieutenant Zhukov?"

"Uh, yeah, I guess so," Zhukov stammered. He seemed off balance. "But the people we are hunting are criminals and escaped prisoners."

"Prisoners?" Micah acted shocked. "I thought they were runaway farmers. Are you saying the emperor was overseeing a prison camp?"

"Huh? No, that's not what I'm saying. Escaped farmers, that's what I meant."

"Are the good people of Isan criminals, Lieutenant Zhukov?"

"Not that I know of."

"Prisoners?" Micah asked.

"No."

"Then you have evidence that they are disloyal to the empire and have conspired against the emperor?"

"What? No! Of course not." Zhukov's confusion was starting to turn to anger.

"Then can you explain to me why you are torturing the good citizens of Isan in that tent over there? Good, loyal citizens that you yourself just said our emperor loves."

Zhukov's face turned scarlet. Micah couldn't tell if it was from anger or embarrassment, and frankly he didn't care.

Micah held Zhukov's gaze. When the lieutenant didn't answer Micah raised his eyebrows.

Zhukov lowered his eyes to the ground. "We may have been a little overly enthusiastic in the pursuit of our mission."

"Hmmm." Disapproval was clear in the sound. Micah continued to stare at the man.

"We'll release them at once," Zhukov said. Micah couldn't tell if the shame in his voice was real or contrived.

"With the emperor's apologies," Micah added.

"Of course."

"Good man." Micah clapped him on the back as if all was forgiven. "Tell me, Lieutenant Zhukov. How would you prefer to inform the men of the emperor's orders? They are your men, after all, it should be your decision. You are a trusted man among General Hamazi's officers, who is one of Emperor Lao's favorite generals. I'm sure you will find a way that will bring honor to both General Hamazi and His Holy Emperor."

*****

"How'd it go?" Joral asked when they were clear of the camp, leaving a somewhat dumbfounded Lieutenant Zhukov behind them.

Micah's sharp look answered the question more than his words.

"This place is a shit show," Micah hissed. "My guess is that Hamazi doesn't know the first thing about our good lieutenant. Some logistics officer under the general's command probably sent Zhukov down here to get him out of the way. He probably assumed it was a relatively harmless mission that Zhukov couldn't muck up too badly. We're going to have to match up units of Night Birds with lancers in order to break them up and instill a little order."

"Patrols of foot and horse wouldn't be that out of the ordinary," Joral said. "You can justify the need."

"I need to meet with his squad leaders to see if any of them is worth a damn. I can't put all of the patrols under the command of my own sergeants, or it will just foster resentment."

"Make sure you pair the more worthless of his men with Garin or Wang. They won't brook any nonsense and will square 'em away quicker than Moab's mom can lift her dress."

"Hey!" Moab complained.

"So serious," Micah clapped the soldier on the shoulder. "Come on, let's settle in. You need a bath."

"Hey!" Moab protested again, then he sniffed his shirt. "Yeah, okay," he said with a shrug.

"Are you sure this is the place?" Micah asked, surveying the endless plains of yellowed grass.

"I only know what I was told," Lieutenant Zhukov answered glumly.

Zhukov's insubordination had returned once it became clear that Micah was dismantling his command and spreading out his troops. Micah had made sure, though, that every order he had given was completely logical and delivered in a pleasant, no-nonsense manner. This had given Zhukov little room to complain, so he had adopted a passive-aggressive pout that had made him about as much fun, these past three weeks, as a badger with a burr in its coat.

Zhukov's men had been more accommodating. Sergeant Garin had implemented daily practice and a sparring board. The friendly competition between the Night Birds and the lancers had helped build camaraderie. Several of Zhukov's men were surprisingly good at spear and sword and the leaders were a good mix from both companies.

Micah rode ahead with Moab and Joral in tow. A collection of buildings appeared on the horizon. A dozen small bunkhouses, not too dissimilar from the barracks Micah had lived in in the Northern Wastes, surrounded a dusty farmyard. A barn and several corrals had been constructed to the west. People gathered in the yard as Micah's column approached.

Two middle-aged men, a little older than Micah's mother, waited at the front of the group.

"Can I help you?" the older of the two men shouted once Micah was within hearing distance.

"Is this your farm?" Micah said politely.

"Aye." The man nodded. "I ask again, can I help you?"

"Well, that depends. We're looking for someone and heard a rumor that they may have been staying here."

Zhukov and the rest of the column rode into the yard. Zhukov sidled his horse up next to Moab's on Micah's right. The other side of the farmyard began to fill as well. Men, women, and children emerged from the bunk houses and formed a crowd behind the two men.

The rancher shrugged. "Maybe, we hired on a bunch of new hands to help during the calving season. Most of them are gone now. Can you be more specific?"

Micah grinned. He could see it in their eyes. *They already know.*

"Well, let's see." Micah decided to play their game. "There's a woman, about your age, with flame red hair. She'd be hard to forget. She has a smile that can light up a room. She's partial to telling campfire stories about the old days. You know, heroes of old, golden cities, grand battles, that sort of thing."

The two men glanced at each other.

"Then there's an old blacksmith who is missing two fingers on his left hand. Horrible accident, that was. His apprentice let the hammer slip while they were crafting a plow blade and smashed the fingers on the anvil. Funny thing though, the blacksmith never cursed once. Didn't even raise his voice. Can you imagine? Smashed his fingers and didn't lose his temper." Micah shook his head as if he still couldn't believe it.

Confusion crossed the face of more than one in the crowd.

"Then there is this boy, about your age," Micah pointed to a sandy-haired boy in the second row. "Let's see. He's blond, built like a blacksmith himself, and has a scar right here." Micah traced a finger from his hairline across his left eye.

"Oh, and a bear. Biggest damn animal I have ever seen. I still can't figure that one out but there would definitely have been a bear."

Micah studied their faces for a minute, letting his words sink in.

"Sound familiar?" Micah asked with a devious smile.

"You're Micah," a low voice sounded from the center of the crowd. It wasn't a question, but rather a statement of certainty.

"Hush up, Anna," the younger of the two men turned his head to quiet the girl.

Micah smiled. "Why, yes I am. Why don't you step out here where I can see you? Anna, is it?"

A girl of about sixteen pushed her way to the front of the group. She wore a blue and white striped dress. Her long brown hair was tied back in a ponytail with a yellow ribbon. She stood defiantly and looked straight at him.

"Why don't you just let him be?" she demanded.

"Whoa," Micah laughed. "You misunderstand my intentions. I don't mean them any harm. They have something that I need, and I would just like to have a quiet conversation with them."

"You want to hurt him just like you did Arthengal."

Micah furrowed his brow and nodded in commiseration. "That was handled poorly. Even if General Alamay were an enemy of the empire that could have been handled better. I truly regret that night, but at the time I wasn't in a position to really affect the outcome."

"And you are now?"

"I am," Micah said. "Look, I just want to talk to them and check some of their belongings. Emperor Lao thinks they may be in possession of some of his property. They may not even know it. After that, they are free to go or do whatever they please."

Anna looked confused and Zhukov shot him a sidelong glance.

"What property?" Anna asked.

"Well now, I can't really go into that. Imperial secrets and all. But, I promise you I don't mean Darius or his companions any harm."

She seemed uncertain. She studied him through narrowed eyes.

"Anna," the younger of the two men said cautiously. "Don't."

She turned to the man with defiance in her eyes. "Daddy, he told us not to do anything stupid. He told us if they came looking to tell them what they wanted to know and not to play hero. And here you and uncle Eban are doing the exact opposite."

Wise advice, Micah though. He had no desire to harm these people. Even Zhukov would have no legitimate reason to cross the line if the farmers answered their questions honestly.

"That's Micah." She pointed. "He already knows Darius was here. He knew as soon as Uncle Eban started playing coy."

Smart girl. Micah suppressed a grin as he watched the family drama play out.

"He went south," Anna finally said, turning back to Micah.

Micah, Joral, and Moab exchanged uncertain looks.

"South? Are you sure? Is he headed to Kasha Amur? I heard he was on his way to Kasha Marka."

"He is," Anna confirmed. "By way of Patel's Rest."

Micah shook his head. "Never heard of it."

"I have," Zhukov growled. "It's up in the mountains south of here. My mother used to tell us stories about the crazy old man that lives there to scare the daylights out of us when she wanted to teach us a lesson. She used to say 'ain't no one return from Patel's Rest that ain't dead or crazy.' She was a mean old bat."

"How do you know that?" Micah asked.

"I grew up on a dirt farm south of here. Ran away when I was fourteen to go join the imperial army in the north."

Will wonders never cease.

"Thank you, Anna," Micah said, sincerely.

"You better keep your promise not to hurt him," she demanded.

"I will," Micah promised. "But why so adamant? What is he to you?"

"We are going to be married."

Damn it, girl. Now why did you have to admit that. Maybe not so smart after all.

Everything happened quickly before Micah had a chance to take control of the situation.

"Anna, no!" A stout woman with brown hair shouted from the back of the group.

"Take her," Zhukov shouted to his men.

Two lancers rode to either side of her and one of them tried to scoop the girl into his saddle. The girl's father tried to wrestle her out of his grasp and the soldier brought the butt of his lance down on the man's head. Blood welled from the wound in his head as he collapsed to the ground.

Anna screamed. The stout woman screamed. Zhukov was shouting at his men. Other lancers were starting to draw weapons. The Night Birds sat in their saddles waiting for his orders.

"Enough!" Micah roared.

The barnyard stilled.

Everyone stared at him.

Micah regained his composure. "Anna, I think it would be best if you come with us. Darius is less likely to do anything rash if you are with us. It will be best for his safety."

Zhukov grinned slyly.

The adults in the group started to protest, but Micah raised a hand.

"She will be safe. I promise you." Micah turned his attention to Anna. "Anna why don't you ride behind Joral here? His mount is strong and can easily handle two riders. And she is gentle and won't jostle you too much."

Anna looked back and forth between the woman, now kneeling by Anna's father, and Micah.

"Please," Micah said gently, holding out a hand. "I really don't want anyone else to get hurt."

Anna nodded, her hands were shaking. It was clear she regretted her final confession. Micah was doing everything he could to prevent violence, but it was clear she really had no choice but to come. Zhukov would not allow otherwise. Anna was an asset that could be used as leverage to get Darius to surrender. If Micah allowed her to go free Zhukov would have justification in overriding his command. Joral helped her mount behind him and turned the horse north. They cantered past the stables and onto the main road.

"That was masterful," Zhukov said appreciatively riding up beside Micah. "You had them eating out of your hand. I see now why the emperor sent you."

"Do you?" Micah muttered sarcastically.

"Yeah. Very well done. You had better intelligence than we did too about the escapees. How did she know your name, though?"

"I was at the battle where we killed Nasu Rabi," Micah explained. "I talked to the boy there. He must have told them the story."

"And all that stuff about not hurting the prisoners, uh - farmers, I mean. I almost believed it myself."

"That's because it's true. The emperor no longer cares about the escaped workers. My orders are to retrieve his property and to try to convince the boy, Darius, to join the imperial army."

"Why?" Zhukov was mystified. "Why would the emperor want a criminal like that in his army?"

As opposed to a criminal like you?

"Because, Lieutenant Zhukov, he is a master swordsman trained by the best swordsman who ever lived, Nasu Rabi."

"Ah," Zhukov nodded. "I guess that makes sense. Is he really that good? I bet I could take him."

Micah laughed despite himself but held back further comment.

"I claim first rights on the girl," Zhukov said casually as if they were discussing the weather.

"Excuse me?" Micah asked. There was little doubt what the man meant.

"When we get back to camp," Zhukov clarified. "I claim first rights on the girl. My men captured her after all."

Bile rose in the back of Micah's throat. Lieutenant Zhukov truly was a discredit to the imperial uniform. How did a man like this ever get command of a unit?

"I meant what I said about that, too. The girl is under my protection."

Zhukov scoffed and heeled his horse into a trot.

*****

As they rode into camp Zhukov and two of his lancers flanked Joral. "Take the girl to my tent," Zhukov commanded.

Micah reined his horse in and vaulted from the saddle as the two lancers dismounted and dragged Anna to the ground.

"Let me go," Anna screamed. She struggled to get free, but the soldiers forced her to her knees.

Micah sprinted the distance to where they held her.

Zhukov got very close to Anna and leaned in with a wicked smile. "You're spirited. I like that. It will make everything more fun."

Anna spat in his face.

Zhukov backhanded her and she dropped to the ground, blood tricking from a split lip.

Everyone froze at the ring of steel.

"Leave her alone," Micah growled.

"I've had just about enough of your self-righteousness." Zhukov turned on him and drew his own blade. "Telling my men how they should run their camp and wasting their time with your silly games."

Several of the lancers shuffled uncomfortably at the comment. In general, the soldiers seemed to enjoy the activities. It had been better than sitting around all day with nothing to do but trade pennies in dice games.

Micah stood in a defensive stance and studied Zhukov. His grip was loose. His feet didn't create a solid base, and his posture was sloppy.

"You don't want to do this, Lieutenant," Micah warned. "Stand down."

A group of men from both companies had started to form around them. Zhukov's pride was on the line now. Micah knew, regretfully, that he wouldn't back down. But Micah had to try.

"Joral," Micah said evenly. "You and Moab take Anna to my tent and set a guard."

The two lancers reluctantly released their grip on Anna's arms as Joral and Moab pulled her away. Micah recognized the two. They had been outside Zhukov's tent the day he had arrived. As Joral pulled Anna aside the two soldiers edged closer to their horses where weapons were secured to their saddles.

Bolstered by the support, Zhukov pressed his position. He stepped forward holding his sword before him.

"I think it's time you and your *Night Birds* were on your way. We can take it from here."

SILLU MITU (NIGHT SHADOW) | 137

This has gone too far, Micah thought. *There is only one way to resolve this without losing control of the men.*

"Lieutenant Zhukov, your insubordination --" Micah knew that would be exactly the wrong thing to say.

Zhukov charged him with a cry of rage.

Micah side-stepped the reckless attack with Willows in the Wind. He followed with The Dragon Whips His Tail. The lashing strike severed Lieutenant Zhukov's hamstring. Zhukov stumbled forward and dropped to one knee. Micah pressed forward with Comet Chases the Moon. He heard a cry from one of the guards as the final thrust penetrated Zhukov's neck from behind.

"Murderer!" one of Zhukov's loyalists shouted as he grabbed a spear from his saddle and charged. The second guard followed closely behind. Micah moved into Dancing Lights. He broke the shaft of the first man's spear in half and then opened his stomach with a vicious back sweep. Micah moved quickly between the two men using Fox Dances with Dandelions. A few quick strikes left both men on the ground beside their commander.

Micah scanned the crowd of onlookers. He saw that Joral had returned and stood at the edge of the crowd, fingers on the hilt of his blade.

"Anyone else?"

Eyes dropped all around the company of lancers and grins crept onto the faces of Night Birds.

Micah searched the group until he saw the face he was looking for.

"Sergeant Minoshka," he called.

"Yes, sir." The sergeant answered uncertainly.

"You are hereby granted a field commission of lieutenant and will act as my second in command. We will make the promotion permanent at the earliest opportunity."

"Yes, sir. Thank you, sir."

"Please form a burial party while I interview our guest."

"Yes, sir."

"Smart," Joral whispered as they walked toward Micah's tent. "The men respect Minoshka, and now he owes you."

Micah grinned. Joral was less gregarious than Moab, but he was better at catching the subtleties of Micah's decisions.

When they reached his tent, Joral joined Moab and two other guards flanking the entrance. Micah lifted the tent flap and entered. Anna was pacing inside. She looked up when he entered. Despite her circumstances he could tell she was more furious than scared.

"Please, have a seat." Micah gestured to a small chair beside a simple wooden table.

Reluctantly, she sat.

Micah cleaned his sword before returning it to its scabbard. He removed the belt and placed it atop a carefully folded wool blanket at the foot of his cot. He sat across from Anna and put his elbows on the table.

"Now," Micah smiled. "Why don't you tell me what my brother has been up to since I last saw him?"

Chapter Thirteen
Patel's Rest

Antu sniffed the air and growled.

"What is it, Antu?" Darius asked.

The bear ignored the comment and searched the sky. He sniffed again and then trotted faster up the narrow mountain road.

Darius glanced up at the blue sky and shrugged. The road followed a bubbling stream as it wound up into the mountains. Darius pulled his horse to a stop and dismounted. He slid down the slight embankment to the edge of the creek. He emptied what was left from his water skin and then bent over to refill it with clear mountain water. As he stood a sudden gust of wind struck him from behind. He shivered and looked upstream in the direction of the wind. The gust died soon enough and the sun once again warmed Darius's skin.

A tiny spark of sunlight reflecting off something caught Darius's eye. He watched as a single snowflake drifted down from an otherwise clear sky and landed on his outstretched hand. There was another brief glint and then the flake was gone, melted in his palm.

*****

Darius leaned into the wind. The blowing snow made it difficult to see more than a few paces ahead. They had been forced to dismount and lead the horses. The slope that led down to the mountain stream was gentle enough with good visibility. However, one misstep in the current conditions could easily break a horse's leg and send the rider tumbling into the rocks below.

"There," Nicolai shouted over the howling wind.

Nicolai looked like an ice devil. His woolen coat and trousers were covered in a thin sheen of white. His normally flowing brown locks were frozen at odd angles taking on the appearance of crystalized horns all over his head. The scarf he had pulled up to cover his ears and nose was also blasted white and the labored puffs of breath that escaped looked like clouds of smoke.

Darius stopped. He used a gloved hand to shield his eyes and peered in the direction that Nicolai pointed. To the left of the path he saw the hulking brown beast. Antu was standing on his hind legs and his mouth was opened in a roar. The sound of it was lost in the howling wind.

Darius nodded and turned his horse in the bear's direction. When he saw them following, Antu dropped to all fours and turned into the trees. They followed the bear into a draw. The ridges provided shelter from the wind and they could hear and see more clearly now. They plodded through ankle-deep snow following Antu's tracks.

Ahead, through the snow, Darius could see the mouth of a cavern punched into the base of a rocky ridgeline. He could not see Antu, but he heard him. Roars and snarls echoed out of the cave. In a sudden flash of fur and fury, a pair of black bears galloped from the cave and ran past Darius and his companions.

Darius turned back to the cave and saw Antu standing at the entrance. Darius clicked his tongue and led his horse forward.

The cave was not deep, and the rocky roof slanted quickly so that Darius could only reach the back on his hands and knees.

"What do you think?" Darius asked the group.

"It's plenty big for the ten of us," Gunnar answered.

"And we can picket the horses near the entrance," Nicolai added. "The ridge will protect them from the worst of the storm and, once we get a fire going, it should warm the mouth of the cave, as well."

The protected vale was further sheltered from the storm by tall fir trees and denuded aspens that decorated the ridge lines and surrounding slopes.

Gunnar and Kal managed to scavenge enough wood along the ridgeline to start a modest fire. The horses pressed deeper into the crevice while the humans huddled around the crackling blaze.

"Where the southern blazes did that come from?" Ander complained loudly.

The group didn't have an answer. The mountain storm had rolled in quickly and with a ferocity that had surprised them all.

"Well, I guess we just as well have our mid-day meal and see if it blows over," Matia said as he rummaged through the bags strapped to one of the mules.

Darius had hired on three of Eban's ranch hands to help with the trek east. Now that late fall had arrived Eban had been forced to cut his staff down to the hands that managed the herd over the winter. Darius hadn't really needed the extra help, but Ander, Petri, and Matia had all been pleasant to work with. The three of them managed the mules and extra supplies. Matia was also an excellent camp cook and prepared the meals.

Darius peered through the mouth of the cave at a roiling gray mass of clouds. "I don't think that's going to happen. I think we'd better work on preparing shelter. I think we're going to be here a while."

"What makes you say that?" Kal asked.

"We'd get storms like this in the mountains surrounding Arthengal's valley. Sometimes it would take them days to blow themselves out."

*****

They huddled in their narrow draw for three days watching the raging storm pile more and more snow to box them in. On the morning of the fourth day Darius woke to blue skies and the chirping of mountain finches.

He crawled from under his bundle of wool blankets and stood with a stretch.

Marku stood a few paces downslope and stared at the wall of snow that had drifted, chest high, across the entrance to the draw.

"You and I are the tallest," Marku said as Darius approached. "And maybe Petri. The three of us will have to punch a hole in this drift to get the horses and supplies out. I sure wish we had bigger shovels."

Darius nodded. The trenching tools they had were great for redirecting water around a sleeping area, but would be little use here.

In the end, it took all of them, in shifts, to open a hole wide enough to get the party back to the main trail. Cordelia and Lianna had tended fires while the men took turns using their bodies and limited tools to shift and trample snow into a path where two of them could walk abreast and lead the mounts out.

They had to repeat the process several times throughout the day to create trails through drifts on the main road. Exhausted, they found a place to camp at the end of the day, having travelled barely a league.

The group sat around the campfire sipping mint and rosehip tea after a meal in which Matia had managed to make jerked beef, corn mash, and dried apricots taste like a porridge from the finest inn.

"How much farther do you think it is to Patel's Rest?" Marku asked that night.

"At this rate, who knows?" Ander complained.

"I'd guess another five or ten days if it's like this the rest of the way," Darius answered as he held his hands over the fire. "We made it most of the way there before the storm hit. I wouldn't have thought us more than a day or two out when the snow started."

"We're going to have to stretch the supplies, especially what's left of the grain," Matia sighed. "We had packed for about forty days, overestimating in case of trouble, we're going to need that excess now, and then some."

"Melt snow every night to replace the water," Darius instructed. "Three-quarter rations for the food until we get there. With progress as slow as it is, the horses should be fine on that. They aren't exerting themselves too much."

"What about your bear?" Matia asked.

Darius searched the snowy hills for the massive brown lump.

"Antu," Darius shouted. A boulder-sized head lifted from the snow. "You're on your own the next few days. Rabbits and fish, if you can find them."

The grunt was audible even at the distance and then the large head flopped back down.

"Do you really think he understood you?" Matia asked.

Darius shrugged. "We'll know if he gets hungry enough to come after the horses." He hid his grin by lifting the tin cup of steaming tea to his lips.

One day followed another of slogging through knee-high snow and pounding through drifts that towered overhead. The group was rewarded on the fifth day by the sight of two triangular pennants flapping in the breeze in the distance. They lost sight of the pennants as the road dipped through a saddle between two ridges.

The pennants never reappeared that day, but they did the next morning as they crested a hill.

"They're close, less than a league away," Darius commented.

They pressed on and, as the sun was settling behind the glacial western peaks, the group rounded a curve. The road climbed a hill after the bend and atop the hill rested two stone towers, built into the cliffs that marked either side of the pass. Narrow, open windows decorated each tower in a spiral winding toward the peak. Gray smoke rose from a chimney at the top of the tower on the left.

Rough-hewn beams, as wide as a man's reach, formed a wall between the two towers. The snow drifted across the base of the tower and wall. A single iron gate, no wider than a single wagon, was set into the base of the wall, but it was shut tight, and snow piled against it.

"Bit late in the season, isn't it?"

Darius was startled by the voice. He glanced around the structure and finally picked out a wiry, bald man poking his head out a window about halfway up the western tower.

"Hello, Tower. We're not traders. My name is Darius. We are on our way through to Kasha Marka."

"Well, that will be a trick, won't it?" The skinny man laughed. "That storm that passed through last week closed the east pass tight."

Darius struggled to follow the accent. The man spoke very quickly and some of the vowel sounds were different. His speech also replaced every th sound with a hard d.

"You think travel up this side was bad," the guard continued. "The mouth of the pass on that side is buried halfway up the wall."

Darius pursed his lips. The wall was at least ten paces high.

"The eastern peaks blocked the worst of the storm and dumped more snow over there than I've ever seen this early in the season," the man continued. "What we got on this side was a light summer flurry by comparison."

Darius's heart sank. "How long before we will be able to move on?"

"Lord MacCinidh might sell you dogs and sleds, but your horses and your—is that a bear? What in the blue devil are you bringing a bear up here for? I'm not so sure his lordship is going to let you bring a bear into the enclave. I'll have to send word back to ask."

"I'm not sure Antu is going to want to go into the enclave. What was it you were saying about the horses?"

"Oh, they're stuck until spring. No way you'll be getting a horse down the mountain to Kasha Marka. You might make it back to Isan if you hurry and are very lucky, before this side is closed for the winter as well. Not sure why you didn't just go the overland route to Kasha Marka anyway. Did someone trick you into believing this way was shorter? Are you dense?"

"No, we're not dense." Darius said, offended. "We have our reasons for coming this way. If you would be so kind as to let us through, I would love to speak to your master about our options. Who do we have the pleasure of speaking with?"

"You don't sound very pleased. Name's Amadan. I'd love to let you in, except the gate is frozen shut," Amadan said. "Don't suppose you want to climb over if I drop down a rope?"

"Our horses—"

"Right, the horses. And the bear. So, the gate it is then. Hold tight, it might take a while." Amadan's face disappeared from the window.

Soon after, the rhythmic ringing of steel on steel began.

Darius stamped his feet, pacing the wall for an hour after Amadan disappeared. Matia decided it was better use of their time to prepare their evening meal while they waited. Darius finally gave up and joined the others.

The ringing continued well after dark. Amadan appeared briefly to swing a large maul at the base of the gate where it joined the ground. He ducked back inside and then the stillness of the night was broken by the torturous groan of rending metal. Slowly the gate moved. Ice and snow fell away from the iron bars as it rose. The portcullis stopped about halfway up.

Amadan's bald head poked out of the gatehouse inside. "Is that enough to get your horses through? I don't know that I can raise it much more by myself."

Darius judged the height. "That should be fine."

Darius led his horse through the opening with Antu close beside them.

Once the party was past the thick, timbered wall and the gate had been lowered, Darius finally got a good look at their rescuer. Bald and wiry, Darius had assumed the man was ancient. To the contrary, Darius guessed Amadan was actually younger than Marku, who was about fifty. Amadan's skin was wrinkled, and his olive complexion was permanently tanned from years in the sun and snow, but his back was firm and his arms looked strong and toned despite being thin.

Amadan offered them a tour of the small outpost. The guard's quarters were in the western tower, but rooms had been built into its twin as well. A small stable was sheltered between the wall and the cliffs. It wasn't large enough to house all their mounts but was well stocked with hay and grain. The outbuildings also included a small shop, a forge, a woodshed fully stocked with split cordwood, and a larder stocked with enough provisions to get Amadan through the winter.

"You're welcome to stay through the night," Amadan said and pointed to the eastern tower. "The hearth's cold in the guest quarters but once you get a fire going it will warm up nicely. Help yourself to the provisions. It's well past time that I was in bed."

With that the old guardsman retired to his tower abode. The door shut heavily and was followed by the thump of a crossbeam settling into place.

Darius woke early the next morning to the smells of burning cedar, stewing apples, and fried bacon. His stomach rumbled. He stumbled down the stone steps from the sleeping quarters to the spacious common area at the base of the tower. Cordelia and Matia were conversing quietly while they prepared breakfast to the light of oil lamps.

Darius stretched and yawned loudly.

Cordelia turned at the sound. "He is certainly well stocked for a lonely guardsman. His master must be very generous."

Darius nodded sleepily. "I'm going to check on the horses."

He stepped out into a brisk mountain morning. The smell of fresh snow and mountain air had a dizzying, nostalgic effect. Darius closed his eyes for a moment and just breathed it in.

In the misty light of dawn, Darius noticed several things about the camp that he had missed the night before. The pass and road were not natural but looked to have been carved through a gap between two glacial ridges. The slopes on either side of the pass were too steep to traverse and the peaks to either side were already packed deep with snow.

The thick, rough-hewn timbers that he had noted the previous evening only formed an outer wall. An older wall built from stone blocks formed a thinner, but still impressive, inner barrier. It looked as if the stone wall had been breached and repaired at some point in the past. There was a section to the right of the gate that appeared to be newer stone.

The road continued uphill beyond the camp. After feeding the horses Darius completed the short hike up to the pinnacle of the pass. He gave a low whistle as he took in the scene below. A large mountain valley opened up below him. A road of winding switchbacks snaked down the mountainside before him. Cairns had been positioned at the more treacherous corners with smoldering signal fires atop each. At least ten leagues to the east he could see the twinkling lights from a similar road rising out of the valley to the twin pass.

The valley was a spectacular site. Mountains surrounded the lush, flat area on three sides. The northern edge dropped sharply, as if cut by a knife, and fell away into a misty darkness. Many streams and rivers poured into the valley from the surrounding peaks. A dozen or more rivers converged as they reached the valley floor. A spider web of waterways wound their way through cultivated fields, areas of vast marshy grassland, and groves of aspen, larch, and cedar alive with the colors of autumn. A kaleidoscope of colors in the valley contrasted sharply with the white and gray of the high mountain peaks that surrounded it.

Darius could see the remnants of the early winter storm but most of the snow had melted in the deep valley. The same could not be said for the surrounding mountains. It reminded Darius of winters with Arthengal when they were often trapped in their little valley until spring.

The rivers converged once more into three grand tributaries at the northern edge of the valley. Thunderous waterfalls spilled into the clouds below. Darius had expected Patel's Rest to be a small mountain outpost not unlike his hometown of Koza. Instead, a pair of elaborate castles filled the bulk of the two islands created by the converging waterways.

A white stone wall surrounded the two islands. Archers' towers rose above the walls at the corners. Inside the walls, the castles rested like twin dragons lounging atop the islands. At the core of each was a stone keep three stories tall. Additions had been made to each that demonstrated the style and work of several generations of architects. There were towers, flat and peaked; bulwarks surrounding elaborate gardens; and a hodgepodge of outbuildings all connected to the center by walkways and walls. Stone archways, decorated with carved gargoyles, spanned the distance between the two castles and allowed passage across the raging river below.

Hundreds of people could be seen on the walls or running about on tasks, like ants on the backs of the twin beasts. What Anna's uncle had described as a small mountain enclave turned out to be a grand highland city.

Chapter Fourteen
The Alchemist

As soon as they reached the valley floor, Antu turned north into the open river lands. Darius watched him go with a twinge of jealousy. The fishing would be good. Now that they had cleared the pass, the temperature in the valley was pleasant. It wasn't as warm as the volcanic valley that had been his and Arthengal's home, but the mountain peaks sheltered the valley from the worst of the mountain weather and wind. A thin dusting of snow was all that remained, in the valley, of the early winter storm that had nearly stranded Darius and his companions. Darius pulled on the reins and led his horse along the north road toward the island city.

"This place is a marvel." Marku stood in his saddle to get a better look at the valley and city. "I can't believe I'd never heard of it."

"The walls and some of the buildings look centuries old," Gunnar said in wonder.

"Master Eban did say that there used to be an imperial outpost here before the war," Ander said. "He said it used to be a well-travelled trade route between Magora and Shalanum. After the war it was taken over by a wealthy nobleman who wanted peace and isolation. Eban said that, while they won't turn traders away, they don't invite travelers as much. People have probably just forgotten about it."

"This was more than just a common imperial outpost," Marku said dubiously. "The craftsmanship on the older buildings is incredible. My guess would be some sort of retreat for the emperor and his family."

They approached a stone bridge that spanned the first of the wide tributaries. It was at least a hundred paces long and was built from carved stone blocks. A stone archway marked each end of the bridge. There were no guards at the near end, but Darius couldn't see the other side clearly. Every twenty paces a marble statue had been mounted to the parapet. The sculptures depicted men and women from an earlier age. It was an eclectic assortment that seemed to have little in relation to one another.

They dismounted and led their horses through the archway. Darius paused to look over the northern parapet. He was hoping to see the waterfall, but the bridge had been built too far back from the edge. He could hear the thunder of the water far below, and a thick mist rose to obscure whatever lay below. Far across the lower river valley the Talia Mountains continued unbroken.

Cordelia stopped to examine one of the statues. "I think this is supposed to be Jasmarana."

"Who?" Darius asked. The statue depicted a young woman in a crouching stance. She held a spear in each hand, the left with its base thrust into the ground for support, and the right held high as if prepared to thrust. Darius could almost imagine the woman pressing down with her left hand to propel herself off the bridge to attack him from above.

"Jasmarana," Cordelia repeated. "You remember the stories. She was a hero from long ago, second or third dynasty, I think, who joined the emperor's forces to battle the legendary dragon Uk'tov Ra. The dragon defeated the entire legion sent by the emperor against him. Only Jasmarana and her spears remained. She battled the dragon for seven days and seven nights. At the end of the week the dragon called for parlay. He was so impressed with her battle prowess that he agreed to grant her three wishes. Her first, and supposedly only, wish was that Uk'tov Ra leave the lands of Chungoku never to return."

Cordelia glanced around at the other statues.

"I think these are all ancient heroes. There is Sadko Novgordov." She pointed to a tall man with a falcon on his left shoulder, an eagle on his right, and a great hawk launching into flight from his extended right hand. "See, you can just see his own wings starting to emerge from his back. The sculptor must have been very familiar with the legends."

The rest of the group had stopped as well and was listening.

"Over there is Hana Rama, the legendary bard with his harp, and there is Jomyo Meishu, the warrior monk. I don't recognize most of the others, but I would bet they are all early Chungoku heroes." Cordelia examined each statue in wonder.

Darius and the others were so engrossed by Cordelia's explanation that they didn't notice the six guards who had emerged on the other side of the bridge and now waited patiently for them to approach. When Darius saw them, he tightened his grip on the reins that had been dangling loosely in his hand and led the horse forward. The others followed.

The guards all had dark hair, cut short to the collar, and the same olive complexion as Amadan, albeit not as weatherworn. They wore crisp powder blue uniforms with brass buttons aligned along the left side. The uniforms bore no heraldry that Darius could see.

In front of the group was another guard, similarly dressed, with the addition of a sharply angled hat the same color as the uniform. All of the soldiers, with the exception of the officer, carried long halberds. The leader wore a sword low on his right hip positioned for a left-handed draw.

Interesting, he fights left-handed, was Darius's first thought. *I'd very much like to spar with him.*

"Good morning." Darius waved a hand.

The lead guard smiled. "Indeed. A bit late in the season for traders." He leaned to the side to get a better look at the contingent. "I don't see much in the way of trade goods. What brings you this way?" He spoke with the same accent as Amadan, albeit not as pronounced.

"We are travelling from Isan to Kasha Marka."

The guard turned his head with curiosity. "Taking the long way about it, aren't you? Why not take the north road out of Isan? It would have saved you half the time."

"There were imperial soldiers on the north road, and we didn't want any trouble."

At that the guard frowned. "What do you mean imperial soldiers?"

"Well," Darius started, not exactly sure how to explain everything.

"Never mind." The lead guard rescued him from further explanation. "Our benefactor, Master Patel, will want to hear this. Follow me, please. You may bring two of your companions with you. Guardsman Jamus, please escort the rest of our guests to the Blind Sparrow. I'm sure Mistress Amon will appreciate the patrons."

Marku stepped forward before Darius could pick anyone else to join him. Rather than create a scene, he relented and then asked Kal to join them. Cordelia led the rest of the party down a cobblestone street after the guard.

"If you please." The guard captain indicated that they should follow him deeper into the city.

"What's your name?" Darius asked.

"Guard Captain Terzi," the man replied simply, leading them on.

Darius marveled at the complexity of the city. If it had appeared disjointed from above, it was even more so from below. Most of the buildings were stone, but that was all they had in common. The architecture varied wildly from one street to the next. The town had been built and rebuilt over centuries. When old structures became unusable it was obvious that the builders of the time knocked them down and erected a newer construct atop the foundations of the old. Houses and shops from multiple eras resided next to each other on the same streets.

Navigating the streets was even more confusing. The captain led them down a once great thoroughfare that ended abruptly at the wall of a shrine that itself looked several hundred years old. Without pause he ascended a stone staircase up the side of a brick wall that bordered the avenue. Atop the wall was an immense garden. Captain Terzi turned onto a narrow path that wound between live oaks and gardenias. The path let out onto another roadway that was so old that the paving stones had been worn nearly to the dirt beneath. The only consistency in their journey was that they were winding ever upward toward the pinnacle of the island.

"All right, it's official," Kal blurted. "I'm lost."

Captain Terzi smiled knowingly. "It's okay, we're almost there."

They passed through an arched wall, a dozen paces thick, with a double portcullis before emerging into yet another garden. This garden was smaller and elegantly manicured. It surrounded a stately stone keep. The main building was three stories high with iron or wooden crossbars mounted in its thirty to forty windows. At the north end of the keep was a taller, square tower, some six stories high. It was windowless, but the walls of each floor were decorated with dozens of narrow slots to let light in and arrows out.

Broad stone steps led down from the keep into the garden. At the base of the steps was a pool, its edges thick with lily pads, decorated with a pair of statues depicting giant, fat fish. Darius saw a heron near the center of the pool surveying the dark, still waters. It thrust its bill down suddenly and emerged with a bright orange fish which flopped twice before disappearing down the bird's gullet.

Captain Terzi led them around the pond and up the steps. They were greeted at the door by a dark-skinned man in his sixties. A brief memory of Arthengal flashed through Darius's mind. Their faces were different, but this man had the same well-manicured beard, the same long wavy hair, and the same rugged look of an outdoorsman. He looked out of place in this castle.

"Master Hudai," Captain Terzi said. "We have visitors. I think Master Patel would be interested in an audience. They bring word of imperial soldiers on the plains."

The doorman raised an eyebrow, but said nothing. He opened the door wider, permitting entrance.

Darius's curiosity got the better of him. "Master Hudai, are you from Kantibar?"

This earned Darius a curious look, but no response.

"You just remind me of a friend of mine and that's where he was from."

"What was your friend's name?" Captain Terzi asked.

"Arthengal," Darius responded.

Hudai's eyes widened and the two men exchanged a glance, but still said nothing.

"Master Hudai cannot speak," Captain Terzi explained. "He has taken a vow of silence."

"Really, why?" Darius asked.

"That is not for me to say," Captain Terzi explained. "You will have to ask Master Hudai." A slight smile played over his lips.

Darius and his companions followed Hudai into the castle. Despite its elegant exterior the inside to the castle was decorated very plainly. There were no tapestries or expensive decorations, only simple furnishings and utilitarian accessories. They were led to a large room in the southern wing of the second floor.

Unlike the rest of the house, this room was a mess. It was a wide, open gallery. The walls were covered with maps and drawings of contraptions that baffled Darius's curious mind. Tables were arranged haphazardly across the floor with barely room to walk between them. Each table was jumbled with curiosities of different sorts. One table held a collection of rocks, every shape, size, and color imaginable. Another table held a complex contraption made of glass. There were bottles, and tubes, and loops of glass. Darius could only guess at their function.

Hudai stopped at the entrance to the room. On the other side, near an open window at the back of the room, Darius could see an old man with white, cropped hair. The man was seated on a stool near a table bent over a pile of parchments studying one through a disc of glass attached to a handle. The man completely ignored them. His complexion was similar to that of Hudai, but not as dark. His face was shaven, but was as dry and creased as the parchments he was studying. He looked like he could have been Arthengal's grandfather.

After several minutes of waiting, Hudai cleared his throat. Apparently, that didn't violate his vows.

"I'm old, I'm not deaf." The man grumbled from the table without looking up. "I'm in the middle of a translation, and I don't want to lose my place."

This seemed to satisfy Hudai, and he resumed his patient wait. Marku and Kal began to shuffle their feet after several more minutes.

Finally, the man set down his glass and looked up. He studied the trio and then rose from his stool. He grabbed a walking staff that leaned against a nearby wall and hobbled with short strides toward them, deftly navigating the maze between tables. He stopped several paces away, leaning heavily against his staff, and examined them some more. Then he walked around them, muttering under his breath and grunting at various observations. Marku, the tallest of the three, was nearly two heads taller than the man.

The ancient examined Marku's hands and poked Darius in the ribs. Darius grunted and looked at Hudai for help, but the silent man's face remained stone except...

Did he just roll his eyes?

Darius was starting to feel awkward being scrutinized so diligently when the white-haired man broke the silence.

"A Merkari and two Shalanazi walk into an enclave." Then the old man paused.

Darius, confused, glanced around. His friends looked similarly confused. Hudai wore a smirk, but the old man's face looked deadly serious. This had to be Master Patel, maybe he was crazy like Eban had said.

"No, you haven't heard that one?" The old man shuffled forward. "That's all right, I can't remember the punch line, anyway."

"I'm sorry," Darius started to say, but was cut off when the old man raised a hand.

"This your first time off the farm, boy?" Master Patel poked Kal in the stomach with his walking stick.

Kal grunted. "Well, yes, I guess it is, sir."

"Mm-hmm," Master Patel muttered.

"You." The old man poked Marku. "You're an interesting one. You are a blacksmith, you're not a blacksmith. Which is it?"

Marku started to answer but was cut off.

"You still work, but your heart isn't in it. You're not sure what you should do so you follow this one around."

This time Patel poked Darius in the ribs.

Darius exchanged curious glances with his companions.

Master Patel moved just in front of Darius and peered up into his eyes. His brow creased and it seemed to Darius as if the old man were trying to read his thoughts. Finally, he bobbed his head up and down in affirmation. "So, it was a good death, then."

"What?" Darius asked, genuinely confused.

"Arthengal. He died a good death protecting you or someone you love."

"How could you possibly know that? Are you a wizard?"

Master Patel laughed. "So, you do have a sense of humor. I was worried that Arthengal's death had left you as dead on the inside as you look on the outside."

Darius hadn't been joking and now he was even more convinced that magic was being used against him.

"Your eyes," Master Patel explained.

"What?" Darius shook his head.

"There's a profound sadness there. Also, dark circles underneath which means you haven't been sleeping well for a long time. You used to smile and laugh, I can see it at the corners of your eyes, but you've also had a lot of worry and pain in recent years. That shows in your brow, between your eyes.

"Arthengal trained you. You wear his swords. You have the calluses on your right hand that show years of practice. You wear his second sword, so his death must have had profound meaning to you. If he had died in his sleep, you would have buried him with the second blade. You continue your training to honor him, but the blisters on your left hand are still forming. He died recently. You still hold the pain of his death inside you. It burns like embers. There is a hardness around your eyes because of it. He was killed by the new emperor or his soldiers."

"How could you possibly know that?" Darius asked.

"I heard you through the window," Patel explained, pointing his staff toward the open window behind them. "Something about imperial soldiers. The old emperor is dead so that implies a new emperor. You want to avenge Arthengal's death, but you have responsibilities holding you back. A mother or a young bride, maybe."

"You are a witch," Darius blurted.

"No, just observant. Come on, it's time for morning tea. Let's adjourn to the parlor, and I'll let you tell your story instead of telling it for you."

Chapter Fifteen
Spies

"That's quite a story," Patel said as Darius finished telling how he and Arthengal had rescued his mother from Emperor Lao's slave camp. "And the new emperor. You say he is Lao Cang Yu's son?"

"That's what my mother said," Darius nodded.

"He would be the most likely heir," Patel said more to himself than the others. The old man rose and shuffled across the floor to refill his cup of tea. "Interesting that Sharav is his protector. If I'm not mistaken, it was Sharav who arrested Lao Cang Yu and brought him back to the capital for trial and execution. I guess it makes sense, though. Sengiin Sharav was a true believer. He was always more loyal to the seat than the man. He believed that whoever sat on the Dragon Throne was ordained by the gods to rule over them and the world of men."

Patel took a sip of his tea and then returned to his seat.

"Even when Chen Bai Jian committed atrocities that would have had old Emperor Chung rolling over in his grave, Sharav was able to justify the actions as the will of a god. 'There is a divine purpose that we mortals are not meant to understand.' He told me that once after he burned an entire city to the ground, killing thousands of people."

"You knew General Sharav personally?" Marku asked.

"Oh yes. I worked with his father. I've known Sengiin since he was a boy. His father was another zealot and raised Sengiin to believe that their position close to the emperor granted them their own divine rights, in a manner of speaking. I think that was one of the reasons Sengiin hated Arthengal so much. He just couldn't reconcile someone who was lowborn being placed above him in the command structure. It didn't matter how effective Colonel Alamay was on the field or how much the men respected him. It only mattered that Arthengal's father was a cloth merchant, and his mother was a weaver."

"I never knew that," Darius whispered.

"Did you ever ask?" Patel narrowed his eyes.

"Pfft." Darius waved a hand. "I gave up asking direct questions about his past. Arthengal told the stories he wanted to tell and avoided answering anything he didn't want to talk about. I didn't even know he was married and had a son until almost a year after I started training with him."

Patel gave a commiserate nod. "I suppose that sounds like Arthengal. He did like to talk about his exploits more than anything that was too personal. With anyone except Sharaea, that is. She was his sun and moon. He told her everything."

"Who is Sharaea?" Marku asked.

"His wife," Darius and Patel answered together.

"She was a remarkable woman," Patel said, rubbing his chin as he remembered. "She was beautiful, well read, and was arguably the best healer in the nine kingdoms."

Marku cocked his head to the side and studied the old man intensely. He searched the room as if looking for the missing piece to a puzzle. Darius noticed Marku's eyes widen slightly as they settled on a ruptured wooden cylinder resting on one of the mahogany bookshelves that decorated the perimeter of the parlor.

"Sharaea knew more about herbs and their properties than even I did," Patel continued. "I could talk to her for hours about—"

"You're Quian MacCinidh, aren't you?" Marku cut him off.

"Who?" Darius and Kal asked together.

"Now that's an infamous name from another time," Patel answered. "What would make you bring up him?"

"Your guardsman at the western pass. He mentioned Lord MacCinidh. He only said it once, but it stuck in my head."

"Damn fool, Amadan," Patel cursed under his breath.

"Plus all your talk about knowing General Sharav and General Alamay when they served under Emperor Chen. Then, just now, you mentioned herbalism. Finally, over there on that shelf. That's a ruptured Light Bringer cylinder if I'm not mistaken."

"I call them shells," Patel corrected.

"Cylinder, shell, whatever you want to call it," Marku said. "You throw it up in the air, it explodes, and showers of sparks light the night sky."

Patel smiled slyly. "You may have more between your ears than one would guess at first glance, blacksmith. I didn't expect any small-town folk such as yourself to have heard the name."

"Who is Keyan McCinnie?" Darius asked.

"I was squire for Lord Simbar," Marku explained.

Patel raised his eyebrows. "A loyalist. You keep odd company, Merkari."

Marku glanced nervously at Darius and Kal. "What? No. I didn't."

"Relax, blacksmith. The war was a long time ago. We've all reinvented ourselves since then."

"Who is Keyan MacKinnie?" Darius said more loudly.

"Quian MacCinidh," Marku corrected.

Darius shook his head. He didn't hear the difference. "Who is he?" Darius repeated the question.

"He was the Emperor's alchemist," Marku said. "He served at least three emperors that I know of. He is credited with inventing the night showers that the Lightning Bringers use, among other things. His creations devastated the rebel troops early in the war until he turned coat and joined forces with Baroness Magora. His inventions were instrumental in helping General Alamay to take the capital."

Patel steepled his fingers over pursed lips.

"Night showers?" Darius asked. "Were those the silver lights that they shot over our heads when we were escaping to the barges?"

Patel shrugged, "Night showers weren't that difficult. The metal flashes white when ignited. The real trick was to launch them high enough into the air that the metal would all burn out before it reached the ground and figuring out a way to slow the descent. The metal will burn through almost anything once fired so definitely not something you want showering down upon your own troops."

Marku nodded. "Incendiaries were his specialty. I've seen what his firebombs do to an enemy when launched from catapults. It was gruesome. When they would explode, they would shower the troops with burning iron, melting holes in armor and body alike."

"Bah." Patel waved a hand in dismissal. "Only with the right combination of iron and phosphorus, and only if you could ignite the sulfur. The key was the correct mixture of charcoal and saltpeter. More often than not, the clay pots would crash to the ground and just shower the enemy with clay and metal dust."

"They were effective enough when thousands of them were hurled into the enemy lines," Marku said as he shuddered at the memory.

"You know that wasn't the original purpose of the night showers. I made them in all different colors. The intention was for battle commanders to be able to give orders to troops across the battlefield through light and color. The generals found a different purpose for my inventions though, as they do. Anyway, as I said, blacksmith, we have all reinvented ourselves since the war." Patel stood and paced the room.

He turned back to the group after a moment. "I don't work with fire anymore. I work with sound." A smile crept across his face and he raised an inquisitive eyebrow. "Do you want to see?"

Darius and Kal looked at each other and juvenile curiosity overtook them.

"Sure."

Patel led them on a circuitous route through the halls of the home until they reached a stone archway that led into the older north tower. They climbed three flights of stairs, emerging onto a flat roof surrounded by a parapet with waist-high embrasures and merlons that towered over Darius's head. Torches were mounted around the parapet and were burning even during the daytime.

In the center of the broad roof were several steel tubes mounted on tripods. The base of each cylinder rested against the stone and the other end was directed over the top of the parapet to the north. Each tube was of different length and diameter.

"I'm still experimenting with the best configuration for launching tubes," Patel explained.

Against the south wall, Darius saw stacks of tightly wrapped bundles, also varying in size. Beside the bundles were neatly piled shapes. Some were spherical, others were oblong, and others still were flattened on one end and narrowed to a point at one end like a large flattened teardrop. These devices varied in construction as much as they differed in size and shape. They were constructed of clay, wood, metal, and porcelain.

"The round bombs encased in iron work the best," Patel said excitedly as he grabbed a cloth bundle from the back and stuffed it into one of the tubes. The tube was the diameter of a large orange and was nearly as long as Darius was tall.

Patel retrieved a wooden staff lying on the roof near the cylinders and stuffed it in after the bundle. He tamped it several times until he was satisfied that the package was packed all the way to the bottom of the tube.

Next Patel opened a wooden case and retrieved a pair of black, waxy ropes that looked like engorged candle wicks. He stuffed one of the wicks into a hole at the back of the tube and made some adjustments to the fit. Patel retrieved one of the torches from the wall and lit the fuse. It sputtered and then began to burn steadily toward the metal cylinder.

Patel picked up one of the metal balls and stuffed the second wick into a hole in the top of it. Darius saw him pack a gummy wax around the base of the fuse to hold it in place. He lit the second fuse and dropped it into the cylinder as the first fuse was reaching its end.

After a brief pause there was a loud thump and a spout of black smoke shot from the hole in the cylinder.

"There," Patel pointed.

Darius looked and could see the metal ball arching over the waterfalls beyond the tower. Both Darius and Kal ran to the edge of the parapet to watch. The ball trailed out over the misty valley and then Darius saw a brief flash of light. Half a second later Darius heard the sound. It was like being inside a thundercloud. The boom of the explosion echoed across the valley floor. Darius saw several people in the city below clap hands to their ears before casting an annoyed glance at the tower.

Patel clapped his hands with glee like a child with a new toy. "That was a good one. Sometimes the fuse sputters out and it just drops into the mist. Depending on which tube I use I can throw them nearly half a league. I made it to the west pass once, but I haven't tried again because when the bomb exploded it triggered an avalanche. The pass was closed for a month while we dug it out. We would have lost poor Amadan if it weren't for the escape tunnels that run below the gate towers."

"It's impressive," Darius said. "But what's it for?"

Patel looked as if Darius had just asked him why water was wet.

"What do you mean, what's it for?" Patel responded. "Discovery is its own ends. Learning how the metals interact. What happens when they burn or when they are ignited under pressure? It's knowledge. The experiments advance our understanding of the world around us."

"But what can it be used for? What benefit does it provide? Is it a weapon like your firebombs?"

"Bah!" Patel waved a hand, clearly disappointed in Darius's question. "Purpose. You sound like Chen or Sharav or even Alamay. Why does everything have to have a purpose? Learning is its own purpose."

Darius looked from Marku to Kal and back to Patel. "Okay. Well, it's very impressive, whatever it does."

"You should go," Patel pouted. "Your friends will be waiting for you at the inn. Captain Terzi is waiting for you outside. He can show you the way."

Patel led them back inside the tower and bade them farewell. Hudai showed them back to the front door where Terzi waited.

*****

Marku trudged through the maze of city streets. His boots slopped through brown sludge, the remnants of the prior night's snowstorm. It had been snowing off and on for the past week. They were lucky in the valley, the snow was usually melted and gone by midday. The surrounding mountains, however, were covered in a thick blanket. Thank the gods they had arrived when they did. Marku shuddered at the thought of being trapped in the mountain passes during this series of storms.

He turned left at the boot maker and finally saw the fruit stand he had been looking for. They were the only grocer in town that still had fresh apples. It was a mystery how he kept them from getting soft or brown but he somehow managed. It had only taken Marku three weeks wandering the streets around the inn, but now he felt confident enough to venture out in the maze that was Patel's Rest without getting lost.

Marku purchased a half dozen apples, stuffing all but one in the pockets of his coat. He closed his eyes and gave a sigh of delight as he sunk his teeth into the one he'd held out. The juices dribbled down his chin as he savored the sweet, crunchy goodness. He ate it to its core, not wanting to waste a bite. Then, wiping a sleeve across his chin, he turned in the direction of the Blind Sparrow.

"…I don't know. He keeps the thing under lock and key. We barely get a glimpse of it when we're not on the road."

The sound of a familiar voice caught Marku's ear as he passed by an alleyway. He stopped for a moment to listen.

"Get it. Bring it to me, and you will have your reward." The response came from a low, gravelly voice. Marku couldn't tell if it was a man or woman. The scraping tone of the sound masked all sense of gender.

"Five hundred gold marks and a full pardon?" the familiar voice said.

Marku turned down the alley in the direction of the sounds.

"That's the deal," the mystery voice responded. "You bring me that box and it shall be done. You will be free to return home without fear of retaliation."

"For each of us?"

Each of them? Marku thought.

"Each of you," the dark voice answered with a sigh.

Marku turned the corner in the alley and saw a dark figure wearing a forest green travelling cloak. The creature's face was hidden by the deep cowl of the cloak. The figure turned to him as he entered the alcove.

"Oh, Marku." A sad voice sounded behind him. "No one was supposed to get hurt. This was supposed to be simple."

Marku turned toward the voice and then felt a sudden, sharp pain in his chest. He looked down in confusion. The knife jutted from his ribs just below his heart.

Marku looked up into the familiar brown eyes and stumbled forward. He clutched at the man's shirt, tearing it, as he fell to his knees. Marku gasped for breath, but was rewarded with spasms of pain as blood filled his lungs instead of air. The man took a step back and Marku heard the cloth tear more as his face and then his fist hit the stone street. Marku gulped again and tears filled his eyes, blurring his vision.

"Damn, I really like this shirt too."

"We'll get you another one. Get your knife and let's get out of here."

Marku felt his body being lifted but the sensation was far way. White lightning shot through his chest again as the blade was jerked free. The blood flowed freely now, and Marku felt warmth beneath the pain. The hammering in his ears slowed and the pain subsided. Only the warmth remained, and peace.

*****

Darius knelt beside Marku's body.

"This is where we found him," Captain Terzi said sympathetically.

Even if Darius had his doubts about the man after Arthengal had been killed Marku didn't deserve this. Marku had always been kind to him as a boy. "And no one saw anything?" Darius asked.

"No, we questioned the local merchants and anyone who lives in the area. A grocer around the way remembers seeing him this morning to buy some apples, but otherwise no one remembers anything."

The apples in question were scattered about Marku's body, ejected from his pockets when he fell. Darius reached out to touch Marku's right hand. It was clenched into a fist, but it held something. Darius pried the fingers apart enough to slip the piece of red cloth from in between them.

He fingered the fabric. It was linen, well-made, and had a splash of white on the edge.

"What did you find?" Captain Terzi asked.

"Cloth." Darius held it up. "From a shirt, I think. There's something familiar about it."

Darius heard cries of alarm from the street beyond the alley.

"There." One of Terzi's men pointed.

Darius followed the direction of the man's finger. A glowing red light floated across the sky. As he watched it, Darius saw another streaming light come from the direction of the western pass. This time the light was yellow.

"By Saridon's glass," Terzi cursed.

"What is it?" Darius asked.

"Invaders at the western gate."

Terzi and the other guards ran off down the street in the direction of the bridge into town. Darius followed. They reached the bridge and scanned the slopes coming down from the western pass. Nothing moved.

A green light suddenly shot into the air from the island castle behind them.

After a moment, a red flare followed, in answer, from the pass.

For a time, there was silence and they scanned the western reaches for movement. Then Darius heard three telltale thumps from the island castle. He turned his gaze skyward and saw three dark round shapes arching toward the mountain peaks above the western pass.

Chapter Sixteen
Invaders

Micah lifted another bite of roast venison to his mouth and chewed meticulously as he studied the girl on the opposite side of the table. She sat glumly, picking at her food but barely eating, just as she had every meal since they had left Isan. The open plains filled with cattlemen and shepherds had transformed into rolling foothills. Still Anna refused to meet Micah's gaze and only spoke when a direct question prevented otherwise.

She didn't complain or make demands. She just acted as though she were a prisoner, which Micah guessed she technically was. He didn't keep her in chains, and she was given the freedom to wander the camp. Two of his men, from Corporal Yanov's squad, followed her to make sure she didn't leave the camp, and more importantly, to make sure the lancers left her alone.

Earlier in the day a thunderstorm had rolled in out of the mountains and drenched the soldiers before they had time to set camp. Anna had stood defiantly in the pouring rain with her arms crossed over her chest waiting for her guards to set up her tent. Even now, her hair was matted to her head and shoulders demonstrating that she hadn't bothered to clean up in preparation for dinner.

"You really should eat something," Micah said in a gentle voice.

Anna remained silent.

"You're wasting away. What will my brother think if I let his bride-to-be wither to skin and bones?"

She shot him a fiery glare across the table.

"Not to mention the rift that it's likely to create with your parents. It's going to make holidays very awkward."

Anna barked a disdainful laugh. "Holidays. You don't think kidnapping your brother's betrothed is going to make family gatherings awkward?"

"That wasn't my choice," Micah corrected. "I'm trying to make the best of a bad situation here."

Anna laughed again.

"Have you been mistreated?" Micah asked.

"No," she admitted.

"Have I denied you the essentials? Food, water, a place to sleep?"

"No."

"Have I protected you from the prying eyes and hands of the soldiers? Did I not risk my own life to protect you from Lieutenant Zhukov?"

Anna nodded.

"I cannot let you go without betraying my relationship to Darius or without looking weak before the men. I command a tenuous situation here between the lancers and my Night Birds. I must maintain a position of strength."

She narrowed her eyes and studied him.

"They don't know that Darius is your brother."

"No," Micah replied simply. "The emperor knows, and he wants me to try to bring Darius into the fold. But it would be complicated to explain that to the men. It is easier to keep them in the dark. For now."

"I could betray you. Let them know that Darius is your brother."

Micah considered. "You could, but you won't. You're a smart girl. Even though you treat me with contempt, you know I'm your best hope at safety and survival. I would never do anything to hurt my brother, and by extension, I will protect you."

Anna's piercing brown eyes dissected him.

Micah cleared his throat and casually ate another bite of venison. "Look. I promise I will keep you safe and make your time with us as comfortable as possible. Will you please eat?"

Anna dropped her gaze to her plate. The venison and roasted carrots were covered with a brown gravy. A bowl of hard rolls sat on the table nearby, intended for use in sopping up the remaining gravy, which by Micah's judgment was the most appetizing part of the meal.

Anna stabbed at a slice of venison. "It's dry," she mumbled as she chewed.

Micah nodded.

Anna sampled a carrot. "They're bitter." She reached for a roll and it crumbled in her hands as she tried to break it in half. She sighed and gave Micah a frustrated look.

"Yeah, but at least the gravy is good," Micah said as he ate another bite, dripping with the stuff.

For the first time the barest hint of a smile crossed Anna's face and she reached across the table for the bowl of brown liquid.

*****

The rain continued for several days, but after the second night it had lightened up enough that Micah decided they could travel. The wagons still moved slowly and more than once had to be freed from mud. As they climbed out of the foothills the air chilled, the ground became firmer, and the rain changed to freezing sleet and finally to snow. Travel became drudging and slow. The soldiers labored in shifts to keep the road cleared ahead of them but the group only advanced two or three leagues a day.

Anna had continued to warm during these days and their meals became more pleasant. The perpetual frost at the other side of the table had thawed to merely a cool breeze.

"How did you and Darius meet?" Micah asked one evening.

"Through Uncle Arthengal."

"Nasu Rabi was your uncle?" Micah was unable to hide the disbelief in his voice.

"Well, not my real uncle. He served with my grandfather in the war. They remained good friends after the war. He was like an uncle to my father and treated my brothers and me like we were family."

Micah sighed in relief. Being a blood relation to Nasu Rabi would have been more dangerous for her than being Darius's fiancée.

"Uncle Arthengal and Darius would stay at our farm outside of Eridu when they came to town to sell their ropes and nets."

"Sell their what now?" Micah asked.

"Ropes and nets. Arthengal was a master craftsman and he was teaching Darius the trade. Once we are married, Father said we can start rotating hemp with the corn. Darius and I can build a house on the north side of the farm, closer to the ocean, but not too far away from the main house. Darius can tend the fields and continue to make rope, and I can tend the house and children."

Micah listened, amazed. This was the life that Darius wanted? A domestic existence similar to how they were raised. With a trade he would be more comfortable and wouldn't be beholden to the next hunt or catch, but still, such a simple life sounded…boring.

"But I thought General Arthengal was teaching Darius to be a weapons master like himself."

"Oh, the sword thing? Yeah, Arthengal was teaching him that too. But that was just so they could rescue Cordelia. Now that she is safe it's time for Darius to settle down."

Micah hid his grin by brushing a hand across his mouth. So, this was Anna's dream, not necessarily Darius's.

"The sword thing?" Micah said bewildered. "You do know that Arthengal was the best swordsman the world has known in several lifetimes and Darius is nearly as good. They are sword masters."

"I do like to watch him practice." Anna said dreamily. "It is certainly masterful." Then, realizing she had spoken aloud, she blushed and changed the subject. "That's all well and good, but swordplay only has one use and it rarely helps put food on the table or raise a family."

"War is coming, Anna." Micah turned serious. "The emperor is going to restore order to the land and free it from the corruption of the land barons, just like Chung Oku Mai did in ancient times. Swordplay could be Darius's most valuable skill in the coming days."

Anna opened her mouth to say something, then thought better of it and took a bite of the pheasant pie on her plate. She chewed slowly, and Micah could tell she was deep in thought. Finally, she swallowed.

"Whether the emperor rules or the barons rule, the only skills that Darius needs are those that will help him care for his family. You speak of war like it is an adventure. I lived with my grandfather after the last great war. I still remember his screams at night when the terrors would take him in his sleep. I don't want that for Darius or our children. I don't want your war, and I will do whatever is necessary to keep Darius free from it."

Micah smiled sadly across the table. "I admire your determination, Anna. And part of me hopes that you are successful. However, I've seen my brother fight. He feels the call in his blood. He will fight, either for the empire or against it. I hope to bring him to the side of the victors because it would break my heart to see him condemned as a rebel and hanged. His best chance to survive this war is on the side of Emperor Lao. When we catch up to him, if you want this domestic fairytale to come true, then you will help me convince him of that."

*****

When the weather finally cleared, Micah's little army made better time. They cleared the foothills and followed the winding road that rose into the mountains proper. The road followed a small river which provided easy access to water and fish. The air continued to cool as they climbed, and Micah could see they were approaching the snowline.

At first, the snow didn't encumber them. It was only ankle deep on the horses and the wagons rolled easily through it. Then they turned a bend in the road where the wind had blown freely down a long canyon. The snow had been piled in chest-high drifts a dozen paces wide. They had been forced to camp for the remainder of the day while they cleared the road. After a similar drift the following day Micah decided to leave the camp intact and send parties ahead to clear the roads. Once a league or so had been cleared they would advance. In this manner they crept up the mountain road toward the summit.

"Lieutenant Kabir." The scout pulled his horse to a stop in front of Micah.

"What is it?" Micah asked.

"Towers, sir."

Micah followed the scout over the next rise in the road. There in the distance he could see two stone towers built into the cliffs. He surveyed the surrounding landscape. The glacial peaks were impassable. Skilled climbers with the proper equipment might be able to circumnavigate the towers, but no army could and certainly not with supplies. The towers were well positioned to defend whatever lay beyond them.

Micah returned to camp and assembled a small force of a dozen of his men and a dozen lancers.

"Why not just take everyone?" Joral asked as they rode east.

"I want to check it out first," Micah explained. "Look at the cliffs around you. Every aspect of the terrain funnels you toward those towers. Not only does it make the positioning of the towers defensible, but it also creates the perfect terrain to lay a trap. If I commanded whatever forces control the tower, I would place archers there and there."

Micah pointed to a pair of angled benches on either side of the canyon they were passing through.

"You can't see the top of the ridge from here. You could easily hide a hundred men in the folds of the mountain."

"Yeah, but how would you get them up there?"

"Ladders and ropes." Micah was surprised by the question. Normally Joral was quicker to catch on. "With time and resources, you could easily create avenues of ascent that you would use to position forces. They could have been observing us for days now and we could be walking into a trap."

"That valley there could hide cavalry." Moab pointed to a long stretch of flat land that spread away from the road and they reached the bottom of a steep dip in the road. The basin turned around a stone outcropping and it was impossible to tell how far it continued beyond. The invisible space could have hidden a lone horseman or an entire battalion.

"Exactly, now you're catching on," Micah congratulated his companion.

They made the final ascent to the towers and Micah admired the construction. They were built into the solid basalt of the cliffs. Huge beams, more than a pace wide, had been hewn square and bound together to form a thick wall between the two towers. The walls were rough and could possibly be climbed, but anyone making the attempt would be at the mercy of the towers and the many, many arrow slits that Micah saw decorating their heights.

Micah pulled his horse to a stop before the lone gate that offered passage through the wall. "Hello gate," Micah shouted.

After a time, a face appeared in a window halfway up the western tower. The old man studied Micah and his men for a moment before responding. Micah's men wore the black leather armor of the Night Birds. The lancers' armor was lighter in color but thicker around the chest and legs. Their long lances were stowed in an upright position. Micah's soldiers each had six or eight spears stored behind their saddles within easy reach.

"Soldiers, then," the bald man from the tower shouted. "I don't recognize the crest. Which baron do you serve? Not Shalanum, nor Magora."

"We serve no baron," Micah reported. "We serve the rightful ruler of these lands, the Holy Emperor Lao Jun Qiu."

Micah let the words settle before continuing. "We mean your master no harm. We are following a band of criminals in from Eridu by way of Isan. We only wish to return them to imperial lands for trial and sentencing."

"Emperor Lao, you say. And where might these imperial lands of yours be? You are a long way from The Wastes and all lands west of here belong to Baron Shalanum."

"No longer," Micah said. "Shalanum Province north of Eridu and Isan has been liberated by the imperial army. The rest of Shalanum will be freed from the tyranny of Baron Shalanum by next summer."

This news seemed to shock the tower keeper. Micah scanned the towers and walls for other signs of movement. Could this old man be alone? Surely not, why would you sacrifice your most defensible position by leaving it guarded so poorly? There must be others still in hiding.

"Are you sure the men you seek came this way?" the man in the tower asked.

"You tell me. They would have had to pass through your gate. A boy of eighteen and his mother accompanied by a blacksmith and a pair of guardsmen."

"You're hardly describing hardened criminals, if you don't mind me saying. What did these people do that warrants this new emperor sending the army after them?"

"The boy was among those who led an assault on a compound north of Eridu. They killed a dozen or more imperial guards and stole valuable imperial artifacts," Micah explained. "The men he travels with were involved in the raid as well."

"Doesn't sound like anyone we've had this way recently—"

"They would have been travelling with a bear as well, nearly the size of my horse."

The tower guard stammered at this and in his eyes, Micah could tell that the guardsman had seen the bear.

"A b-b-bear, you say. Why would -- *how* would people travel with a bear?"

"There's no need to lie," Micah interrupted. "As I said, we mean your master no harm. I don't even need to march my men into your valley. Bring me the criminals and all they possess and we'll be on our way."

"Your men?" The tower guard surveyed the small party at the base of the towers. Micah glanced over his shoulder toward the pass where they had entered and gave the barest nod of his chin. The gatekeeper seemed to understand. "Ah, I see. Let me send a message to the main castle. I'll be right back."

The old man disappeared inside the tower. A few minutes later Micah heard a thump from the top of the tower. It reminded Micah of the sound when the Lightning Bringers launch their night showers. He looked past the tower and saw a red light streaming toward the valley beyond. A moment later the sound repeated, and Micah saw a yellow light trailing through the sky to the northwest.

"That's an odd way of communicating," Joral observed.

"No odder than flashing lights or flags to communicate between ships," Moab noted.

After a time, they saw a green light arcing through the air in the distance. The tower responded with another red streamer. Three loud thumps echoed up the canyon walls originating from somewhere beyond the wall.

"There." Moab pointed.

Three dark round shapes traced a path across the blue and white sky. Two of the shapes flew toward the peaks to the east of the pass and one to the western peak. Just before the shapes struck the mountain they exploded.

Micah clapped his hands over his ears as the sound reverberated across the cliffs and canyons. He felt the vibrations of the noise in his chest. Micah half expected to see blood on his fingers as he pulled them away from his ears.

"Ride!" Moab shouted suddenly. He wheeled his horse and thundered down the road in the direction they had come.

Micah and Joral turned and followed without questioning Moab's order. The rest of the Night Birds followed quickly behind. The lancers were slower to respond. Micah glanced back as he crested the next rise. His men galloped past as he reined in slightly. Too late, the lancers recognized the danger they were in. They whipped their horses and raced up the hill for all they were worth.

Micah watched as billowing clouds descended toward the riders. A sound like a thousand galloping horses echoed off the mountainside. Showers of ice and gravel pelted the soldiers and their horses.

A boulder bounced off the cliff and carried the lead rider off his horse into the cliff wall. A wave of white followed the boulder. The horses were pushed a half step to the right by the flood of snow then all disappeared. Debris bounced off the road behind him, and Micah heeled his horse, charging forward once again.

It took an hour for Micah, Moab, and Joral to pick their way across the debris of the avalanche after the snow and dust settled. Finally, they were able to see the destruction beyond the hill. The road, the towers, and the wall were all hidden from view, buried under a turbulent sea of snow, rocks, and twisted trees.

On the opposite shore Micah saw an assemblage of men in blue uniforms forming up. There were about thirty men in all. As one, they raised their bows and fired. The arrows all struck the snow a hundred paces from where Micah and his men stood. It was three hundred paces across the avalanche plain to the archers. If they tried to charge it would be a killing field.

"How many men did we lose?" Micah asked.

"The Night Birds all made it clear, but all twelve lancers were lost. Bloody shame, some of them were good men. Seems like an extreme reaction," Moab quipped. "Wipe out your tower and walls to prevent a few dozen soldiers from entering."

"The defenses are probably not as damaged as you might think," Micah responded. It was a shame about the men. Had they reacted immediately at Moab's warning some of them may have made it. "But this road is surely blocked until spring. There is no way we could get the horses across."

"What do we do now?" Moab asked.

"A few of us will find a way in somehow," Micah said absently as he studied the surrounding landscape and the archers that guarded the approach. "I think a small group can get in. I need to find out if Darius and his group are still here, and if they have the box."

Moab and Joral watched silently.

"We are the Night Birds, after all," Micah added with a wink. "They can't keep us out."

His men shared a smile before all three turned back to their camp.

Chapter Seventeen
Traitors

"Come with me." Captain Terzi waved a hand to get Darius's attention.

Darius looked back at the scene in the alley and the still body of his companion. He was torn between finding out more about whoever was attacking the western gate and who had killed Marku.

"My men will finish up here. They'll take his body back to the keep. They will let you know if they find anything else. Master Patel will want to talk to you about what's going on at the pass." Captain Terzi urged Darius to follow.

They wound through the streets until they reached the castle. Hudai was waiting for them at the door and he led them to Patel's study. To Darius's surprise, Amadan, the tower guard from the western gate, was seated in a chair talking to Patel.

"How did you get here?" Darius asked. "I figured you would be buried under a couple hundred paces of snow."

"There are tunnels that run from the gate towers back to the main city," Patel explained. "Amandan, tell Darius what you were telling me."

"They said they were with the imperial army," Amadan explained. "Their flag and crest showed black dragons. I've never seen the like before."

"It is the crest of the Lao family," Patel explained. "They were lords of the eastern isles and Kasha Kyoshu in the Yappon province. I'm surprised you don't remember. It was the death of Lao Cang that triggered the civil war."

"That was a long time ago, m'lord. There were too many sigils to remember in those days. Now, with only nine, it's easier." Amadan shrugged.

"The Lao family would have been next in line after the Chens. So, not only a new emperor but a new dynasty, it would seem." Patel turned to Darius. "Do you recognize the crest?"

"Two black dragons intertwined on a field of blue?" Darius asked.

Amadan nodded.

"That's the same flag that flew over the emperor's house where we rescued my mother. She told me that the leader there called himself Emperor Lao Jun Qiu."

"Yeah, that's the name they used," Amadan confirmed. "Said they was tracking criminals that attacked the emperor, killed his guards, and stole some sort of treasure."

"I admit to the attack, but we didn't steal anything. We only freed a bunch of slaves, including my mother. They've been chasing us since we fled Anbar Ur," Darius explained.

"They also said Eridu and Isan have fallen to this new emperor and that the rest of Shalanum will fall by summer," Amadan added.

Patel leaned back in his chair considering. When he spoke, it was more to himself than the others. "If the emperor is trying to wage a war against Shalanum it seems unlikely that he would send a detachment into the mountains after a few escaped slaves. Our data is incomplete. If not the slaves, then the boy. Why the boy? Arthengal's apprentice. Not something the boy stole, something Arthengal stole."

Patel turned his full attention to Darius.

"Did Arthengal give you a box? It would have been made of dark oak, simply carved, and banded in iron. There would be two locks."

"How could you possibly know that?" Darius blurted without thinking, caught off-guard by the old man's apparent ability to read his mind.

"I saw the box many times during my years at Kasha Esharra. The items that are inside are said to be touched by the gods and were given to Chung Oku Mai by Antu, the sky father himself."

"What is in the box?" Darius asked.

"So, you haven't opened it?" Patel sounded surprised.

"No." Darius shook his head. "Arthengal asked me to take it to someone named Saria in Kasha Marka."

Patel laughed.

"Am I missing something?" Darius asked.

"No, just the cliché of one living legend passing accoutrements of the gods off to another living legend for safe keeping." Patel chuckled again.

Darius looked even more confused.

"You probably are more familiar with Saria Oberman's *nom de guerre*, Sillu Mitu, the Night Shadow."

Darius was dumbfounded. Another character from his mother's stories seemingly come to life.

"So, what's in the box?" It was Amadan who asked the question this time.

"For lack of more descriptive terms I guess you would say a crown and a scepter, but they are much more than that," Patel explained. "When worn together they make the wearer appear to be 'bathed in the light of the heavens.' A glow surrounds him. They are a major part of how the emperors were able to convince the common folk that they were gods."

"So, they're magical?" Darius asked.

"The emperors would have you believe that. I've had a long-held suspicion to the contrary," Patel said. "I suspect they are adorned with specially cut crystals. When paired together and held at the proper angle, they reflect the light of the sun and make the wearer seem to glow. I have never been allowed to examine the artifacts to confirm my suspicions. I have seen them in use several times. It's quite spectacular to observe. I can see why the small folk thought the emperors were gods."

"So, they aren't magical?" Darius asked.

Patel shrugged and then winked. "What is magic? Illusion? Alchemy? Allurement? Because they are certainly all of those."

"Well, it's, uh, I don't know, magical. Otherworldly, I guess."

Patel laughed again. "That would be in the eye of the beholder, now wouldn't it? They certainly seem otherworldly when you observe the phenomenon."

"So, then we can destroy them?" Darius asked.

"That depends on if you believe in the old gods and if you believe in the mysticism that they will curse you and all your future generations if you destroy them. It certainly could be legend, but if even Arthengal, the least pious person I know, couldn't work up the nerve to toss them in a volcano somewhere, I don't know who can."

"What about you?"

"What *about* me?"

"Well, you seem devoted to science and alchemy. If you don't believe in the gods, then you can destroy them."

"You misunderstand my motivations, young man. While I am devoted to improving my understanding of the world around me, I have seen too much to believe there isn't some sort of intelligence behind the design of our world. I am definitely not inclined to test the will and the wrath of the gods."

Darius sighed. "So, we continue to Kasha Marka."

"Where is the box?" Patel asked.

"Hidden in my rooms back at the inn."

"The box and its contents are extremely valuable. We would not want them to fall into the wrong hands. This new emperor would pay handsomely for the box and I'm sure he has spies everywhere if he is making a move on the baronies."

Darius nodded. "There have been men pursuing me since I left Eridu. They carry bounty notices. I assumed it was because of the attack on the compound, but it makes more sense if he is after the box rather than me."

"What's the bounty?" Amadan asked with a twinkle in his eye.

"They've gone up all summer. The last one was three hundred marks." Darius said.

"Bah," Amadan spat. "Hardly worth the trouble. Wait until the reward is over five thousand marks and you are forced to move into the mountains and change your name." He laughed.

Patel coughed. "In any case, you should probably put it in safe keeping here until you are able to leave. Would you object to moving it to our vault? It would also give me the opportunity to study the objects and confirm my suspicions about their properties."

Darius considered for a minute. "No, but I'll keep the keys with me if you don't mind."

"Whatever you want," Patel said.

A soldier dressed in blue with red lapels entered the study. He held a brief exchange with Captain Terzi and then left.

"What do you have to report, Captain?" Patel asked.

"A small scouting party was seen investigating the opposite side of the avalanche field. We have three squads of archers keeping watch."

"Will thirty archers be enough to hold the line?" Patel asked.

"We have two more companies of archers waiting and the lancers are assembling if they need to defend the base of the pass. We don't yet know the full size of the imperial detachment."

"There weren't more than thirty at the gates," Amadan said. "But the officer that was leading them made a show of implying there were a lot more over the hill."

"Two hundred and thirty archers should hold long enough. The snow will be too unstable for horses and it will take them a while to cross, should they come. Keep me posted, Captain. Now, if you wouldn't mind escorting young Darius here back to his room so he can retrieve that box."

*****

Darius entered the inn. There was a small dining area for guests on the main floor, as well as the kitchens and living quarters for the innkeeper and his family. The guest rooms, six in all, were upstairs. Lianna and his mother shared one of the rooms. Darius shared one with Kal and the other six men were paired off in what remained. Ander had been sleeping with Marku. Darius decided that he should tell the others about Marku before he moved the box.

Darius knocked on the door of his mother's room.

"Just a minute." The call came from the other side of the door and then his mother, wrapped in a shawl, opened the door just wide enough to glance out. "Oh, Darius. What is it? Can it wait? I was just about to have a bath. It's taken poor Millicent nearly an hour to set everything up."

"I have some bad news, I'm afraid," Darius said. "I was going to assemble everyone downstairs to tell you all at the same time."

"What is it?" Her face looked worried.

"Marku is dead."

"Oh my," she gasped and covered her mouth with her hand, nearly dropping the shawl. She looked over her shoulder regretfully. "I'll make it a quick bath. Round up the men and I'll be down in less than an hour."

Darius found Kal in the main room having a lunch of fish stew and oat cakes. Ander had been in his room reading. The other four men were out. Darius asked Master Abel, the innkeeper, to send his sons out to see if they could find them.

"Is this about the explosions in the mountains?" Nicolai asked as he and Gunnar entered the common room.

Cordelia and Lianna entered the room just behind the brothers. One of Abel's sons, Jesop, was still out looking for Matia and Petri, but Darius decided not to wait.

"No, but we can discuss that, as well. First, I have bad news." He addressed the group. "A few hours ago, one of Captain Terzi's city patrols found Marku. He had been killed, stabbed in the chest.

They are still trying to figure out what happened, but it looks like he was robbed."

"How could this happen?" Kal asked, dismayed. "I thought this city was supposed to be safe? Are the rest of us in danger?"

"It is," Darius reassured him. "There hasn't been a crime like this in years. Captain Terzi and Master Patel both send their deepest sympathies and assure us that they will uncover the truth. There wasn't sign of a struggle, so Captain Terzi surmised that Marku was taken by surprise."

"Poor Marku," Cordelia sniffed. "After everything he had been through."

Lianna stifled a sob and then turned her face into Cordelia's shoulder.

The innkeeper's son, Jesop, entered the room. "I'm sorry, Master Darius, but your men have left the valley."

"What do you mean they've left the valley?" Darius asked. "There must be some mistake."

"No, sir. I spoke with Master Eran, who raises the dogs who pull the sleds. He said that Master Matia and Master Petri were at his shop not two hours ago. They bought supplies, sleds, and dogs for a trip over the eastern pass. They said they was following your orders and that they had to get to Kasha Marka as soon as possible."

Darius ran his fingers through his hair. This didn't make sense. "Kal, go check their rooms, please."

Kal ran up the stairs taking them two at a time. Darius paced the small room. Cordelia comforted Lianna. The other three men remained seated, but wore expressions of varying degrees of concern.

Kal returned clutching a red shirt.

"Empty except for this." Kal held the shirt out. It was a simple red shirt with white striping. It was open at the top with leather laces that could be tightened to close it. The shirt was torn down the left side and all of the leather laces dangled uselessly. A patch of the shirt had been torn free.

Darius fished in his pocket. He fingered the red cloth in his hand.

"What is it?" Ander asked.

Darius held out the cloth. "When we found Marku, he was clutching this in his hand."

Ander took the cloth and held it up against the shirt that Kal held. It was a match.

"But why?" Ander seemed as baffled as the rest of them.

"I can't think of a thing. I thought they got on well with Marku." Darius shook his head. Then something from his earlier conversation with Patel struck him. "Unless."

Darius sprinted up the stairs and thrust the door to his room open. He lifted the blankets to reveal the space beneath his bed. Empty. He flipped the mattress and searched all around the small room.

Nothing. The box was gone.

Chapter Eighteen
Manhunt

Darius retraced the path back to Master Patel's keep. This time his entire entourage was in tow. He banged on the door with a hint of impatience. Hudai answered, taken aback as Darius tried to push through the door. He held a firm hand against Darius's chest. He would not disregard propriety.

Darius met the Hudai's steady gaze and took a long breath to calm himself. "Is he still in his study?" Darius asked.

Hudai glanced uncertainly at the large party then nodded reluctantly. He stepped out of the way and waved a hand to invite entrance into the keep. He led the party through the silent hallways to a large oak door.

Darius burst into the study. "It's gone."

Patel looked up from his book in surprise. He paused before responding, then gave a nod. "The box. It was taken by some of your men, who are responsible for killing the blacksmith."

"How do you do that?" Darius complained in frustration.

Patel smiled slightly. "Have they escaped the valley yet?"

"They purchased sleds, dogs, and supplies a few hours ago. So, they can't have gotten far." Darius said.

"They will have gone east. The western gate would have been blocked by then. It will take time to get gear together for you to follow. How many of your companions will you be taking with you?"

Darius hadn't thought that far ahead. He considered briefly. "Three. Ander and the twins. Kal will remain here with my mother and Lianna. They will follow behind with our horses after the pass clears."

Patel nodded.

"And Antu, of course," Darius added.

"Ah, your bear. I would very much like to meet him someday. Would you mind if I sent some of Captain Terzi's men along with you? They will be more experienced with the dog sleds and you will make better time that way."

Darius shrugged. "That's fine. How quickly can we leave?"

Patel eyed the sun through the western windows of the study. It was settling low over the mountains.

"It would be better if you wait until morning. We can get the supplies and men together this evening and you can set out at first light."

Darius sighed.

*****

"I most certainly will not!" Cordelia burst out as Darius explained the plan back in the common room of the Blind Sparrow.

"Mother, it makes the most sense for you and Lianna to stay here."

"Why?" Cordelia huffed. "Because we are women?"

"You are, but that's not the reason." Darius said patiently. "Lianna is still a child and has no business being there if things turn ugly once we catch up to Matia and Petri. She would either be in the way or be in danger if she comes. She won't stay if you go. So you have to stay, too."

"And why do I have to stay?" Kal's expression was as grumpy as Cordelia's. "Why not Ander? Or Nicolai and Gunnar?"

"Because Ander knows these men. He's worked with them off and on for years. He is our best chance of ending this without a fight. If it does end in violence, I know Nicolai and Gunnar can handle themselves."

Kal looked hurt at the last.

"Look," Darius said impatiently. "Somebody has to come with me, and somebody has to stay back with the supplies. This is what made the most sense to me. If anyone has a strong argument why I should change my mind speak up now. Otherwise we need to pack our things and at least try to get a few hours of sleep."

Cordelia's mouth moved silently as she tried to put words to a plan that wouldn't come. Kal glanced anxiously between Darius and his mother.

Finally, Cordelia sighed and dropped her gaze to the floor. "No, I can't think of a better plan," she said, her voice barely a whisper.

Kal's face was crestfallen. Darius felt bad for his friend, but this was the best way. They had to travel quickly and be prepared to fight.

*****

Darius and his three companions met Captain Terzi at the eastern gate to the city just before dawn.

"This is Ensign Kaya, and Guardsmen Anat, Osman, and Klein." The captain introduced Darius to the four soldiers who would be accompanying them. "They will handle the sleds. Each of you will be paired with one of them and will ride in front of them on the sledge. They can get you situated."

"Thank you, Captain," Darius said.

"Come along then," Ensign Kaya directed. "We've already hauled the dogs and sleds up to the snowline past the gates."

When they arrived at the gate there were eight dogs harnessed to each of five sleds. Two boys, introduced as Wilem and Prat, were checking the harnesses.

"Why five sleds?" Darius asked.

"The fifth is just for supplies. The boys will bring it along behind us. Give them any gear you want to stow and then we'll get you situated."

The sleds looked nothing like what Darius had imagined. In his mind he had pictured something like the sleighs described in books he and Arthengal had read. The dogs were harnessed to a flat length of lacquered wood. It curled slightly in the front. Wooden supports had been added to keep the passenger or supplies from tumbling out the sides and to give the driver something to hang on to. All in all, they looked very flimsy and he couldn't imagine they would be comfortable to sit in.

The boys, Wilem and Prat, spread a blanket of wolf pelts on the sled and instructed Darius how to sit.

"Don't hold on to the sides," Wilem warned.

"Why not?" Darius asked.

"You'll break your wrists if the sled flips over.

Instilled with even more confidence Darius took his place on the sled. He stored his swords on one side of his legs and hooked the belts around the frame of the sled so they wouldn't become lost in the snow if they did tip over. On his other side he secured his bow and a quiver, a leather cap secured tightly over the end to protect the fletchings from moisture.

Wilem offered Darius another blanket to place over his legs once he was situated. He was more comfortable than he imagined he would be.

The dogs started barking wildly as Darius settled himself. He turned his head to see the massive shape of Antu lumbering up from the eastern gate. The bear paused as the dogs began to franticly pull at their bindings.

Darius leapt up and approached the bear. He scratched Antu's head and then leaned in. "I don't think those dogs like you," he said quietly.

Antu grunted and then a low growl resonated in his chest.

"And you don't like them much, either," Darius laughed. "Maybe it would be better for everyone if you followed a little further behind. We need the dogs to get us where we are going, and I wouldn't want any of them to injure themselves trying to test their mettle."

Antu growled again and then plodded north, around the howling dogs.

*****

Snow spread out before them. There was no sign of a road beyond the eastern gate. The gate itself was all but buried from the storm. The lee side had knee-deep drifts but only the very top of the wall was visible on the side where the storm had struck.

Once everyone was in their places, Wilem and Prat went around to each group of dogs and untied the lead dog from a stake that had been driven into the snow. The dogs began to bark and prance. They were excited to get underway.

"Hike, hike," Ensign Kaya shouted, and Darius's sled lurched forward. They picked up speed quickly and soon were shooting down the slope away from the gate. Darius felt an exhilaration unlike anything he'd ever felt. It was like riding a horse fast across a meadow but because he was so low to the ground, he felt more stimulated by the motion. He also felt a little bit uneasy given he had no control over the dogs or the sled.

"Lean into the corner," Kaya shouted over the sound of the dogs as they approached the first bend.

"Gee, gee," Kaya ordered to the dogs. Darius did as he was told, and they glided around the turn.

He glanced back and saw a sled behind them about ten paces. He couldn't see much beyond that from his vantage.

"Whoa, whoa," Kaya shouted as the slope began to steepen. The dogs slowed to a trot and Kaya worked the sled to keep it from overtaking the animals as they careened down a steep incline.

"Hike, hike," Kaya commanded again as they neared the bottom of the dip. The dogs took off again gaining momentum to climb the rise on the other side. Kaya jumped off the back as the sled climbed and pushed, running behind, while the dogs pulled. As soon as they reached the top, he stepped back into position.

The dogs rounded a left turn as Kaya hollered, "Haw, haw."

They made great time through the snow-covered pass. Soon Darius noticed an icy scar trace across the serene white of the hills from the right. It joined their trail and ran parallel to their course. He remembered the river that had flowed out of the mountains along the road they had entered. That mountain stream had been much more inviting than this blue-white crevasse that followed them now.

They stopped around midday for a meal. The dogs were ravenous and thirsty. Half the provisions on the supply sled seemed to be devoted to the dogs.

Darius inspected the placid landscape. The snow was unbroken, with the exception of the ravine to their right.

"Are you sure they came this way?" Darius asked. "It doesn't look like anyone has come this way since the storm."

"The path has drifted over, but I can still make it out. Look for a slight depression in the snow. It is very subtle."

Darius studied the plain of snow before them. Then he kneeled and looked at the horizon of the snow where the trail turned downhill again. He could make out two very slight breaks in the otherwise flat line separating snow from sky.

"How far ahead of us are they?" Darius asked.

"It's difficult to tell," Kaya said. "Their track is even, unusual for amateurs. So, either they have experience, or they hired guides."

"More likely the latter," Ander commented as he approached from behind. "These are cattlemen. I've worked with them for almost five years. They are never very far from a ranch."

"Were they from Isan? Where did they work before Eban Malik hired them on?" Darius asked.

Ander shrugged. "No, they came into Isan about five years ago. They had experience though, you can tell. They either grew up on ranches or worked another one somewhere else. There is no shortage of ranches on the Taspin plains. It's the best sheep and cattle land I've ever seen."

"They came together? So, they knew each other before?" Darius asked.

Ander nodded.

"They were decent men and hard workers." Ander said. "It just doesn't make sense why they would do this."

They found where their quarry had camped the night before about an hour past their midday break. The following day they came upon a similar campsite about an hour before they planned to stop.

"We're making up ground at least," Kaya commented. "They may not realize they are being followed so they may not be pressing their teams. At this pace we should catch them in five or six days."

Darius thought back to their ascent into the mountains. "Will we still be in the mountains or will we have dropped into the foothills by then?"

"Hard to say," Kaya said. "It will be close. The eastern side of the mountains drops more gradually than the west. We'll be out of the major passes for sure, but we won't be in the lowlands. There will still be plenty of snow to run the sleds, provided they don't catch on and speed up their pace."

"Do we have enough provisions to last for a trip that long?" Darius asked.

"The boys will set snares after the evening meal. There is usually no problem supplementing our needs, as long as you aren't too particular regarding the type of meat you eat." Kaya said.

Darius thought about the various types of varmints that might populate high mountain passes and didn't inquire further.

*****

Once they left the passes a few days later the ground was more open. Darius had expected evergreens and tree-covered slopes like the mountains near Anbar Ur. Instead the white terrain continued, broken only by the glacial lakes and the occasional bushy tree poking through the snow.

One day, after the midday meal, Kaya called Darius to the edge of a nearby hill. The ledge looked out over a wide winter plain below them. Stark white hills rose out of the valley on the other side. Kaya knelt down.

"Do you see there?" He pointed across the valley.

Darius saw three black lines cutting across the alpine hills.

"Is that them?" Darius asked.

Kaya nodded. "They can't be more than a few hours ahead of us. We'll wait until they crest that hill to get going again. They would be able to see us just as clearly and I don't want to spook them. We should catch them by tomorrow night. We should go without fires tonight. They would be able to see the light for miles."

By noon the next day they could hear the barking of the dogs in front of them.

"If we can hear them, they can hear us," Kaya commented. "We should press a little harder."

Darius nodded and was rewarded with a spray of snow in the face as dogs churned the snow.

An hour later Darius sat up tall in the sled. He could see a dark shape cresting the hill in front of them. Kaya jumped off his perch and ran behind the sled pushing. His breath became more labored and by the time he stepped back into the driver's position he was panting as loudly as the dogs. The sled slid over the precipice of the next downhill slope and Darius could see the other sled clearly and another two sleds not too much farther beyond.

Two men rode what appeared to be Matia and Petri's provisions sled similarly to how Darius and Kaya rode. One of the men glanced back and saw Darius. The driver cracked a whip over the top of the dogs' heads and his sled pulled away.

"That was unnecessary." Kaya said disapprovingly.

Darius and Kaya's sled fishtailed down the mountain as Kaya let off on the brake. At the base of the hill the terrain was flat and wide for leagues in all directions. Darius heard a groan and crack as their sled hit the flat space.

"It's a mountain lake," Kaya explained. "Normally the trail would run over that way along that ridge." He pointed south.

"Will it hold?" Darius asked.

"I sure hope so," Kaya responded. "It's a bit early in the season, but I've come here ice fishing later in the winter. The lake gets a good thick sheet most years. They seem to think it will hold." Kaya indicated their quarry. "We'd lose two days on them going around, though."

The ice below them groaned again.

Darius glanced back. Their other sleds had stopped at the edge of the lake and they seemed to be discussing their options. After a moment or two they spread out. Each took a slightly different route across the lake. Darius started to ask why but his thoughts were broken by a loud crack that echoed across the valley.

Darius turned quickly just in time to see the driver of the sled in front of them flail briefly and then disappear. He only had a moment to ponder their disappearance before a series of loud cracks and pops drew their attention. Water was seeping through the ice and edging toward them.

"Gee, gee," Kaya shouted and immediately turned the sled south. Darius leaned into the turn, and soon they were driving perpendicular to their targets.

Darius looked back questioningly at Kaya.

"The lake is shallower on the southern end. The ice will be thicker." Kaya shouted his response to the unspoken question.

Darius nodded and then searched the bleak landscape for any sign of the closest sled. Dogs, men, and sled had all disappeared. Darius's heart ached with guilt, especially for the loss of the dogs, but for the men as well who were probably just hired hands and had had no part in the theft or the death of Marku.

As their elevation had dropped, Darius began to realize that what he had assumed were bushy scrub trees at the beginning of the trip were actually scraggly pine trees. At their current elevation the infrequent conifers towered three or four paces above the snow. The eastern edge of the lake was home to a forest of these trees. Hundreds of them, no more than a span across and at most five paces tall, covered the bank and hillside beyond. Darius could see the remaining two sleds disappear into this forest as Kaya once again urged their dogs to turn after them. Darius and Kaya were just over halfway across the lake and their targets were almost a league ahead of them now.

"We won't catch them today," Kaya sighed. "We should regroup at the other side of the lake and find a good place to camp. We'll start early and make up some ground. They won't be able to travel as fast now that they've lost their supplies."

*****

"There they are," Ensign Kaya pointed.

Darius scrambled to his knees. He shaded his eyes against the afternoon sun. He could see the two sleds about two hundred paces ahead coming out of the trees. They were travelling about the same speed. It would be a long chase to close the distance unless they could figure out a way to slow them down.

Darius retrieved a bow string from his belt pouch. He strung the bow and then removed the leather cover to his quiver. He drew out an arrow and then carefully he stood on the sled.

"What are you doing?" Kaya said worriedly.

Darius spread his feet creating a solid base. The rocking of the sled made him feel unbalanced as the sled rocketed across the uneven ground. He repositioned his feet in opposite corners and felt a little better.

He nocked the arrow and drew it back evenly, judging the distance. His breathing steadied and he released the string like parting silk.

The arrow flew the distance and landed a good fifty paces behind the rear sled. They were moving faster than he had thought.

Darius knelt gingerly, trying not to rock the sled, and retrieved another arrow.

His second shot landed in the snow a few paces to the left of the sled. The driver looked back nervously and cracked his whip over the top of the dog's heads.

Darius didn't want to hurt anyone, but he feared he might actually have to shoot one of them.

He tried a third time, aiming for a spot between the two sleds. Just as he released, Ensign Kaya guided the sled over a snow-covered tree. The sled lurched and Darius's bow dipped. The arrow soared through the air and stuck into the wooden railing next to the driver's hands.

"That was amazing," Ensign Kaya applauded the shot.

"Uh, yeah. Thanks," Darius said, blushing.

The driver screamed then guided his sled to a stop.

"I surrender, I surrender!" He was shouting as Darius and Kaya pulled up beside them. The driver dropped into the snow with his hands stretched out before him. Matia looked up meekly from the seat of the sled.

"Do you have it?" Darius asked.

Matia shook his head and pointed. "The box is in Petri's sled."

Darius turned. Petri and his sled were reaching the edge of Darius's range. He notched another arrow and pulled the string back as far as he dared. Angling the shaft toward the tops of the trees he released. The arrow fell uselessly a dozen paces in front of the sled just before it angled around a knoll and disappeared from view.

Ander's sled pulled up from behind.

"Secure these two," Darius ordered. "We're going after Petri."

Ensign Kaya shouted and they were off again. He encouraged even more speed out of the team and the dog's paws churned the snow.

They rounded the bluff where they had last seen Petri's sled and were greeted with a scene of disaster.

"Whoa, whoa." Kaya slowed the sled to a stop.

The back side of the hill dropped away sharply as a stream swept in from the northeast. There had been enough room for the dogs to run along a narrow ledge but as the sled had reached the trail it had slipped down the slope and toppled.

The harness had twisted as the sled had rolled. While the driver had been thrown clear Petri must have grabbed onto the sled for support. The sled had rolled over the top of him, more than once by the look of him, and he was trapped under the bulk of it. Four of the dogs had been tangled in the harness. The rear two looked severely injured and lay still in the snow whining softly.

The lead dog and others were trying to scramble up the slope to get away from the sled. The harness was pulled tight against the lead dog's chest and Darius could see blood on the white fur.

Kaya leapt from their sled and sprinted the distance. He pulled his belt knife loose and cut the straps freeing the lead dog. The dog gave a yelp of appreciation as it bounded free. Ensign Kaya was already working on the third dog by the time Darius was able to extricate himself from the sled and join him.

The driver recovered in time to join them in cutting the final two dogs free of their trappings. Both dogs had broken legs and one had a severe laceration across her chest from the harness straps.

Kaya and the other driver inspected the injured dogs.

Darius turned his attention to Petri. His body lay in the snow, but his legs were trapped under the weight of the sled. His right arm and left leg were both twisted at odd angles. Red froth bubbled on Petri's lips. His eyes gave Darius a pleading look. Darius walked around him, and then knelt to examine the man's injuries.

"They will survive but will never pull a sled again," Kaya explained as he rejoined Darius.

"I think that's more than we can say for Petri here," Darius nodded to the man. "He is bleeding on the inside. Even if I had the right herbs, I'm not sure I could stop it in time. The arm could be straightened and set but that leg worries me worse than the internal injuries."

The leg was broken above the knee and the lower half was still tangled in the sled.

"Even if he didn't have the other injuries, I'm afraid we'd have to amputate the leg." Darius continued.

Petri gurgled a frantic response.

"I think the best we can do is try to free him and make him comfortable for the night. I don't think he'll survive until morning."

Fear and then resignation passed through Petri's eyes.

Darius bent into the wreckage of the sled and cut the leather bindings that held the dark wooden box and the blanket that still partially wrapped it. He carried the box back to his own sled and carefully secured it in place.

Kaya returned to the rest of their group. Petri rested in the sled while Darius walked beside. The other driver and dogs trailed behind them.

Ander had a nice fire going and even though it was early was preparing an evening meal. Nicolai and Gunnar stood guard over Matia and his driver.

They arranged Petri on a bed of blankets near the fire. Darius retrieved some rose hips and nightshade from his bags on the supply sled. He ground the mixture into powder and then stirred it into a little water that Ander had been heating by the fire. Darius knelt beside Petri and offered him a sip. At first Petri refused.

"It will help with the pain," Darius explained.

Petri cringed as he drank. He finished the tea and then sank back onto his blankets.

That done, Darius turned his attention to Matia.

"Why?" Darius asked the man.

"They were going to give us five hundred gold marks each." Matia pleaded as if that should be enough to forgive the betrayal.

"That's a lot of money." Gunnar gave a low whistle.

Nicolai gave his brother a sidelong glance.

"That's it. You betrayed me for money," Darius growled.

"A ranch hand could work his entire life and never see half that," Ander commented from the fire.

"And a full pardon," Matia added quickly. "See, Petri and I ran into some trouble some years back down in Sidia. The man said the new emperor would pay us five hundred marks each and give us full pardons. All we had to do was deliver the box to Eridu. We could return home and see our families again."

"And why did you kill Marku?"

"That was Petri!" Matia exclaimed. "I didn't want to hurt no one. It all seemed so simple. You weren't doing anything with the box except taking it to Kasha Marka. Why did it matter who had the box? We get paid more money than I ever dreamed, and we get to go home, and no one gets hurt. That was the way it was supposed to be. It all went to Saridon when Marku showed up in that alley. Then that avalanche blocked our way west." His voice faded.

Darius stomped away. He spotted a flash of brown on the hillside to the west.

"I'm going to go check on Antu," Darius grunted. "I'll be back by nightfall."

Winter 35 A.E.

Chapter Nineteen
Backtrack

Micah pulled the hood of his cloak tighter around his face. He shrank back slightly into the shadows of the alley as he watched the woman examining the cloth. The girl beside her looked distracted and didn't seem to enjoy shopping nearly as much as the woman did. The girl had mousey brown hair and thin elfin features. Her eyes danced curiously from one distraction to the next.

The woman looked much as Micah remembered her, but older. The lustrous red hair showed a few streaks of gray at the temples. She looked strong, though. Healthy. It made his heart warm to know that she was okay. Micah longed to go to her but to do so would jeopardize his mission.

A soldier, dressed in blue, approached Cordelia. He was speaking to her, but Micah couldn't make it out from this distance.

I have to get closer, he thought.

Micah drifted behind vendors' stalls and found a place near a milliner's stall where he could hear the conversation.

"…sent the others back to be tried here by our magistrate," the soldier was saying.

"What about Darius and the others?" Cordelia asked.

"They were so far down the mountain by the time they caught up they decided to continue on. They said to meet them in Kasha Marka once the passes clear, and you can safely travel with the horses."

"Did they recover the box?" Cordelia asked.

Micah leaned in closer, straining to hear the answer.

"Yes," the soldier replied. "Your man Petri had it. There was an accident, and Petri didn't survive, but Darius did recover the box. Ensign Kaya reported that it was undamaged. Master Patel was disappointed that he won't have the opportunity to study the contents further."

Micah reclined against a nearby post with a dissatisfied sigh. So, both Darius and the box were gone and on their way to Kasha Marka. That was unfortunate. To make matters worse, he had learned during the past weeks scouting the city that the eastern pass was snowed in. They also hadn't lightened the guard at the western pass. So, it was unlikely he could move his men through this route. They would have to backtrack.

Micah rejoined Moab and Joral at the King's Table and filled them in.

"So, what's the plan now?" Joral asked.

"I think we have to head back to Isan and circle around to Kasha Marka by way of the main road."

"Won't the criminals have passed the emperor's box off to the rebel agents in Kasha Marka by then?" Moab asked.

"Maybe," Micah said. "But I don't know what other choice we have. Hopefully, we can pick up the trail there and recover the emperor's property. In either case, that is the mission, and we have to try."

PART II

City of Wonders

Alive with the sounds of the streets;
Hawkers call, musicians play, water splashes under it all
Vibrant

Awake with the smells of the world;
Cinnamon, lavender, meat roasting on the spit
Enticing

Alluring with the sights of life;
Statues tower, buildings soar, color abounds all around you
Elegant

Ambrosial with the tastes of desire;
Chocolate melts on the tongue, anise stirs the senses
Delectable

Animated with feelings of passion
Dancing, fighting, loving, laughing, your body pulses
Kasha Marka

-City of Wonders
Ye Foa Wen

2890 Imperial Era

Chapter Twenty
Ullani

The Grand Market of Kasha Marka was world renowned. The three-story stone building stretched the length of the city block. It faced the *La Dame de Miracles* fountain on the east and the Grand Palisades on the west. The more prosperous or politically influential merchants had permanent shops inside the market building, where only the wealthiest of clientele shopped. The rest of the populace was relegated to the red and brown brick courtyard of the market square. Farmers and other merchants would sell their wares in stalls set up around the palisades.

Ullani wondered, not for the first time, how the Palisades got its name. There was nothing defensive about the architectural marvel. Tall stone towers rose every fifty paces the length of the stone building. Ornately carved buttresses connected the market proper to the towers. Colorful canvas and silk hung between the buttresses not only provided patrons with cover from the sun or rain but also served to further the majestic reputation of the Grand Market.

Ullani relaxed in the crook where one of these buttresses met its tower. From this vantage she could easily scan the crowd. The market was near the Merchant's Gate in the southern wall.

Originally the weigh station for all goods coming from Kantibar and the port of Basara, the market had grown, due to its reputation, to be the center of trade for the entire city. There was still an active market at the Spice Gate, more than a league away on the other side of the city, but the goods coming in from Kasha Haaki had greatly diminished in recent decades. Merkar Province had been hit hard by the War of the Barons and Kasha Haaki had been slow to recover. Improvements in shipping had reduced the need for overland trade and caravans that could cross the Ziyandi Desert were expensive to outfit.

The Grand Market thus remained the best place in the city for Ullani and her gang to scout for fresh marks. She had followed the rules, worked hard, and had proven herself a valuable and loyal member of the guild. Her rewards had been concordant with her performance. By ten, she had been made a member of the gang at the Spice Gate. She had been transferred to the Merchant Gate by sixteen. Last year when Meritas, the former gang leader, had been killed in a duel, Ullani had been promoted to lead the Merchant Gate gang.

A tall, blond man dressed in a dark blue wool shirt and matching pants had entered the market. His clothes were travel stained and ragged. He wore a gray, hooded cloak over his clothing. A traveler's pack hung from his shoulders. Something heavy rested in the bottom of the pack, but otherwise it appeared to be empty. He also carried a long bundle across his back wrapped in a fur blanket. At his waist she could see a belt knife and pouch. She couldn't tell from this distance what else he might have under the traveling cloak. He stopped at the edge of the market and looked around. His face said he was stunned by the size of the crowd.

Outlander, Ullani thought. *First time in Kasha Marka.*

Ullani scanned the crowd. It was temple day, so the crowd was comparatively small. On market day, at midweek, the crowd would be ten times the size of what milled around below Ullani's dangling feet.

The man almost seemed ready to turn around. Instead, he waved to a couple other men in the crowd. Four men joined him at the side of the market building. They huddled together and the blond man began giving orders. The group was an incongruous lot.

The first had dark hair and was tall, like the man, and broad shouldered too. The pair looked like they were used to physical labor. They were similarly dressed. Had Ullani encountered them together she would have assumed they were kinsmen. The second man was older, at least twice the younger man's age, but he obviously deferred to the younger man's authority.

Outland noble? Or maybe a landowner's son and his father's foreman?

The next two men fit with that assumption. They were shorter and older than the boy by at least ten years. They appeared to be brothers, twins maybe. Each carried a thick walking staff and they were dressed in fur-lined leathers.

Guardsmen?

The final man was who threw Ullani out of sorts. He didn't fit with the group at all. He was obviously a soldier, the uniform said that much, but what would he be doing with this group? Normally, she would have just assumed the group had met on the road and had travelled this far together. However, it was clear that the soldier also answered to the young man's direction. What sort of outlander, dressed like a bumpkin, would command soldiers?

As she considered the puzzle, the man retrieved a pouch from his belt. It was fat and filled his large palm.

Mistake pulling that out in the open, she chided even as she grinned at her newest mark.

He doled out a small handful of coins to each of the men. The sunlight reflected off the handfuls of copper. Ullani didn't see a single flash of silver or shimmer of gold.

Maybe the boy's not such a rube after all. The purse was an obvious distraction. The size and weight of it would tempt almost any thief and distract them from looking farther. She considered the purse, still visible in his hand. A couple hundred pennies, at least. It would be an honest score for any hard-working thief, but it would also get you laughed at by the more experienced pickpockets.

Ullani scaled the buttress and darted along the raised cornices until she could get a closer look. She settled into a new perch only a few paces away as the traveler was giving his final instructions to the group. She scanned his clothing more carefully. At his waist he wore a sword. She hadn't seen it under the cloak from her previous vantage. This changed her assessment of the boy, but only slightly.

Just because a man wore a sword didn't mean he knew how to use it and, based on his dress and his age, it was unlikely that he did.

Ullani noticed that the inside of his left boot bulged more than the right.

Ah-ha, that's where the drachs are. Smart. Won't be easy to get those. I guess the pennies will do. She doubted a man of his obvious station had any gold marks on his person, but a pouch of pennies the size of this one almost certainly meant he had silver.

The stranger stowed his belt pouch as his companions drifted off in different directions, each intent on whatever mission he had assigned. As he readjusted his cloak, she also noted a leather thong tied around his neck. She couldn't see what sort of jewelry hung under his shirt but whatever it was had to be more valuable than the bag of copper. She was just about to drop down and quietly relieve him of his necklace when she saw a group of men approaching from the shadows closer to the building.

Ullani glanced around. The boy had stepped far enough away from the market to deliver his instructions and coin that most of the market's patrons wouldn't notice him. She studied the approaching group. She didn't recognize any of them, so they weren't part of the guild. Their manner indicated ill intent. She unhooked the cudgel from her belt and loosened one of her hidden knives. She may be forced to defend this country hick.

The guild master would not be happy if out-of-town cutthroats brought down the attention of the guards. The rules were in place for a reason. The guild was allowed to operate under certain conditions and one of those expectations was that no one was killed. It was the guild's responsibility to prevent what looked like was about to occur below her. If they didn't, the city guard would crack down on their operations as punishment. The severity and term of that punishment would depend on the station of the victim. An outlander, landowner's son would mean at least a week of lost wages.

She counted the assailants as the blond man looked up with a smile. Five. He greeted the newcomers as if they were old friends. Ullani dropped lithely to the ground and crept behind the stall backs along the market wall. She could hear him talking to the strangers.

"Hello!" His voice was friendly and unconcerned.

Is he really so naïve? Ullani thought.

"You fellows look like locals. Maybe you can help me. I'm looking for an inn called The Bard's Tale."

Ullani's steps faltered. The Bard's Tale had burned down when Ullani had been a girl. In its day, it had been a common meeting place for the guild master's eyes and ears from across Magora and beyond. Since the accident, the rendezvous had been moved to The Pike and the Rose. It was odd that a man as young as this would use the name.

I wonder if he is connected to one of the master's old contacts.

The question seemed to make the cutthroats hesitate as well. Or maybe it was the outlander's demeanor in general.

"Uh, no. Never heard of it," the leader of the thugs answered. He was a thick-necked man with short-cropped hair. His hand gripped a short, but wicked-looking dagger loosely at his side.

"Huh, so I guess I was wrong. Are you new to town, like me?"

"Yeah, I guess you could say that," the hoodlum said with an unfriendly smile. "We're, uh, travelling tax collectors."

The other gangsters laughed at the joke.

"You tell him, Aven. Tell him how much he owes in taxes."

"Well, let's see, there's the highway tax, and the…"

Ullani was watching the outlander. He stood casually, his hands near his waist, thumbs lightly hooked in his belt. His face was calm.

"Look, friends. I'm sure you are doing a great job. See, the thing is I'm not from Magora. I pay my taxes in Shalanum. So, if you'll excuse me, I really need to find The Bard's Tale." The outlander turned to go, but the leader of the group stepped in front of him, placing his left hand on the traveler's shoulder. The thug's right hand gripped the knife more menacingly now.

"Look yourself, friend. Our taxes aren't optional. Now, we'll be taking that bag of coin you got there."

"Please take your hand off of me," the outlander said in a low, dangerous voice.

The cutthroat either didn't hear the tone or chose to ignore it. "Or what? There's five of us and only one of you. Make it easy on yourself and just give us the money."

Ullani started to move to come to the boy's aid but she wasn't fast enough.

The outlander slapped his left hand over the thief's and then twisted, ducking under the man's arm. The thug gave a gasp of pain as he was flipped onto his back. Ullani heard the ring of steel as the outlander completed his turn, and he ended facing the other four with his sword drawn.

They hesitated; he didn't. They obviously hadn't expected him to draw a weapon and the momentary delay cost them. The outlander glided smoothly between and around his assailants. It reminded Ullani of the time she had snuck up to the castle to watch one of the Baroness's galas. The men and women dancing together had looked so beautiful, like a poem played out before her eyes. The outlander moved like that. His partners, the thieves, moved like a crude limerick sung in a seedy dockside pub.

He always struck the hooligans with the flat of his sword, never drawing blood.

That's good, Ullani thought. The city guard wouldn't go any easier on him if he killed someone, even if he was defending himself. The magistrate would likely let him off with a warning, but he'd spend a week in the cells before a magistrate ever saw him. The cells were rough no matter who you were.

Ullani returned her cudgel to its belt loop and sat back on her heels to watch the brilliant swordsman work. The fight would be brief, but was drawing the eyes of other onlookers, nonetheless. One of the thugs rose from the paving stones rubbing his head. He drew a rather wicked-looking dagger from his belt. The outlander, busy with the others, didn't notice him. The thief raised the dagger and prepared to plunge it in the blond boy's back. Ullani's wrist twitched. Momentary surprise filled the boy's eyes as her throwing knife whisked past his head and sunk into the palm of the brute. Her target cried out in pain and dropped his dagger. He sank to his knees clutching his damaged hand.

Ullani stepped from her hiding place. The outlander turned at her approach, raising the sword. Ullani surveyed the men. All of them lay or knelt on the ground groaning and nursing wounds. Aside from her attack, blood had not been drawn. There were a few broken fingers and wrists and a couple of cracked heads, but nothing they wouldn't recover from. She held out her hands, palms facing him, so he could see she meant no harm.

"Not looking for trouble," she said evenly. "I saw what happened. I'm just here to help. The guards will be on their way soon. If you don't want to lose that sword you should be gone by the time they get here. I can explain what happened. So long as no one gets killed, the guards tend to move on if the fight was fair."

Ullani glanced around at the pitiful lot then at the man clutching his hand.

"Was that you?" he asked.

"Aye," she replied. "I couldn't have him stabbing you in the back."

The man grinned and sheathed his blade. "Well, you have my thanks."

"I heard what you asked them," Ullani changed the subject. "The Bard's Tale burned down some time ago. I think you'll find what you're looking for at The Pike and the Rose."

Concern furrowed the stranger's brow. "I was told to go to The Bard's Tale. I'm supposed to meet someone there."

Ullani took a step closer and spoke with a knowing tone. "Like I said. Pike and Rose is where you want to go." She placed a hand gently on his shoulder and pointed down a cross street. "It's down that way. You'll follow that street until you reach the soap district. You'll know you're there from the smell. Then turn right on Crownsgate and keep going north until you reach the bell foundry. The Pike and the Rose is just around the corner to the left."

He looked at her, uncertain. Then he smiled.

"Thank you." He extended a hand.

"You're welcome." She returned without grasping his hand. "Now be off with you before trouble arrives."

She watched him go and then turned back to the would-be thieves. A couple of them were just getting back to their feet. She approached the man she had struck and grasped his wrist. Without ceremony she jerked her blade clear from his hand, and the man cried out.

Ullani crouched, holding the bloodied knife under his chin.

"I want you to listen carefully because I'm only going to say this once." Her tone was quiet and dangerous, like the outlander's had been. The thug definitely heard it this time.

"This is Red Shadow territory." Ullani waved a hand at the market. "And Kasha Marka is under the protection of The Guild. You and your men are going to leave quickly and quietly out the Merchant's Gate as soon as you can stand. If we ever see you in the city again, they could search a lifetime and not find where we will scatter your bones."

Terror filled the eyes of the thug.

"Nod if you understand," Ullani said darkly and exerted a little more pressure on the knife for emphasis. A thin trickle of blood ran down his neck.

The man nodded.

"Good." She patted him on the cheek and stood.

Ullani fingered the leather thong as she walked away. The boy hadn't even noticed when she took it, distracted as he was. It hadn't contained the valuables she had hoped for. There was an ivory medallion etched with the image of a roaring bear. The only other thing dangling from the cord was an iron key, but a key without a lock was about as useful as a coin purse with a hole in it.

Ullani sighed. *I should have just gone for the coppers.*

Chapter Twenty-One
The Pike and the Rose

What a nice girl, Darius thought to himself as he trotted across the market square. Everyone else he had talked to since arriving at Kasha Marka had been either dismissive or rude. The guards at the gate had looked the ragtag group up and down as if considering whether or not they should be allowed into the city. A few had waved a hand dismissively in the general direction of the market, but Darius was pretty sure they weren't actually listening to him. Then, of course, the last lot had tried to rob him.

And those eyes. The girl's eyes had been pale blue. The contrast to her dark skin made them all the more captivating.

Darius's nose began to itch as he navigated a turn in the road. The air was thick with myriad smells. Individually none of the smells would have been unpleasant: rose and lilac, butter and mint, chamomile and citrus, and underlying it all a faintly gamey scent from rendering animal fat. Together, the smells were an assault on his senses. He sneezed and scratched his nose. Tears formed in the corners of his eyes. Unconsciously, his stride lengthened to move more quickly past the shops.

Darius idly scratched his neck as the air began to clear. His fingers played along his shoulder, searching for something without realizing it. Suddenly his mind snapped to awareness. He felt along his neck and chest. He looked inside his shirt. The leather thong and pendant that Arthengal had given him for his eighteenth birthday were gone. They must have come loose in the fight. He turned and ran back down the roadway.

The girl and the men were gone by the time he returned. He searched all around behind the stalls and along the market building looking for the scrimshaw necklace. His heart ached as he searched frantically. The pendant was not the only thing he had left to remind him of his dead mentor, but it was his most treasured. It connected the memory of Arthengal with his relationship with Antu, the bear.

The necklace also bore one of the two keys needed to open the oak box that he was tasked with taking to Saria. However, he worried less about the key than the charm. Saria could always figure out another way to open the box, that wasn't his concern.

Darius finally gave up and with a heavy heart plodded back to the soap district. Lost in sullen thoughts, he barely noticed the smell upon his return. He wasn't sure what he had been expecting, but as he rounded the last turn past the bell foundry his expectations were shattered. The Pike and the Rose sat opposite a small collection of stalls selling meat pies, ales, and cider. It was not so much an inn as sort of an outdoor fair. There was a large shabby two-story building off to the side which Darius expected held rooms for rent, but the main structure of The Pike and the Rose was a circular arena surrounded by wooden stands. Darius couldn't see the arena floor, but the benches were filled with shouting patrons.

As he approached, a great hurrah echoed through the stands. He saw men raise pewter mugs and ale sloshed across their hands and down their arms. None of them seemed to notice. Curious, he edged closer to the stadium trying to get a better look. A guard that he hadn't noticed previously stepped in front of him.

"That's two pennies fer the rockpile, or five fer the center."

"Rockpile?" Darius questioned.

"The stands down on the ends there. Can't see a damned thing from there but the ale's better."

Darius fished five coppers out of his purse and pressed them into the man's palm.

"Go on up with ye, then." The guard waved a hand toward a rickety set of stairs.

Darius climbed the stairs and shouldered his way through the crowd until he found an opening big enough to stand. He could see the grounds more clearly now. There was a sand-covered field about fifty paces wide and a hundred paces long. All of the action was in a twenty-pace circle in the center of the field.

Four men circled each other. Two of the men had blue sashes tied around their biceps and the other two had red. The blue men were both armed with spears. One of the red men carried a weighted net and the second wielded a chipped sword.

The spearmen jabbed clumsily at their opponents, who circled just out of reach looking for an opening. The fighters looked like they had no more training than the thugs that had assaulted

Darius near the market. The crowd roared as the man with the net stepped too close and was marked along the ribs with a spear thrust.

"Who are the fighters?" Darius shouted at the man next to him.

The man shrugged, taking a second to examine Darius's attire. Darius noticed that the rest of the crowd in the center of the field was well dressed. He must look out of place in his sweat-stained woolens and tattered travelling cloak. Hopefully, Ander found them all more suitable clothing. Mistress Elsie would have burned all their clothes without a second thought.

"It's open pit night," the man shouted back. "Anyone can sign up at the pit master's stall before sundown. It's a half-drach to enter. The top three finishers split the pot, providing they survive, and the winner gets an extra gold mark."

"How many fighters enter?" Darius asked.

"Last temple day there was more than fifty. The matches went well into the night. Today there's only twenty, so far. Half have already been eliminated. It's been a bloody day so far. There may be a few latecomers but it's looking like an early night."

"Do they fight to the death?" Darius asked.

The man looked at him like he was daft.

"Nah, five stripes or a pin? Death matches were outlawed when the barons ousted the old emperor."

Darius started to ask his next question, but the man saw the confusion on his face and took pity.

"A stripe is any hit that draws blood. See, blue already up three stripes to one against red."

Darius examined the fighters. In addition to the bloody mark on the net man's chest he saw a nick on the cheek of the swordsman and the man also seemed to be limping from a wound in the leg. One of the men wielding spears had a cloth wrapped around his left hand where he grasped the shaft. The swordsman must have gotten a lucky strike.

"A pin is when you disable someone so they can't fight anymore. That might mean tangling them in a net or knocking them unconscious. The pit master has to make a ruling on pins. There haven't been any pins today and a lot of the stripes have run deep. Once a fighter starts to lose too much blood, they can't fight anymore. If they don't drop out themselves, the pit master may disqualify them."

Darius nodded his understanding.

Satisfied, the man turned back to the fight and joined with the roaring crowd as another spear thrust marked the swordsman's thigh.

Darius certainly didn't need the money, but it looked like fun. First, he had to find Saria, though. Maybe another day he could come back and use the pits to practice.

He shouldered his way back to the entrance.

"Who is the proprietor here?" he asked the guard.

The man grinned at the term. "Jarvis runs the pits, if that's what you're asking. His wife Norrie runs the inn." He pointed to the two-story ramshackle building.

Darius decided to start at the inn. He walked along the side of the stadium until he reached the entrance. The building was brick and ran the width of the field. Darius could see another side entrance that let out onto the field. Crumbling gargoyles decorated the roof of the building. It looked like it could have been a fancy retreat in its heyday, but the building had fallen into disrepair.

Inside there was a broad common area with a fireplace. The fire was blazing, and it was uncomfortably warm inside. Tables and chairs were arranged haphazardly around the area. Men occupied most of the chairs. Some were moaning and seemed barely able to sit upright. Others were getting wounds tended to. A pair of young women ran back and forth from the back to the common area carrying basins of water and bundles of torn cloth.

Darius shrugged his pack and gear off his shoulders and removed his cloak. Several of the men and their companions looked up as he entered and the sword around his waist earned a second glance from many. He wrapped everything in his cloak and carried it under one arm.

Darius spied a tall, willowy woman in a blue dress and white apron. She had gray hair and her face was etched by hardship. She was older than his own mother, but not as old as Arthengal. More than that he couldn't say.

She was shouting instructions to the girls. A young man exited from the kitchens carrying several steaming bowls. She directed the boy to a pair of tables near the back of the room.

"Excuse me," Darius said as he approached the woman. "Are you Mistress Nellie?"

"Ha!" She laughed. "Ain't no one called me Mistress in a devil's age. But yes, I'm Nell. Are you here to secure rooms before you enter the pits? We have plenty of singles left."

"Maybe another time. Today, I just need information --"

Nell continued as if he hadn't spoken. "The rooms are for fighters only. Seven pennies for the room, bandages, and all the mutton stew you can eat. Pay for the room and your pit fees at once and we'll call it even at a full drach. I'll give you a chit to present to that no-good husband of mine. If you pay him direct, I won't see half of it. He can't buy ale with my chits."

"No, really, I'm not here to fight today. I'm looking for someone."

She finally paused and looked him up and down. "Are you sure? You have the look of one of them. A bit down on his luck, looking to make an easy mark."

"I'm sure. I'm looking for Saria."

"Never heard of her." The woman turned around and marched toward the kitchen.

Darius chased after her. "Look, I was told by a friend of Saria's to go to The Bard's Tale. But when I got here someone told me that the inn had burned down, and that I should inquire at The Pike and the Rose."

She turned back around. "Inquire? You certainly don't talk like one of them." She jabbed a thumb at the common room. "Bard's

Tale burned down, that's for sure. Must be five years now, at least. Who was it told you to come here?"

"I didn't catch her name. She was tall, for a girl. She had curly black hair and blue eyes. She had a dark complexion, like silk chocolate."

"Like silk chocolate," the proprietress laughed uproariously. "Aren't you fancy? I think I had chocolate once at a festival day ten years ago. Back when Jarvis was still trying to impress me. Where did you see her?"

"At the market square. I had just finished fighting off a bunch of muggers. She told me to leave before the city guards arrived, and that she would take care of explaining things. She gave me directions to here."

Nell eyed him suspiciously. "I might know the girl that you speak of. She goes by the name Ullani. Sound familiar?"

"No." Darius shook his head. "My friend only told me to come find Saria. I have a package to deliver to her from him."

"That it?" She pointed to the bundle he carried under his arm.

"No," he lied. "This is just my gear and my weapons."

She raised an eyebrow at the mention of more weapons than what he wore at his waist.

"Tell you what," Nell said. "You can leave the package here with me. I have a lot of contacts around the city. I'll find Saria for you and deliver your package. Only charge, say, two pennies for delivery. What do you say?"

Darius shook his head. "No, I have to deliver it personally. The package is back with my men. They are finding lodging for the night."

"Your men? Who are you, boy?"

"I'm sorry, I'm Darius." He held out a hand to the woman.

"That doesn't tell me spit."

Darius took a gamble. "My friend's name was Arthengal Alamay."

That got her attention. She grabbed him by the shoulder and drug him through the kitchen door. Darius was surprised by her strength. Nell's grip was like iron. He weighed over thirteen stone and she moved him like a child. He stumbled along after her as she ducked into an alcove in the kitchen.

"You have a message for Saria from Nasu Rabi?" Nell hissed in a low tone. She glanced over her shoulders as if spies were hiding in the shadows of her kitchen.

"A package," he corrected. "And a message, I guess."

"Show me," she demanded.

"I told you. I can't."

"Then show me you are who you say you are. If you come from who you say you do then you'll know how to use that sword you carry. Enter the pits. You convince me and I'll get word to Saria. You don't and I'll still get word to Saria, but you won't like the result."

Darius sighed. "Do you have someplace I can store my gear? Someplace with locks."

"Rooms are for fighters only. It's seven pennies for a room, a full mark for a room with locks." She repeated her earlier instructions.

Darius counted twenty pennies out of his pouch. "For the room, one with a lock, and the pit entry."

She counted the coins while she considered him. She fished a wooden token out of her apron. "Give this to Jarvis and he'll let you fight. I'll show you to a room, and make sure your belongings aren't disturbed."

Nell led Darius up the stairs to a room in the back. A ring of keys appeared in her hand. She found the right one, opened the door, and then removed it from the ring.

Handing him the key she said. "Now don't you lose this. It's expensive to replace locks."

Darius closed the door behind him. He started to throw his gear on the bed but then had second thoughts. There was every likelihood that fleas or lice infested the bunk and he didn't need either. Instead, he hung his cloak and pack from a spike on the back of the door. Unwrapping his bow, arrows, and second sword from the blanket, he draped the fur blanket over the only chair in the room and leaned the bow and arrows in the corner.

He strapped the second sword belt on. If he was going to spar, he might as well practice with both blades. Working forms was one thing and he was getting better. Testing his forms against a live opponent was entirely different.

Darius locked the door as he left and dropped the key inside his right boot. The left boot was uncomfortable enough with the bag of gold marks crammed into it.

Jarvis was a portly man with a bald head and a thick brown mustache draped over generous jowls. He gave Darius a disappointed look when he handed over the wooden coin.

"You've been talking to that wife of mine, I see." He shook his head. "I suppose she talked you into a room as well. You'd have saved half your coin if you'd just come to me right off. You could have chucked your gear in the shed there if you had any."

Darius shrugged.

"You know how to use those or are they just for show?" Jarvis nodded to the swords.

"Just for show," Darius winked.

Jarvis laughed.

"All right then. In you go. Luc will get you sorted out inside."

Darius passed through a small gate at the side of the arena into a long hallway below the bleachers. He followed the passage to the end where it opened up into a dimly lit room. A bench ran the length of the room on both sides. Sweaty, bleeding men looked up at him disdainfully as he entered. They had been fighting all afternoon and didn't appreciate the fresh fighter joining near the end.

Only six men were left, plus the four that were currently on the field.

The pit master approached Darius as he entered.

"Coming in a bit late, aren't you?" Luc asked.

"Sorry, I only just arrived." Darius blushed. "I've been travelling all day."

That seemed to satisfy some of the men sitting close by. At least he wasn't well rested.

Luc turned to survey the fight.

"Four to two, red," he announced. There was a general grumbling from the men on the benches. "We'll be down to singles after this by the look. New guy, put on the red, you'll be fighting Arlo."

A muscular giant of a man grunted at the end of the benches. He stood and moved to the gate. Darius was tall but this man towered over him by more than a head. His shoulders were half again as wide as Darius and his thighs were nearly as wide as Darius's waist.

He picked up a spiked maul leaning against the wall of the cage and gave Darius a wicked grin. The head on the weapon was almost the size of Darius's own.

I wouldn't like a stripe from that thing. Darius cringed.

Darius reminded himself that he didn't have to kill the man, only nick him a few times, and stay out of the way of that giant hammer.

"What's your name?" Luc asked.

"Darius."

The crowd roared again, and shortly after, the four fighters tumbled into the stall. Luc examined one of the men wearing a red badge. His eyes were watery, and he seemed barely able to stand.

"You're done for the day, Jessop. Go on in. Nellie will get you a nice bowl of stew."

The man nodded weakly and stumbled out the rear exit.

Darius followed Luc and Arlo out onto the field. He squinted. Even the weak winter sun was bright after being in the darkness of the stalls.

Luc introduced them to the crowd as Arlo the Giant and Darius Double-blade.

The crowd appeared more massive from the floor of the stadium. Darius found himself getting nervous. He hadn't sparred in front of a crowd before, only a few friends and family. He drew his first sword but then fumbled the second. Too late he realized he hadn't freed the hilt from the buckle, a mistake he hadn't made since he was a boy.

The crowd erupted in laughter and Darius's face grew hot. Meanwhile, Arlo paraded around the stadium, pumping his arms and the gigantic hammer, riling up the crowd further. The noise was deafening.

Darius finally freed the second blade and turned to face his opponent. He took up a relaxed stance with his right blade forward and his left blade back, ready to defend.

Arlo charged with the hammer held high and then swung it crosswise aiming for Darius's head.

The less stable footing of the sand combined with his nervousness and made his movements awkward as he moved through Dancing Lights. He also made the mistake of trying to block the hammer and nearly lost his second weapon. The crowd laughed again and began to chant Arlo's name.

Darius learned from his mistake. He moved onto the balls of his feet and adjusted into an offensive stance.

Arlo charged again, this time striking downward. Darius didn't try to block. This time he moved more nimbly to the side and lunged forward with Striking Adder. Sand erupted around the head of the maul, showering Darius with debris. His blade found its target and a thin line of blood appeared on Arlo's left bicep. The crowd erupted and Darius thought he heard his name a few times through the uproar.

Arlo backed away and then adjusted his attack. He advanced steadily, swinging the hammer back and forth at waist level. A few swings like that, with the weight of the hammer, would have exhausted Darius, but the giant seemed tireless. Darius stepped back, watching the swings to get the timing. Then, when he was ready, he lunged just as the head of the hammer passed his chest. Using a variation of Boulder Crashes Down Mountain he rolled inside the arc of the swing, twisted as he completed the roll and stood, and scored twin slashes along the giant's right thigh. He cut more deeply than he had intended, and Arlo stumbled as Darius danced away.

The crowd roared, as much for the theatrics of the maneuver as for the fact that the score was now three to zero in Darius's favor.

Arlo was limping now and didn't seem able to charge. The brown wool of his trousers was growing dark with blood. Darius felt badly. He hadn't meant to injure the man that seriously. It was only sparring, after all. He decided to end it quickly so the big man could get his wounds treated. Before he could execute his next move, however, Arlo stumbled and fell. The crowd went silent.

Darius ran to the man's side, skidding to a stop in the sand. He examined the leg wound, just above the knee, and a spurt of blood hit Darius in the arm.

"Rat spit," Darius cursed.

He worked quickly. He used his sword and cut the braided rope that Arlo used as a belt. Darius pulled it free from the man's pants and wrapped it around the giant's leg. He pulled it tight and twisted it several times. The blood flow slowed, and Darius twisted the rope again until it stopped. He held it in place but knew that it would unwind as soon as he let it go.

The crowd watched in amazement. Luc arrived with a couple of the other fighters.

"I need something to tie this to so we can carry him inside," Darius said.

One of the fighters from the first match Darius had watched stomped on the shaft of his spear and broke a length of wood off. Darius let go of the tourniquet long enough to tie the rope to the wood and then twisted again. Using lengths of torn cloth from Arlo's shirt he tied the wood down to the man's leg so it would stay in place.

"Help me," Darius instructed.

It took five of them to carry a now limp Arlo back to the inn. They lay him on a table. Luc retrieved a glowing red poker from the fireplace and laid it across the sword wound. Arlo moaned and woke briefly.

Darius cringed as Nell's daughters packed salt into the lesser wounds and the cauterized wound, covered both with folded linen towels, and tied them down with ribbons of cloth.

"That's not—" Darius started before Nell stepped in and guided him away.

"Let the girls work," Nell said. "They've fixed a sight more wounds than you have, I'm sure."

Darius started to argue but then allowed himself to be led away.

"Let's get you cleaned up. You can't go back into the city looking like that."

Darius looked down at himself. His hands and shirt were covered in blood.

"That was quick thinking," Luc said to Darius as they stepped away. "Arlo would have died for sure without your help."

"I didn't mean to cut him that deeply," Darius apologized.

"Eh, accidents happen," Luc said. "We see it every day. Most often Nell's girls are able to help. They don't lose many."

"You better get back out," Nell said. "The crowd will be getting restless. Disqualify these two and keep on with the rest."

Luc nodded and returned to the arena.

Nell led Darius into the back of the inn. Behind the kitchens there was a wide, open area with sunken pools of water. Faded and broken tiles decorated the pools and the landings surrounding them. Stone benches lined the walls of the room. Additional rooms exited off to the sides of the bath, but their doors were shuttered, adding to the appearance of general disrepair of the ancient building. The water was by no means clear, but it looked clean.

"We don't often open this area up to the fighters, but I think you earned it. I won't even charge you extra. Do you have a change of clothes? I can get it from your rooms if you give me your key."

"Not on me, no. Our extra supplies are at the stables with our mule."

"I'll find you something of Jarvis's. They might be a bit tight on you, but they'll do until you get back to your men."

After Nell left, Darius disrobed and stepped into one of the pools of water. It was surprisingly warm. It reminded him of the bathing pool that Arthengal had built in their valley back home. Upon further examination, Darius noticed water flowing into the other pool from some unidentified source. The water then flowed into the second pool via a tiled channel between the two. He found a drain along the wall near the bottom of his pool that gently sucked the water away into the depths below the city.

Darius washed away the blood and grime from weeks of travel. Once he was clean, he found a submerged shelf near the inlet between pools. He relaxed against the wall and let the warm water cascade over his shoulders. He closed his eyes and let the waters sooth away his aches and pains.

"Well, you just settled right in, didn't you?"

Darius opened his eyes, expecting the unfamiliar voice to belong to one of Nell's daughters.

An older woman wearing a red coat brocaded with gold and silver flowers sat casually on one of the stone benches opposite the pool. Her legs were crossed. She stood to circle the pool and Darius saw that she wore black, silken breeches that clung to her shapely legs. The coat had a tail that fell to the middle of her thighs obscuring her backside.

While Nell and this woman looked nearly the same age, time had been much kinder to the stranger. Her lustrous red hair cascaded around her shoulders and her green eyes pierced him to his soul. She moved with the grace of a cat. Her beauty was primal and timeless. Despite her age, Darius found himself reacting to her beauty as she moved closer. He shifted uncomfortably, becoming acutely aware of his nakedness, even though he was obscured by the blue-green waters.

"I heard you were looking for me?" the stranger purred. She kneeled by the edge of the pool an arm's length from where he sat. A thin but dangerous looking dagger appeared in her hand as if by magic.

Darius suddenly felt very vulnerable and alone, but somehow still aroused.

"Care to tell me why?"

Chapter Twenty-Two
Magora

Darius cleared his throat. His eyes flickered to the steel blade. "Arthengal sent me to deliver something to Saria."

The woman eyed him suspiciously, twirling the knife in her fingers. "That's a dangerous name to use as a reference, in certain circles. Actually, I guess both names could be dangerous, in certain circles." She laughed. "Tell me exactly what you were told."

"I was told to take a box to The Bard's Tale in Kasha Marka and ask for a woman named Saria."

"And why would the legendary Nasu Rabi entrust a farm boy with a mission such as that? Why wouldn't he bring it himself, if it was important?"

"He was killed," Darius said. Sadness and anger edged his voice. "He asked me just before he died, because…" Darius considered for a moment. "I guess because I was his apprentice, sort of."

"Hmm," the woman mused. "I think I need to hear the whole story. Why don't you start from the beginning?"

She sat back and Darius felt his tension ease.

As the woman made herself more comfortable, Darius started his story. He began with the raid on his village. Then he told of his journey north, meeting Arthengal, and of their years together. He described the rescue of his mother, their escape to the south, and the nighttime raid by the emperor's soldiers which resulted in Arthengal's death.

At first the woman listened patiently, relaxed by the edge of the pools. She eyed him dubiously as he described Antu and his conviction that the bear was, in fact, the embodiment of the Sky Father sent to guide and test him. By the time he reached the point of describing the imperial camps and the soldiers they faced during the rescue and escape, she was pacing the length of the bath flipping the dagger absently from one hand to the other.

"There have been all sorts of rumors out of Shalanum since the baron was killed last spring," she interrupted. "Everything from marauding hordes from the north to Chen Bai Jian returned from the grave to seek his vengeance."

"Not Chen Bai Jian," Darius corrected. "Lao Jun Qiu"

She gave a distracted nod and continued to pace, talking half to herself.

"We have sent scouts on the road north and have been able to confirm that an army is camped at the gap between the Talia and Shahin ranges. It flies the dragon sigil of house Lao so that tracks. Their patrols have been effective at turning our scouts back so we haven't heard anything from the interior. Merchants returning from Kasha Amur report general unrest and political infighting but nothing about imperial armies."

"When we were in Patel's Rest we heard that they had taken Eridu and Isan," Darius offered. "We didn't hear anything about the capital."

"Ah, so there is more to your story. Please continue." She waved a hand.

Darius told her about the attacks on the Taspin Plains while they travelled to Isan and the bounty hunters that followed. He briefly summarized his summer working on the cattle ranch before moving on to events that led to their escape from Isan to Patel's Rest and their journey to Kasha Marka.

"So, you met the old alchemist, then?" she asked.

Darius nodded.

"I always found him to be a bit of a coot. He was a genius, of course, but always a bit odd."

"Like how he guesses everything about you before you've even exchanged pleasantries?" Darius asked.

"Yes," she said. "That always unnerves me. But, also his fascination with rocks and oils and clouds, basically anything in nature that he can use to create fire or explosions. He loves his explosions."

"Clouds?" Darius questioned.

"Oh, he didn't talk about clouds? He couldn't stop talking about it during the war. He was convinced he could harness the power of storms to rain fire and lightning down upon the enemy. Maybe he finally gave up. What's he working on now?"

"Sound, I guess," Darius said. "Making his explosions loud. When we were there, he used them to create an avalanche in the western pass when the emperor's soldiers arrived."

"Sound..." She shook her head. "Quian MacCinidh always was an odd one. So, where is this box?"

"You are Saria?" Darius asked. The woman never had introduced herself. "I need to be sure first. Can you answer a few questions?"

She laughed and then waved her hand. "Ask away."

Darius tried to think of something on the spot that would make him sure this was the right woman.

"What name did you go by in the war?"

She hesitated briefly and then caught his meaning.

"Sillu Mitu. A silly name given to me by soldiers, much like Nasu Rabi."

"What is your last name?" he asked.

"Oberman," she answered quickly.

Darius nodded sagely at the response. A third question occurred to him that very few people were likely to know the answer to.

"What was the name of Arthengal Alamay's son?"

She let out a long, low whistle. "That's a good one."

"He said you would know the answer," Darius lied.

"Let me think. That was almost forty years ago. I only met Sharaea and the boy once. What was his name?"

She paced, muttering names under her breath. "It was a Basari name, what was it? Noah? No something with a W."

"Walden," she announced.

Darius started to open his mouth to protest.

"No, Wilem," she corrected.

Darius nodded. He couldn't think of any other questions and not sure how else to verify the woman's identity decided to be satisfied with the answers.

"I have the box upstairs with my things," Darius admitted.

"Let's go."

Darius looked down at himself. "Do you mind if I get dressed first?"

"I'm not stopping you." She smiled slyly.

Darius blushed from head to toe.

Saria rolled her eyes but retrieved a towel from a nearby bench and tossed it in his direction. Darius had to lunge out of the water to keep the towel from getting wet, exposing himself to the waist in the process.

Saria chuckled. "You didn't learn everything from your mentor. Arthengal was never shy when it came to baths. And he did love his baths. Hurry up. I'll wait in the hallway."

*****

Darius unwrapped the box and set it on the bed. Saria examined it carefully, inspecting the craftsmanship and the locks.

"This matches the description of the reliquary of Chung Oku Mai." Saria turned the dark box over in her hands. "Have you opened it?"

Darius shook his head.

"Where are the keys?"

"My mother has one of them," Darius explained. "The other one is lost."

"Lost? What do you mean lost?"

Darius blushed. "I was attacked when I first got to town. I lost my necklace during the struggle. The key was attached. I went back to look, but I couldn't find it."

"Bedria will want to see this and hear your story. Here." She handed him the box. "Put this in your pack. We'll go back to my grotto and I'll send word for her."

Darius followed Saria, not into the streets as he had expected but deeper into the baths. She opened a door in the back of the building to expose a staircase that led into the darkness below the building. She lit a lantern atop a table near the door and continued down the carved steps.

They emerged onto a stone walkway that ran beside a subterranean stream. Arched ceilings rose above them. The entire tunnel seemed to be constructed of lacquered brick. Water drained from inlets built into the wall opposite the walkway. Sometimes the water came in via slow, algae-covered trickles and elsewhere it poured in a steady stream.

"Welcome to the sewers of Kasha Marka." Saria spread her arms expressively.

Darius took an involuntary step back from the stream. A trench carved into the center of the floor contained the water and kept it from spilling onto the walkway, but he didn't want to take his chances by getting too close.

The smell was not unpleasant under the baths but as they advanced into the heart of the city Darius found that he was holding his cloak over his nose to block the stench. Saria seemed not to mind in the least. She navigated the warren of tunnels as if she were out for a country stroll.

Eventually, they turned and the tunnels began to rise. Darius tried to remember the layout of the city as he'd seen it from outside.

They had first sighted the towering walls that surrounded the city almost three hours before they had arrived at the Merchant's Gate. He remembered seeing a hill, almost a plateau, that rose from the center of the city. As they approached, they had only been able to clearly see two structures atop the bluff, an ornately built castle on the east end and a pyramidic temple to the west. Darius guessed that they were climbing toward one of those structures now.

The underground leveled out and the stream broadened into pools. A web of causeways and pillars supported a vast ceiling overhead. The brickwork here was painted red and yellow. Every so often Darius spied a shield set into the wall with a yellow eagle painted onto a field of red. He remembered from his years selling rope in Eridu that this was the coat of arms for Baroness Magora.

Saria pulled the latch on a banded metal door at one end of the pool room. Darius followed her down the adjoining hallway and left the water, and the stench, of the sewers behind. The hall widened and wove between a series of interconnected rooms. Diaphanous curtains hung in the entrances of each room obscuring his view of the inside. He looked back as they passed and saw curious eyes peeking out from more than one room.

They finally entered a large room at the end of the hallway. Half a dozen similar halls branched out from the central room. Large stuffed cushions and pillows decorated the floor. Young men and women lounged in groups of three or four eating fruit and sipping a dark liquid from colorful ceramic cups. The murmur of their voices stopped as Saria entered the room.

She bent to whisper in the ear of one of the men who then sprang up and jogged from the room.

Saria climbed the few steps to a simple dais in the center of the room and lowered herself onto a pair of red cushions embroidered with gold flowers. She indicated for Darius to sit. He did so and scanned the crowd of faces all looking at them curiously.

"Ullani," Saria called out across the room.

"Yes, mistress."

Darius turned at the sound of the voice. It was the same blue-eyed girl that he had seen near the market square. The girl who had helped him with directions.

The girl sipped from her cup.

"This is Darius," Saria continued.

"We've met," Darius interrupted.

"You have?" Saria asked, curious.

"She gave me directions to The Pike and the Rose after I was attacked."

Ullani smiled. "I'm glad you found your way." She took another sip.

"Good," Saria stated. "Then you know where to look. Darius lost a necklace at the square. It's very important that we find it."

The girl coughed as she sipped too much of the liquid in. "I'm sorry, a what?"

"A necklace," Saria repeated. "It has a key and…" She turned to Darius. "What else?"

"A pendant," Darius added. "It's ivory with a picture of a bear."

"Scour the market," Saria instructed. "Look for any sign of it. Check with the merchants, too. It's possible someone has already sold it. Find out what you can."

"Of course, mistress." Ullani rose smoothly and glided from the room.

Darius heard the stomping of boots as the girl left. He turned his attention to a tunnel to the left.

Guards wearing red leather under their polished breastplates fanned out as they entered the room. They stood at attention: spears held erect. At the head of the group was a formidable man wearing a full suit of red lacquered armor. Atop his head he wore an ornate helmet. Leather flaps, lacquered like the rest of his armor, extended to protect the sides of his neck. A crown of pure white fur decorated the top, and at his brow a golden eagle adorned the vertical bill. He wore a pair of swords, one at his hip and one on his back. Darius considered the positioning. It would be easier to draw if both blades weren't at his waist.

"Lord Captain Misrak," Saria whispered to Darius. "Captain of Bedria's guard."

"Who is Bedria?" Darius asked.

Saria ignored the question. Instead she snapped her fingers to the group of youth in the room and they began disappearing down disparate hallways. The guard captain coughed as the last of the youths left and a shrouded figure entered the room from behind them. The figure was tall, dressed from head to toe in a shimmering red cloak with a deep hood pulled down to hide the face.

The figure glanced around the room and then, satisfied that they were alone, raised the hood and thrust it away to spill down her back.

The woman was the embodiment of elegance. She pulled her hair free from the cloak and let the torrent of black ringlets cascade down her back and frame her face. Hawkish black eyes scanned Darius and seemed to assess him in an instant. High cheekbones and full lips rose in a smile as she prepared to greet them. Her smooth, ebony skin radiated power and beauty.

"Darius, may I present Bedria Kess, Baroness of Magora province. Baroness, this is Darius Kabir, Arthengal's apprentice. He brings us a very interesting gift and an even more interesting story."

"Baroness?" Darius stammered. "But you look younger than my mother. You can't possibly be…"

Bedria's laugh sounded like the chime of festival bells, deep but musical. Her voice, too, was deeper than he had expected.

"I knew Arthengal when I was a girl, but if he sang the praises of the Baroness of Magora, he spoke of my mother."

"He always spoke very highly of her. So, your mother is—"

"Dead," she said with a hint of sadness. "Almost ten years ago now."

"I'm sorry for your loss," Darius said.

"And Arthengal?" Bedria asked.

"He was killed last summer by Emperor Lao's soldiers."

"It seems we have a lot to discuss."

She lowered herself onto one of the cushions and her guards spread out to cover each of the entrances and guarantee their privacy while they talked.

Chapter Twenty-Three
Life at the Palace

"Do you remember the time when Arthengal bet the Mortikai commander that he could smack every member of his squad on the nose with a spoon before one of them could lay a hand on him?" Baroness Magora interrupted Darius's story again.

Saria rolled with laughter on her pillow. "Yes. He was so drunk."

Darius was bewildered. This was not the Arthengal he had known.

"Did he do it?" Darius asked in wonder.

Both women were overcome with peals of laughter. Even the Lord Misrak chuckled.

"Of course not," Saria said when she could speak. "The commander was so offended that he grabbed the serving tray from the hands of a nearby porter and thrashed Arthengal, driving him from the room."

"But Arthengal kept trying to hit the commander on the nose even as he stumbled backward out of the dining hall," the baroness added.

A soldier emerged from one of the side passages and whispered in Lord Misrak's ear.

"Baroness," he said quietly. "You have an appointment with Magistrate Oni."

"Oh my, is it that time already?" she said, wiping her eyes. She rose and smoothed her cloak. "Darius, you simply must continue your tale at a later time. Will you and Saria join me for dinner tomorrow?"

Saria rose as the baroness did and pulled Darius to his feet.

"Uh," Darius was taken aback by the invitation.

"Of course we will," Saria interjected. "It is late anyway, and his men are probably wondering what has become of him. They must be worried by now."

"Your men?" The Baroness seemed intrigued. "Where are they staying? You must move them into the palace."

"I'm not sure, actually," Darius said. "They were to secure lodging while I searched for Saria."

"Follow us then," Bedria commanded. "I'll have rooms prepared in the palace and a servant will fetch your men, wherever they have settled."

Saria gave Darius a slight shove on the back as Baroness Magora and her contingent turned to leave. The two of them fell in behind the last of the guards.

Lord Misrak moved beside Darius as they walked.

"Did Arthengal teach you how to use both of those blades?" the guard captain asked.

"No," Darius answered. "He only taught me how to fight with one sword, but I've been trying to adapt his forms to two."

Misrak gave him a sidelong glance. "You've adapted single-blade forms for use with two blades? How is that going for you?" He seemed amused.

"It's difficult. The forms that pair with a shield work best, but the others are more challenging."

Misrak laughed. "I'm not surprised. I'm impressed that you were able to adapt at all. Two-weapon forms are very different from single-blade forms. I would be happy to teach you a few if you have time."

"It would be my honor, sir," Darius sputtered.

"Bah," Misrak waved a hand. "The honor would be mine. I would love the opportunity to spar with Arthengal's apprentice."

*****

Ullani emerged from the shadows after the group had left. She felt ashamed that she hadn't followed Saria's orders. But what was the point, really? She already knew where the pendant and key were. She fingered the leather thong in her pocket. The question remained whether she should turn them over to her master.

The conversation had been both enlightening and educational. She had seen a side of Saria and the baroness that few were privileged enough to witness. And the young man, Darius, was even more intriguing still. She was once again forced to reevaluate her opinion of him. She would have to figure out a way to get closer to the man. Ullani saw opportunity here and Saria had always told her to never pass up a good opportunity. She patted her pocket having decided to turn over the pendant but keep the key for now.

*****

"I can't believe we're staying in the palace," Ander said, not for the first time. "It doesn't seem right." He sat on the floor in Darius's room, afraid to sit on the furniture for fear of breaking it or getting it dirty.

"Seems right enough to me," Gunnar laughed from where he lounged on a cushioned chaise. He retrieved another piece of the fried yellow fruit from the tray near the couch. "What did they call these again? They are delicious."

"Plantains." Darius looked up from the bench where he was oiling his sword, a chore that was long overdue after weeks on the road.

Nicolai entered the room carrying armfuls of silk shirts and cotton breaches. He dumped the pile on the feather bed. "Gifts from the baroness. There should be something here to fit all of us. I, for one, will be happy to get out of these woolens. They smell like mildew and a month of sweat."

The others nodded in agreement.

"We're instructed to leave our clothes in the baskets in our rooms. Someone will be along to fetch them and have them cleaned."

"Burned, more likely," Darius commented.

Ander rose and inspected the clothing on the bed. The bed was as large as six or more bunkhouse cots arranged together.

"I can't wear any of these," Ander complained. "One day on the road and these would fall to pieces."

"We won't be going on the road for a while, Ander," Darius said. "At least not until my mother and the others join us."

"Still, it wouldn't feel right. Give me a good wool shirt and a sturdy pair of rawhide trousers any day. We'll freeze to death in these, they're too thin."

"I think we're supposed to wear these coats over the top." Nicolai held up a red coat with brass buttons and yellow pinstriping. He held it against his body. The front was cut to end at the belt, but the back extended nearly to his knees. "This will be interesting."

The sound of a woman clearing her throat near the doorway caused all of the men to jump and turn their attention.

The woman from the marketplace stood in the doorway.

Darius stood and set his weapons aside.

"Ullani, isn't it?" Darius asked.

The girl nodded.

"Thank you again for your help earlier. Let me introduce you. This is Gunnar, Nicolai, and Ander. Everyone, this is Ullani. She helped me find directions to Saria."

"My lady." Ander bowed his head.

The brothers laughed.

"Pleasure to meet you, Ullani," Nicolai said.

"Where is your fourth man?" Ullani asked Darius.

Darius was confused by the question at first. "You mean Guardsman Klein?"

Ullani shrugged.

"He's off checking out the city," Darius answered.

"Which brings me to the point of my visit," Ullani said. "Saria has asked me to show you around Kasha Marka."

"Oh." Darius was surprised. "Okay, that would be great. Just me or any of us?"

Ullani shrugged again.

"Can we do it tomorrow?" Darius asked. "We're supposed to have dinner with the baroness tonight."

"Oh." Ullani seemed disappointed.

"Do you want to join us?" Darius asked. "I'm sure she wouldn't mind."

Ullani brightened. "Are you sure? That would be amazing. I've never dined with the Baroness before." She glanced down at her attire and frowned. She wore simple yellow pants that flared at the hips and a long red jacket with gold stenciling on the sleeves. Under her jacket Darius saw a tightly laced yellow corset. Her cleavage was clearly visible when she turned, and the jacket opened slightly. "I will need to go change first. This wouldn't be appropriate for dinner with the baroness."

"That's fine." Darius smiled, meeting her crystal blue gaze. He blushed slightly as he realized she had caught him admiring her corset. "We're still trying to figure out what to wear ourselves."

Darius grabbed a red shirt and blue cotton pants from the pile of clothes and held them up. "What do you think?"

"You'll need a jacket," Ullani said.

He grabbed the red coat out of Nicolai's hands.

Ullani wrinkled her nose. "Too much red."

She crossed to the bed and started picking through the clothes. She held several jackets up before settling on one that was dark blue with ornate patterns stenciled on the chest and sleeves. It was open at the chest and long enough to fall nearly to his knees. She selected a green shirt with ruffles at the chest and sleeves and a pair of light beige trousers.

"That'll do." She held her choices out.

Darius hesitated. "Are you sure?" None were choices he would have made for himself.

Ullani nodded. "Yes. Trust me."

Darius glanced at the others who were trying to hide snickers.

Ullani looked at his companions with narrowed eyes and shook her head. "That won't do either." She selected equally garish costumes for each of the others. Their grins faded with each new selection until each of them looked as uncomfortable with Ullani's choices as Darius felt.

Finally, she gave a satisfied nod. "I will meet you there. What time are you expected?"

"Seventh bell," Darius said.

Ullani looked aghast. "That's only two hours from now. I must hurry. See you there."

*****

Darius and his companions arrived at dinner and were announced into the dining hall. They were led to seats by ushers. The dining hall was vast. In its center was a wide oak table. Nearly forty people were already seated around the table and several seats remained vacant. A dozen or more servants stood at attention around the perimeter of the room while servers kept wine glasses full around the table.

Darius was led toward the head of the table and was seated in the place of honor next to the head of the table. To his right sat a teenage version of the baroness. She was a statuesque beauty, a couple years younger than Darius. She filled out her purple dinner gown admirably. She gave a polite smile as Darius sat.

"Aisha Kess." She held out a downturned hand which Darius shook gently.

"Darius Kabir, it's a pleasure to meet you. Are you related to the baroness? You look just like her."

"I'm her daughter. My brother, Kofi, is seated across from us."

Darius drew his attention to the tall young man seated opposite her. He was handsome, with closely cropped hair and a broad smile. His dark eyes shown as he chatted with the woman seated next to him in hushed tones. The woman laughed aloud and fanned her face with her hand as he finished his story.

"Kofi," the woman whispered loudly. "You are terrible."

"Kofi," Aisha got his attention. "This is Darius. He is mother's guest."

"Very nice to meet you," Kofi said in a voice that was both deep and harmonious. Confidence radiated off the young man.

Cordelia was shown to the seat opposite Darius. He quickly made introductions to the baroness's children.

"Baroness Bedria Kess," the chamberlain's voice echoed through the dining hall. Bedria strode across the room. Lord Misrak trailed a few steps behind her and took a position behind her right shoulder as she arrived at the head of the table.

Bedria reached for a crystal goblet of white wine resting near her plate. She raised it. "Beloved guests. It is with great honor that I welcome you to dine with us this evening. We are doubly blessed this evening by our guest Darius and his mother Cordelia. Darius was, until recently, apprentice to the late, great General Alamay, former marshal general to the realm."

Whispers and gasps echoed around the table and Darius felt all eyes fall on him.

"Please raise your glasses in a toast to our guests and their health." Bedria raised her glass and took a sip. Cheers of welcome reverberated through the hall as the other guests followed suit.

As the baroness was finishing her toast the chamberlain cleared his throat near the entrance to the dining hall. He announced the newest guest. "Ullani Hailu of Kasha Marka."

Bedria raised a curious eyebrow to Saria who gave the briefest shake of her head.

"My apologies, Baroness," Darius said. "I invited her. She was so helpful to me when I first arrived. I hope you don't mind."

"Of course not," the baroness answered with a gracious smile. She signaled to the chamberlain who led Ullani into the room.

Darius watched Ullani approach the table. She was dressed in an elegant red dinner gown. She looked beautiful. Her blue eyes sparkled with wonder as she tried not to be obvious glancing around the room. Uncertainty flashed across her face as she arrived at the table and she gave an awkward curtsy. "Baroness," she said shyly. "Thank you for the honor of attending your dinner."

"Of course, child. You can sit next to Lord Darvin. I'm sure you will have much to talk about."

A lanky man wearing a green jacket and a curving gray mustache looked curiously at the girl as she sat. It was obvious he had no idea who she was.

Dinner was a spectacular event unlike anything Darius had ever experienced. First servants placed a porcelain bowl before each guest. Still more staff followed behind with large tureens of soup. Darius, taking his cue from the Aisha and Kofi, waited until all of the guests were served before taking a taste of the thick, meaty broth.

It was spicy, with hints of cumin and garlic and several flavors Darius couldn't identify.

The bowls were cleared away and the second course was served on delicate plates. Darius studied the small bird that rested atop a bed of mint and rice. Chopped red and yellow peppers had been sprinkled over the top and there was a drizzle of reddish-brown sauce. He poked the bird with his knife.

"Stuffed quail," Aisha leaned close to whisper in his ear.

Darius nodded. "How do you eat it?" he whispered back. He was tempted to tear it apart and eat it with his hands like he would goose or chicken but that seemed wrong.

Aisha demonstrated. Pulling off the tiny legs first she delicately nibbled the meat from the bone. She cut the wings off and moved them to the side of her plate with a two-tined fork. Then she cut the bird in half, down the middle. Inside, it was stuffed with bread and onions. She cut the rest into bite-sized chunks and used the fork to raise small bites to her mouth.

Darius tried to mimic her etiquette. By the end of the course Aisha's plate bore a tiny pile of bones and scraps. Darius's plate looked like the dogs had caught the poor bird unaware in the grass.

The third course was a selection of spiced meat, baked fish, and roasted venison. Darius was much more comfortable with this course, cutting chunks of meat and spearing them with his knife. The silver dinner fork that most guests used remained untouched next to his plate.

The fourth course was slices of rich cheese, strawberries, and stewed plums. By the time the fifth course arrived Darius could hardly breathe, his stomach was so full. The final course was a variety of bite-sized pastries. Darius sampled a date and walnut roll, a tiny little pie topped with a pecan, and a sticky triangle shaped dessert with layers of thin dough and nuts topped with honey.

"Baklava," Aisha whispered. "It's my favorite."

"It's good," Darius mumbled through a full mouth.

After dinner was over the guests were redirected to a broad gallery where they could mingle and sip brandy. Saria grabbed Ullani by the elbow and guided her to the edge of the room.

"That was bold," Saria admonished.

Ullani blushed. "Darius invited me. He is the honored guest. I couldn't rightly refuse, could I?"

Saria narrowed her eyes. "I suppose not."

She glanced around the room to make sure no one was within hearing distance. She stepped even closer to Ullani and whispered, "Did you find the key?"

Ullani lowed her gaze to the floor. "No. I'm sorry. I searched everywhere around the market," she lied. "I found the pendant, discarded in a trash heap, but no sign of the key."

Ullani pulled the ivory disc from her pocket and showed her mentor.

"Hmm, that is a shame." Saria seemed disappointed. "Hopefully Bedria's smiths will have better luck."

Ullani nodded. "I sure hope so."

"I'm going to retire for the evening," Saria said. "Stay if you like, but mind what you say to the nobles. You should return the trinket to our new friend."

"Of course," Ullani said. "Thank you. I think I will take the time to get to know our honored guest a little better."

Chapter Twenty-Four
Playing with Fire

The moon was rising into view over the tops of the buildings as Ullani led Darius through the warren of streets. It was the fourth night in a row that she had taken him out. She had taken him to her favorite spots in the city. At each new location he was filled with wonder like the country rube that he was. She found his naivete refreshing and the more time she spent with him the more she realized that she genuinely liked him. He had a kind heart, but there was also a fire in him, especially when he talked about the imperials. She still intended to use him to advance her own social standing, but nothing said she couldn't enjoy herself while she did it.

"Where are we going again?" Darius asked.

"Madam Beyene's," she answered. "It's my favorite bistro in the distillers' quarter. I can't believe you have never tried ouzo."

Darius shrugged. "I've had a cup of wine or two during festival, but Arthengal didn't make a practice of keeping spirits in the valley."

"Oh, ouzo isn't like wine, farm boy. It is so much better. You are in for a treat."

They turned a final corner and the alleyway opened into a plaza decorated with a small fountain. She guided him to a small café with a handful of tables scattered near the entrance.

"You pick a table," Ullani instructed. "I'll get the drinks and food."

She returned several minutes later carrying a tray. Darius was sitting at one of the tables studying the passersby. She watched him for a moment. He was wearing a purple coat tonight. It went well with the blue trousers and new black leather boots. She set the glasses, a carafe of ouzo and a pitcher of water on the table.

Darius picked up the small glass and turned it in his fingers. He examined the bulb in the middle and the curved bowl above it. "This is it?" he asked. "It's so small."

"It doesn't take much," Ullani smiled.

She placed a plate of assorted meats and cheeses in the center of the table then took her seat. She filled each of the glasses to the top of the bulb with the liqueur and then added a little water until the clear liquid turned milky.

Darius picked up his glass and gulped it down. He immediately started coughing.

"No, you fool. You sip it." Ullani shook her head. "Rube," she added under her breath.

Darius blushed.

She mixed him another drink and then demonstrated. She took a small sip, savoring the flavor, letting the cool liquid dance over her tongue before sliding down her throat. Then she selected a piece of sharp white cheese and took a bite allowing the two flavors to merge in her mouth. A sigh of satisfaction escaped her lips.

Darius tried to imitate her. He took a small sip and then crudely swished the liqueur in his mouth.

"It's sweet," he said. "It has an unusual flavor. What is that? I've never tasted it before."

"It's anise," she said as she took another sip. "And maybe a hint of coriander."

Darius took a bite of cheese and then sampled the prosciutto. "Mmm, this is good." He pointed to the salty meat.

Ullani leaned back in her seat enjoying the warm feeling that was growing in her chest. The crisp nighttime air was refreshing by contrast. She sipped her drink and smiled as the farm boy tried different pairings of ouzo, meat, and cheese.

A warm sensation coursed through her body as they slowly drained the carafe. He told her stories of growing up in a small fishing village and of his adventures with Arthengal. She told him of her upbringing on the streets of Kasha Marka.

"You're a thief?" he said a bit too loud.

"Hush," she admonished. "We prefer Red Shadows, and don't be so judgmental. We provide a valuable service to the city."

He looked at her dubiously. "How is thievery a valuable service?"

"This is a big city," she explained. "Crime will happen. It's a fact. The Red Shadow makes sure that criminal activity doesn't get out of control. We also make sure no one gets killed in the process.

Anyone acting outside the bounds of the Red Shadow is punished severely."

"By the city guard?" Darius asked.

"Sometimes," Ullani said. "We tip off the city guard, and they get to look good for the people. But most times we take care of the problem ourselves."

Darius shook his head. "You would end up in the pillory back home."

"Aye, and we'd likely lose a hand if we were in Kasha Haaki. But here in Kasha Marka we operate with relative freedom. It is not the perfect system; no province has mastered the art of managing criminal activity. Still, the freedom of the barons to enact their own laws over their people is better than it was before when you could be hanged merely for stealing a loaf of bread to feed your family."

"Does the baroness know about the Red Shadow?"

"She does," Ullani nodded. "A portion of our *salaries* always makes it into the city's tax coffers and another portion is devoted to keeping the city's impoverished fed. And like I said, crime remains manageable. The people feel safe and trade remains prosperous."

When the moon was high in the sky above them, she looked at the empty bottle. "Should I buy another?"

Darius nodded enthusiastically.

She bought another carafe of the liqueur, this time with a hint of cloves.

"Oh," Ullani exclaimed as if suddenly remembering something important. "I found something for you."

"For me?" Darius looked confused.

Ullani fished the ivory pendant out of her pocket. She had been looking for just the right time to return it to him.

"I wasn't able to find your key, but I found this near the market." She extended her hand, palm up.

Darius's face brightened when he saw the etched carving of the bear. "Thank you so much. This means more to me than you know."

Darius reached across the table and retrieved his most treasured possession. Arthengal had made him the pendant for his eighteenth name day. It was an ivory disc bearing the scrimshaw likeness of Antu.

His elbow bumped the tiny glass and tipped it over. Ouzo spilled across the table.

"Rat spit," Darius cursed and jumped back before the liquid could spill into his lap.

Ullani nearly choked with laughter. "Rat spit?" she chuckled "Is that the best curse you have? Rat Spit? What's next 'noodle sticks'? You curse like a ten-year old girl."

Darius blushed. His mother would have slapped him and Micah silly if they had said anything more provocative when they were children, and Arthengal hadn't been much for curses so Darius hadn't learned much in his sheltered life. Even the sailors that they sold their nets and rope to seemed to instinctively guard his tender ears when he was around.

"What would you suggest?" Darius said grumpily.

"I don't know. How about 'son of a banshee' for something with a little more flare? 'Fire and brimstone,' if you want to give it a religious edge. 'Sludge fudger' is a simple alternative, 'sweet mother of pearl' if you want to sound like a proper farm wife. My personal favorite is 'flaming scrotum of a near-sighted sea dog'."

Darius's cheeks reddened further, not from the salty language, but rather from his obvious lack of experience. "Would you teach me?" Darius asked meekly.

The timid request brought further peels of laughter.

For the next hour Ullani and Darius traded curses back and forth across the table. Had they not been the only patrons the proprietor probably would have asked them to leave.

Once they tired of the game Ullani purchased a third round of ouzo that tasted like the first but with the aftertaste of fennel. They turned their conversation back to their pasts. Darius talked about his bear, Antu, and she listened in rapt terror. Ullani entertained him to tears of laughter with stories of hijinks from the many festivals that Kasha Marka hosted. The moon had sunk below the level of the rooftops again when she drained the last drop from her glass.

Darius found that he enjoyed Ullani's company immensely. Even though Darius had travelled more, Ullani seemed more *worldly*. Her life growing up on the streets of the largest city on the continent gave her a perspective on life that Darius found intriguing. She was attractive, to be sure, but he had Anna. He wasn't looking for romance. Ullani was dangerous, and funny. She talked like a rogue and drank like a sailor. She was unlike any friend Darius had ever had.

"We had better head back. It will be morning soon." Ullani stretched and yawned.

Darius stood to go and nearly toppled over.

Ullani laughed. "Easy, big fella." She held out a hand to steady him.

"Sorry," Darius apologized. "I hadn't realized how strong the drink was."

Ullani escorted him back to his room in the palace. The hallways were abandoned at this time of night and the stillness in the palace made it seem like they were the only two inhabitants.

"Thank you, I had a great time, again." Darius turned when they reached the door to his room.

"You know," Ullani reached out a finger to touch his coat. "I don't have to go." She traced the finger down his chest.

"I think I've had enough for one night and probably need to sleep," Darius said, clearly not catching her meaning.

Ullani leaned in and spread her fingers so her hand was on his chest. "No," she spoke softly in his ear. "I mean I could stay the night."

Darius leaned back slightly and looked in her eyes.

He's blushing. How cute.

"I told you, Ullani, I'm engaged to be married."

"I know, to your farm girl," she said dismissively. She leaned in again, closer this time. Her breath tickled his ear as she spoke. "I could teach you things that your farm girl would never have dreamed."

His face turned crimson.

"I think I should go," he choked.

"Okay," she said casually and stepped back. "Your loss. Have a good sleep. I will see you tomorrow."

"Thank you again," he stammered. He turned the knob on his door and backed into his room watching her as if he expected her to charge in after him.

I don't give up that easily, farm boy, Ullani thought to herself after the door closed with a quiet click. Her plan to get closer to him was working perfectly. She was surprised by his resistance to her attempts at seduction. It was unusual for a man, but she was content to play the long game. Already her standing in court had advanced as she was becoming recognized by several of the merchants and minor nobles. Such connections would be important if she ever wanted to take over for Saria. Her mentor was getting old. She was nearly sixty after all. Saria couldn't plan to run the guild forever.

*****

Darius groaned. His head pounded and his mouth tasted like a family of squirrels had camped in it for the night. He stumbled out of bed, bleary eyed, to the chest of drawers near the bed. He reached for the pewter mug and the pitcher of water. He sloshed as much water on the lace covering on top of the chest as he got in the cup.

He drained the water in a single gulp and then poured a second. He emptied the rest of the pitcher into the ceramic basin beside it and splashed his face with water.

What time is it?

The heavy satin curtains were still drawn over the windows. He stepped toward them and pulled them aside. The midday sun felt like hot pokers in his eyes. His stomach turned and he belched. The effect was not pleasant. He decided that he needed food.

On his way to the kitchens, he passed Lord Misrak. The guard captain turned to follow him.

"You look like death warmed over, if you don't mind me saying. Did that sewer girl introduce you to the seedier sections of our fair city last night?" There was a grin on his face as he said it.

"She introduced me to ouzo," Darius mumbled.

"Ah, nothing better, but you do need to watch yourself. It's stronger than it seems."

Darius nodded.

"I was just on my way to find you, actually. My duties are light today, and I was wondering if you would like to learn some of the dual-weapon forms I had mentioned."

"I think I need to eat. And then I think I might go back to my room and die."

Misrak laughed. "A good workout will do you good. Best cure for too much drink is to sweat it out of you. Go get some bread and eggs and ask Margarite to mix you up a batch of *the cure*."

"What's that?" Darius asked.

"Oh, you won't like it. It's a mixture of tomato and pickle juice with ginger and a spot of brandy." Lord Misrak laughed again. "But Margarite swears by it. I make her give it to all of my new recruits if they have found themselves too deep in their cups the night before."

Darius groaned and his stomach turned again.

"Meet me in the practice yard after you've eaten. You'll feel better after an hour or two of practice, I promise."

*****

Darius entered the practice yard, a broad expanse of grass on the north side of the palace surrounded by tall hedges. On the north side of the yard several soldiers were firing at straw archery targets. Lord Misrak waited in the middle near a patch of short grass encircled by paving stones. An assortment of weapons was arranged on racks near several wooden practice dummies.

"You're looking better, at least," Lord Misrak commented.

"Food helped," Darius said. "But my head is still pounding."

"We'll work that out of you, don't you worry. Did you bring your swords?"

"No. Should I have? I thought we would use practice weapons."

"We will," Misrak agreed. "I was just going to show you the proper way to wear two blades. We have extra weapons and harnesses over here. The way I noticed you wearing them before will make it difficult to draw them both at once. You had one at each hip, correct?"

"Yes. That is how Arthengal taught me how to wear my sword, at the hip."

"Which is fine for a single blade. It doesn't work as well for two blades, as I'm sure you've found. I prefer one at my hip and one over my shoulder. Here, let me show you."

Lord Misrak retrieved two swords and a collection of belts and straps from a weapons rack at the near side of the practice yard.

"First, I find it easier to draw my off-hand from the hip." Misrak fastened a belt and blade around Darius's waist and adjusted it so the hilt was just above his right hip. "Try that."

Darius drew the blade with his left hand a bit awkwardly.

Misrak made a few additional adjustments to the positioning and made him try again. This time the blade slid cleanly from the scabbard.

"We'll adjust the harness next." He fixed a longer belt diagonally across Darius's chest. "You can adjust it here at the side."

The guard captain adjusted the gear until Darius could feel the hilt of the blade resting right to left between his shoulder blades. The hilt extended just past his right shoulder.

"Now reach up with your right hand and draw the blade," Misrak instructed. "Watch your ear."

Darius did as instructed.

"Up and then away from your body," Misrak coached as Darius carefully drew the sword.

"Putting it back takes a bit more practice." Lord Misrak held up a twin to the scabbard he had strapped to Darius's back. "It requires a different type of sheath on the back. See how it's open on the side here partway up?"

Darius nodded.

"That allows you to draw it more easily but can also help you guide it back into position."

They practiced the technique several more times, sheathing and unsheathing the blade. Once Darius had some success, Misrak had him try both blades at once.

"Good," the soldier clapped him on the shoulder. "You will need a bit more practice, but you have the idea. I can have our leather smiths take your measurements and craft one that fits a bit more snuggly. You don't want it to be too loose or it will get uncomfortable on the shoulder. How about a bit of sparring first with a single blade so I can assess your technique before I introduce you to the dual forms?"

"Sure," Darius agreed.

Darius took the practice sword he was offered and took a defensive posture. Misrak attacked with Searching the Sea, a common first attack when assessing a new opponent's strengths. His movements were a bit slow and Darius easily blocked and counterattacked with Comet Chases the Moon. Lord Misrak increased his pace and attacked more quickly. Darius quickly forgot his headache as he got into the flow of the forms and found that he was enjoying himself. The guard captain was really quite good.

After fifteen minutes of attacking and countering, Darius increased his own pace and went on the offensive. He soon had Misrak backstepping across the field. Darius transitioned from Wild Horse Leaps into Striking Adder and finally landed the first blow in the captain's middle.

"Hold," Lord Misrak called and lowered his blade.

Darius returned to a defensive stance and waited.

"That was amazing," Misrak said once he had caught his breath. "You have incredible skill for one so young."

Darius grinned. "You're not too bad yourself."

"Thank you, but I have twenty years' experience on you so forgive me if I don't take as much pride in the result as you should. Okay, why don't you show me what you have with two blades?"

Darius picked up a second practice sword and entered his modified defensive stance, his left hand slightly lower than the right and turned so the blade guarded his center.

Lord Misrak attacked, still using only one weapon. Darius blocked with his new version of Lazy Viper.

"Impressive adaptation," Misrak said and then countered with Scooping the Moon.

Darius dropped both blades to block and Misrak quickly changed his approach to take advantage of the lowered guard and rapped Darius on the head.

"You have two weapons. You should never have an excuse to leave an opening like that."

Misrak launched several more attacks and Darius countered with his adaptations but each time the captain was able to breach his defenses and score a strike.

"Okay, that's enough," Misrak said. "I like some of what you've done, they're really quite ingenious improvisations. You would do well against an untrained opponent. However, you are still fighting with one sword. You just happen to have a blade in each hand. Let me show you the first novice form. It's called The Hawk and the Dove."

Misrak retrieved another stave and moved slowly through the form. The left and right weapons created their own dance. The left was always low, and the right was always high. When he would thrust with the right, he would block with the left. A low slash was paired with a high counter, and so on.

"Move through it with me."

Darius stood next to the man and mimicked his movements. The exercise reminded him of his earliest sessions with Arthengal. Soon he was moving through the form at practice speed.

"Good. I'll show you Sun and Moon next. You can practice those two for a while and I'll show you two more forms next week. How does that sound?"

"Sounds great," Darius said with a smile.

While he was practicing, he noticed Ullani entering the far side of the practice field. She leaned against the wall and watched the two men until sweat was running down their faces and their shirts were soaked through. When Misrak finally called an end to the practice she sauntered toward the men.

"It's like watching a moving work of art," Ullani purred. Her grin was wolfish as her eyes traveled up and down the length of Darius's sweat-soaked body.

"Thank you," Darius said, wiping his brow with a towel Misrak had tossed him. He ignored her flirtatious tone and ogling gaze. She must be teasing him after last night. But he had been clear, they were just friends. He was promised to Anna.

"You should come practice sometime," Lord Misrak offered to Ullani. "It is good for a lady in your trade to be able to defend herself."

"Oh, I can take care of myself all right," Ullani smiled.

"Oh, really?" Lord Misrak raised an eyebrow. "Lady Saria has trained you in the martial arts?"

"Of a sort," Ullani replied.

"Shall we have a brief demonstration of your skill?" Lord Misrak tilted his head. From the tone of his voice Darius didn't think Misrak believed her.

Ullani shrugged. She moved several paces away from the practice dummies. Suddenly her hands moved in a blur as her feet completed a quick sequence of steps not unlike Dancing Lights. When she was through a short, but surely fatal, knife protruded from each of the six mannequins in both the heart and the head.

Lord Misrak laughed and clapped his hands. "Nicely done. I do stand corrected."

"That was amazing," Darius said with awe.

Ullani retrieved her throwing knives which disappeared deftly into the folds of her clothing. A look of pride shown on her face as she returned to the two men.

"How are you feeling today?" Ullani gave Darius a sly grin.

"Good, now. I wasn't when I woke, but the practice helped."

"You certainly smell like you sweated out all the alcohol." She wrinkled her nose.

Darius sniffed his shirt and it almost made his headache return.

"You should take a bath," Ullani grinned. "Soon."

*****

Darius entered the palace baths. He glanced around nervously. He still wasn't used to public baths. So far, he had managed to come only early in the morning or late in the day when the room was abandoned. There were two large pools in the tiled room, similar to the baths at the Rose. Two older stewards occupied one of the pools, but the other was vacant. He set his towel on a bench near the edge of the pool and quickly disrobed. He hurried down the stairs into the heated water and in his nervousness almost slipped on the wet tiles.

Near the edge of the pool were several cakes of soap and folded clothes. He started to move toward them when the sound of the door opening and closing drew his attention.

Ullani stood by the door holding her own towel.

"I figured as much as we drank last night, I could probably use a bath of my own," she said casually.

"Now?" Darius squeaked.

"What better time?" she shrugged.

With a single motion she pulled her loose-fitting red top over her head. Her mocha skin was flawless, her taut abdomen transitioning with perfection to the smooth curves of her breasts. She stooped as she pulled off her pants and Darius glanced over his shoulder nervously at the old men. They were ignoring the girl as if this happened every day, which, Darius supposed, it probably did.

"You're getting in with me?" Darius asked. His gaze darted left and right making him feel like a trapped rabbit looking for an escape.

"Why wouldn't I? You are in the women's pool, after all."

"I am? I didn't know."

Ullani shrugged, "I don't mind, you can stay. They don't look as interesting as I am anyway." She nodded her chin toward the ancient stewards. "Besides, it's not uncommon for friends or even family to bathe together."

Somehow the statement of cultural tolerance didn't make Darius feel any more comfortable.

Ullani glided smoothly into the water. Darius felt more guilty with each slow step that she took, but he found that he could not tear his eyes away from her naked form until she was submerged up to her chin and sliding through the water toward him.

She positioned herself on one of the underwater benches and lay her head back against the edge of the pool. The water lapped gently just below her shoulders as she stretched out with a satisfied sigh.

"Nothing better than a hot bath to ease the muscles, is there?" she asked.

"Nope," Darius squeaked again.

What is wrong with my voice?

Darius found a seat for himself and tried to act casual as he lay his head back and closed his eyes. He heard the two old men talking as they left their pool and walked to the exit. Then the room was silent.

"Want me to wash your back?" Ullani offered.

"What!"

"What?" Ullani seemed confused. "It's quite common. It's so hard to reach on your own."

"I'm not so sure about that," Darius stammered.

"Come on." Ullani slapped his shoulder. "I'll be quick. Then maybe you can help me with mine."

She reached for a bar of soap and pushed him into the center of the pool. Before he could protest again, she began lathering his back and shoulders. He had to admit that the massaging pressure of the bar felt good after a long morning of sword practice. He allowed himself to relax a little and enjoy the sensation.

She continued to the tops of his shoulders and his outer arm. He felt the tension leave him as tight muscles relaxed. She leaned against him as her hand drifted over his shoulder to massage his chest. He could feel the warmth of her body extending the length of his back.

A shiver ran through him as Ullani pressed even closer to reach under his arm to grab the soap with her other hand. She drew circles across his chest and abdomen with the cake of soap. The heat of her body coalesced to two fiery, hard points just below his shoulder blades. Her hand continued to circle lower and lower until, --

Darius jumped away. "Okay, I think I'm good and, uh, clean. Thank you for your help. I, uh, think I'm going to. Oh, I just remembered I was supposed to meet Nicolai and Gunnar for lunch. Okay, well, bye." He paddled quickly across the pool as he spoke and practically ran to his belongings. He pulled his clothes on without bothering to dry himself. He glanced back once and saw Ullani lounging against the back wall with a devilish grin on her face.

Maybe she didn't get the hint that we are just friends after all. Darius thought as he stumbled from the room. He promised himself that he would be more direct next time.

Spring 35 A.E.

Chapter Twenty-Five
Captain Zima

Micah rose in the saddle to get a better view of the camp spread out across the valley. The remnants of snow were stained brown from mud and refuse. Most of the soldiers were busy breaking down tents and packing gear onto wagons.

"You've been travelling all winter?"

Micah turned his attention back to the sentry guard who had stopped Micah's column.

"Mostly," Micah reported. "We had to stop to make camp when the winter storms were at their worst." Micah trailed off when he realized the guard wasn't really listening. He was inspecting the pair of documents Micah had given him.

The first parchment was Lieutenant Zhukov's orders to find and capture the escaped prisoners and the second were Micah's orders, countermanding the first, demanding the capture and return of unspecified stolen property of the Emperor Jun to the pro tem imperial capital in Eridu.

"And you didn't capture the prisoners?"

Micah sighed. This was the second time the guard had asked the question. Micah waited for the guard to look up at him before responding.

"As I mentioned previously, they escaped into the Talia mountains and we were unable to pursue them due to an avalanche."

"Okay, you'll want to check in with Captain Zima. He will tell you how to align your columns with the rest of the army. We have orders to depart for Kasha Marka at dawn. Captain Han is the quartermaster. You can check in with him to resupply if you need it before we set off."

"Thank you, and where is General Hamazi? My orders come directly from Emperor Jun and I need to brief him on their importance."

The soldier looked at Micah like he was daft. "Check in with Captain Zima. He will give you your additional orders, Lieutenant."

Micah sighed and then heeled his horse. The rest of his ragtag column advanced with him. The winter had been rough. They had been snowed in several times and more than twenty men had died from exposure. At the beginning, Micah had refused to allow his men to pillage the villages or farms that they passed insisting that they forage for supplies. As the winter wore on and their circumstances became more severe, he had sacrificed his morals for the sake of his men. He regretted the circumstances of the poor farmers whose homesteads had been stripped bare, and regretted even more the lives of those who had tried to protect their belongings, but it had been a necessary evil to guarantee the survival of Micah and his men. Much of their gear was in disrepair and they were in desperate need of supplies, but Micah followed his orders and sought out Captain Zima.

*****

Micah's stomach growled as he stood beside his horse and waited outside the tent. The sergeant on duty had taken Micah's orders inside more than an hour before. Moab and Joral waited patiently by his side. Lieutenant Minoshka also waited nearby, checking the straps on his saddle.

Micah had ordered Sergeant Han to take the rest of the men to resupply as soon as they had arrived at the tent. He hoped that his men, at least, had managed to find a good meal.

A short man with a thin blond mustache and stringy brown hair exited the tent. His uniform was neatly assembled and bore the rank of captain. He scanned the four of them and then addressed Lieutenant Minoshka.

"*Sergeant* Minoshka. Can you please come in and provide me a briefing of what became of Lieutenant Zhukov?"

"Of course, Captain Zima," Minoshka answered smartly and followed the captain into the tent.

Another hour later Minoshka exited looking somewhat chastened and flashed Micah an apologetic look.

Captain Zima exited again and held the tent flap open.

"Lieutenant Kabir." Zima gestured to the inside of the tent.

Micah followed him inside.

The captain sat down behind a simple wooden table. Micah stood at attention in front of him and waited to be addressed.

"Lieutenant Kabir. It is my understanding that you murdered Lieutenant Zhukov, a distinguished officer with a long career serving under General Hamazi and myself. Before we proceed with your official trial and execution, I am obliged to allow you to offer your account of events."

"You have been misinformed, Captain," Micah said simply.

"In what way, Lieutenant? You did kill Lieutenant Zhukov?"

"Yes, sir. I executed him in fair combat for the crime of mutiny," Micah explained.

"Excuse me? You did what?"

"Emperor Jun placed me in charge of forces at Isan. Lieutenant Zhukov resisted the orders of the Emperor from the day I arrived. His mutiny came to a head when he tried to seize command from me because I refused to allow him to rape the local village girl that he had kidnapped. He challenged me to a duel and tragically lost his life. I promoted *Lieutenant* Minoshka to the command of the lancers following Zhukov's death."

Captain Zima's face was like stone.

Micah continued to stand at attention while the Captain chewed on his cheek.

"Thank you, Lieutenant," Captain Zima said after some time. "You have given me a lot to consider. That will be all for now. Please see to your men."

"Thank you, sir. If I may, sir," Micah asked, still standing rigid.

"What is it, Lieutenant?" Zima grunted through clenched teeth.

"Sir, Lieutenant Minoshka has served admirably since his appointment. Discipline has increased significantly within the ranks of the lancers and their performance in drills has been commendable. I promised him that I would argue on his behalf to make the promotion permanent."

"I will take the recommendation under consideration." Zima's stone face relaxed only a fraction. "Will that be all?"

"Unless you consider it otherwise, sir, I believe my orders from Emperor Jun are still valid. I believe the fugitives escaped to Kasha Marka with the emperor's property. My understanding is that General Hamazi is preparing to lay siege to the city. I would like permission to take the Night Birds inside and continue our pursuit."

Captain Zima studied Micah. Zima's right hand rested on the table clenched tightly into a fist. The knuckles of his left hand strained and the fingertips were white from the pressure he was exerting on the closed fist.

The captain forced a smile. "I cannot think of anything that would countermand those orders at this time, Lieutenant. You may proceed as you see fit once we arrive at Kasha Marka."

"Thank you, Captain." Micah clicked his heels. "Have a blessed day, Captain. May the light of his Holiness Emperor Jun shine upon you."

Micah spun on his heels and exited the tent. His heart continued to hammer in his chest while he mounted his horse.

"How did it go?" Moab asked.

"Fine, why do you ask?" Micah said casually. *Well, that was close.*

Moab grinned. "No reason, you know two lieutenants go out, one comes back. I'm sure it happens all the time."

"That's two drachs," Joral interjected.

"For what?" Micah asked.

"Oh, nothing," Moab answered, digging in his pouch. "Just a little bet on whether or not you'd leave the tent on your feet or in shackles."

"Oh, ye of little faith." Micah punched Moab in the arm. "Come on, let's get the men settled."

Chapter Twenty-Six
Reunited

Cordelia saw the towers first, peaking over the hills in the distance and then disappearing as they crested each rise in the road. They rose like brown and gray sentinels above the trees in the distance. Soon enough they saw the wall connecting the looming giants.

Cordelia and her small band merged with the road from Kantibar about ten leagues south of the city. Their quiet mountain road suddenly became a bustle of activity. Merchants hurried their caravans along, trying to beat their competitors to the spring markets. Some traders didn't bother to try. They erected stands alongside the road selling everything from meat to wool; from produce to liquors. Farmers from the numerous homesteads that surrounded the city flocked to these roadside vendors rather than making the longer journey into the city.

Cordelia took a bite out of an apricot while she perused the colorful bolts of cloth arrayed at one roadside vendor. She absently wiped the juice from her chin with the back of her hand. The craftsmanship of the cloth was as good as anything she had seen back home. She fingered a length of dark green cloth with her left hand, not wanting to stain it with juice.

"That color would go beautifully with your hair." The vendor was a short graying woman in a handsome blue frock.

Cordelia stroked her red hair and cringed. She hadn't washed it in over a week and the normally lustrous red was dingy and brown from days of road dust.

"You are too kind," Cordelia said politely.

"Here, let me hold it up for you," the merchant said with a smile.

Cordelia tossed the apricot pit into a bush behind the stall and spread her arms to allow the woman to hold the cloth in front of her. She handed Cordelia a polished bronze mirror so she could inspect herself.

"See, what did I tell you?" The trader gently lifted Cordelia's auburn locks so that they spilled across the green fabric. "It goes perfectly with your hair and your eyes."

Cordelia smiled. It would be nice to have a new dress once they reached the city. She let out an exaggerated sigh.

"Fine, you have convinced me," Cordelia said as she inspected the width of the bolt. "I think twenty span ought to be enough. I'll give you one drach."

"That's wonderful, m'lady. It will make a fine dress. Twenty span will be two drachs and five, though, if you please."

"It is a fine cloth," Cordelia said. "But I still have to sew the dress. I couldn't possibly pay more than one drach and three."

"And a fine seamstress you are judging by the quality of the beautiful dress you are wearing. You will need thread that matches, of course. I'll add on two spools of the perfect color and we can call it a deal at two drachs."

"What? This old thing?" Cordelia held the hem of her dress away from her body. "Just an old farmwife's dress. You raise a good point. A cloth of that color will need some highlights. Throw in the green thread and two spools of yellow and all will be well at one drach and eight."

"Done," the merchant smiled.

Cordelia was carefully stowing her wrapped package in her saddle bags when Kal rode up beside her.

"I've gotten word to Darius," Kal panted. "He will meet us at the Merchant's Gate. We should be there by nightfall."

"Thank goodness," Cordelia exclaimed. "I can't wait for a good bath and a real mattress."

Cordelia inspected the height of the sun. "Kal, round up the others if you would. We've spent enough time shopping. Let's see if we can't beat the sun to the gatehouse."

*****

Cordelia marveled at the city. Her father had regaled her with stories of Kasha Marka from his time spent there during the war. She had retold those stories to Micah and Darius a thousand times. But her father's narratives paled in comparison to the real thing.

The walls stood the height of six men and the towers stood half again as tall. As they approached the towering gates, they rode across an arched limestone bridge. The bridge crossed a grass moat covered in a luxurious green carpet. The bronze doors of the gate were flung open to admit the flood of travelers and merchants into the city. Each door bore a gilded eagle, wings spread in flight.

"Mother!"

Cordelia turned at the sound and saw Darius approaching as they dismounted and led their horses through the bustle. She stroked the neck of her mare to keep her calm in the crowd.

Darius threw his arms around her in an all-encompassing embrace. She still couldn't believe how much he had grown. It wasn't too many years gone by when she could envelop him in a hug. He gave her a squeeze that made her ribs hurt and then released her quickly.

"How was your trip?" he asked.

"Good." Her voice sounded tired in her ears, but Darius seemed not to notice. He chattered on like when he was a boy who had discovered some new curiosity in the woods.

Darius's words flooded over her and around her as she walked in a daze. She admired the buildings that rose four and five stories above the road. Marble porticos marked the entrances of each building and decorative balconies marked the upper floors. She peered down alleyways and noticed ropes strung between the balconies to opposite buildings. Clothing hung drying in the sun over the crowded lanes. The crowd seemed not to notice the occasional drip from above.

Darius led them past the Grand Market, a spectacle that overwhelmed Cordelia's senses. The cacophony of sound that drowned out Darius's voice was matched only by the miasma that made her eyes water. The air was thick with overlapping smells of cinnamon, citrus, roasting meat, cumin, flowers, and a hundred unidentifiable smells was overwhelming.

The crowd began to clear as they passed an ovular marble fountain depicting Nammu, the mother goddess, on her center pedestal directing an orchestra of water nymphs. Each nymph held a gilded fish aloft and water streamed from the fishes' mouths. The streams of water converged on statues of Antu and his sister Kisha struggling to emerge from the sea that was their birthplace. Cordelia's father had described the fountain to her in detail when she was a girl. He had told the story of the birth of heaven and earth, from The Mother of Miracles, for whom the fountain was named. Seeing it in person brought back a flood of memories and emotions. Cordelia casually wiped away a tear and smiled at the memory of time spent with her father and story times with her sons.

"It's a beautiful fountain, isn't it?" Darius asked, noticing her smile, if not the tear.

She smiled back and reached out to caress his cheek. "It certainly is."

Darius led them through a maze of streets. As they retreated from the market square the noise faded to a persistent buzz. She had a feeling that the city was never totally quiet. She had gotten so used to the serenity of Patel's Rest that the noise, more than anything, was difficult to adapt to. She thought back to quiet nights on a high balcony staring out over the waterfalls into the abyss beyond and the silence that only a snow-covered mountain valley can provide. There the rushing water had blocked out other sounds with white noise that deepened the stillness. Here, in the city, the constant hum felt like needles piercing the flesh behind her ears.

"When we get to the palace, you'll be able to settle in and relax. The Baroness wanted to host a dinner in your honor but—"

Cordelia was snapped back to awareness. "What are you talking about?" She was tired from the journey and distracted by the clamor around them. She heard the edge in her tone and immediately regretted it.

Darius looked at her queerly. "Haven't you been listening to me?" he asked, mirroring her irritation.

"I'm sorry, honey." Cordelia smiled. "The noise and all the distractions of the city, it has been hard to pay attention. Please, what were you saying? Something about a palace?"

"Baroness Magora has invited us to stay in the palace," Darius repeated with feigned patience. "We moved in there soon after we arrived. She wanted to keep the box in her vault, and she has locksmiths working to reproduce the key I lost."

"You lost your key?" Cordelia gasped.

Darius rolled his eyes. "Yes. They haven't had any luck yet, but they are hoping once they get the chance to examine your key, they will have a better idea of how to craft a replacement.

"In the meantime, we are staying at the palace so that we and the box are safe. I told her about the imperial troops that have been following us and she didn't want to take any chances."

Cordelia nodded. "That was kind of her."

"Arthengal was an old friend. I think the gesture is more to honor him than us. In any case, I'll take it. The palace is amazing. We all have our own rooms and each one is the size of the meeting hall in Koza."

"Sounds incredible," Cordelia mused.

"The bath chambers are a little awkward."

Is he blushing?

"They have public baths so you might have to share. I try to go in the middle of the night when no one else is there."

"That shouldn't be a problem." She smiled and patted his arm. "It sounds lovely."

He always was a bit sensitive about such things.

"Well, I'll show you the way as soon as we get you settled in your rooms. I'm sure you'll want to clean up after weeks on the trail."

Subtle.

"Once you've had a bath, I'll take you to dinner at one of the outdoor cafes that Ullani showed me. They have the best mutton stew."

"Who's Ullani?"

"Just a girl who Saria assigned to show me around the city. She's been very helpful."

He is blushing! I'll have to find out more about this Ullani. He better not be doing anything that would break poor Anna's heart.

"That sounds fine, dear, but maybe tomorrow night. I think after I bathe, I want nothing more than to sleep for a week in a real bed."

Chapter Twenty-Seven
Dragons and Lions

"You've come with news?" Jun asked the general officer standing crisply at attention opposite the emperor's field desk.

"Yes, your Majesty." The general stared at the floor, going beyond what was customary, refusing to meet his emperor's gaze even when spoken to.

He's nervous. He doesn't want to deliver this report, Jun thought.

"General Sharav has positioned his forces along the ridgelines north of Port of Giselle. He wishes to report that forces of Shalanum, while late in assembling, have arrived and have encamped south of the port.

"They number nearly eighty thousand with a quarter of that devoted to cavalry. Your Majesty, they outnumber us nearly two to one, even with the reinforcements that we have en route from Eridu." Concern marked the officer's tone.

Jun waved a hand dismissively. "Relax, General Kalin. Our men may not have the superiority of numbers, but they are better trained. They have endured the hardships of the Northern Wastes while the southern armies have gotten fat and lazy. I also wouldn't worry too much about the Shalanazi cavalry. I have a feeling their numbers are not as distressing as you might think. Now, tell me. How are their horsemen positioned?"

"They are divided between the vanguard and the flanks with some held in reserve," the officer recited.

Jun shook his head. "Show me."

He rose and strode across the tent to the long table erected across the room. A general terrain map had been rolled out and a large wooden building had been placed on the left side near the midpoint of the map. Jun picked up a wooden dowel from the table. Boxes of wooden figurines rested on the edges of the table. The wooden carvings depicted horses, soldiers, knights, ships, and all other manner of military figurines.

"This is Port of Giselle." Jun tapped the rod on the house. "Here are the hills to the north." Jun placed a line of plane wooden blocks on the map.

"Show me," Jun repeated.

General Kalin inspected the figures. He selected six soldiers holding bows.

"Our archers are here, along the ridgeline." He placed three of the pieces behind the wooden blocks. "The Shalanazi archers are here, south of the city with a clear shot at the battlefield.

"Shalanum has placed two regiments of light infantry in the city to protect it and has barred the gates." The general placed a pair of soldiers next to the house.

"Our infantry are positioned at the base of the hill below the archers." Two soldiers went on the map in front of the blocks. "And our cavalry are ready to charge from the east." Two horses were placed to the right of the blocks.

"As you are aware, Your Majesty, our heavy infantry were delayed and are still en route from Eridu. They should arrive by tomorrow evening." Kalin placed two knight figurines at the top of the map well behind the imperial archers.

Jun studied the placement of his forces. He grunted with satisfaction and then gestured for General Kalin to continue. "And where are the rest of the Shalanazi forces?"

"Five regiments of light infantry are prepared to engage. They are led by two regiments of heavy infantry and the vanguard which is comprised of heavy cavalry." He placed a row of five soldiers in front of the Shalanazi archers. Then he placed a mounted knight in front of the soldiers and a standing knight to either side.

"They have light cavalry on the flanks." A horse was placed on either side of the line of archers. "And in reserve they have two regiments, one of light infantry and one of light cavalry." The final two figures were placed at the foot of the map behind the archers.

"Our scouts also report that a fleet of Shalanazi ships left Kasha Amur with close to fifty thousand mixed infantry. They should arrive within a matter of days." General Kalin placed ten ships on the left edge of the map.

Jun considered the placements. "It would seem they are determined to wipe us from the map. They hold almost nothing in reserve."

"Neither do we, Majesty," Kalin commented.

"Yes, but we don't have the necessary reserves. The bulk of our forces are either in the north, making sure Magoran forces can't surprise us from behind, or are still sailing south from Tuding Harbor."

"They await your arrival on the field to engage, Majesty."

Jun studied the map a moment more and then nodded.

"Lead the way, General."

Jun mounted the horse that was waiting for him outside the tent and rode the fifteen minutes south to the battlefield. The air was heavy with the scent of sweat and anticipation. The officers' horses stamped their hooves and shifted from side to side. The animals seemed as anxious to engage as their riders.

Jun rode up beside General Sharav who was conversing with several of his officers.

"Everything is ready, Commander General?" Jun asked.

"Of course, Majesty. We await your order."

Jun surveyed the scene across the broad fields of grain that spread out east of the city. The size of the Shalanazi forces arrayed against them certainly looked intimidating. His own forces were dwarfed by the size of the enemy army.

Jun glanced east. The sun was an hour above the horizon.

"Sound the advance, General," Jun said.

A horn sounded behind him. The imperial bowmen notched their bows but waited to draw. The light infantry below the hill began to march forward, slowly. Across the green expanse there was a noticeable shift as the Shalanazi forces began their advance. The armored soldiers tramped across the field in three shining rectangles. The lines of conscripts with their short spears and peasants' clothing marched somewhat less confidently behind the regiments of knights. The Shalanazi light cavalry trotted slowly at the flanks, lances held high.

Jun's forces stopped after marching only five hundred paces, as they had been ordered to do. They intended to tire out the heavily armored enemy by making them march the greater distance.

Soon, the heavy forces had outpaced the conscripts by fifty or more strides. They were almost in range of Jun's archers.

"Steady," Jun heard the artillery general urge. The command was echoed down the line in both directions.

"Ready." There was a whooshing sound as thousands of bows were drawn at once.

"Take aim." Bows raised and steadied.

"Fire."

The air became black with arrows. A torrent of steel and wood rained down on the advancing enemy. The Shalanazi infantry stopped and raised their shields over their heads. Most of the arrows shattered or ricocheted off of the heavy shields and armor but a few made it through the gaps and found targets.

Jun's bowmen waited for the heavy infantry to start their advance again before ordering a second round. By then the Shalanazi light infantry had caught up but were still out of range.

A horn sounded across the battlefield. The enemy archers, seeing that Jun's forces were determined to stay out of range, had decided to advance. They were picking up their staked arrows and advancing behind the line of infantrymen at a trot.

The Shalanazi light infantry finally entered bow range. Jun's artillery general called for a third assault. The sea of black darkened the sky again. The marching knights stopped again and raised shields, expecting another barrage. The arrows flew past them, however, into the center of the advancing conscripts. Hundreds of men fell and a great wailing arose from the battlefield.

Another horn sounded and a cry rose from the enemy vanguard. Dust rose from thousands of hooves as horses began to run. Then chaos descended upon the enemy ranks.

The light cavalry, which had been milling about well behind the advancing line of infantry suddenly broke into a charge, lowering their lances. They charged headlong into their own flanks trampling and skewering their own men. Cries of dismay and alarm could be heard across the field.

Jun smiled to himself. Minister Cray had come through. At least two of the cavalry regiments had been turned to his side.

The smile broadened as he watched the reserve cavalry charge at the back ranks of archers with devastating effectiveness.

Make that three regiments.

The three regiments of horsemen wheeled for another charge at their own ranks. During the second charge some of the soldiers had regained their wits enough to defend themselves but it was not enough, and the damage was severe. The second charge broke the light infantry and they began fleeing. Some ran south while others tried to bang on the gates of the city demanding admittance.

Jun's archers changed targets again and aimed at the Shalanazi heavy cavalry. Enough arrows found the less protected flesh of the horses to create disorder in the lines.

The enemy general had finally been alerted to the chaos in his back ranks. A bugle sounded and the heavy cavalry halted their advance and turned to engage the traitors. However, it took them time to organize and before they rode toward the easternmost brigade with lowered lances, the light cavalry had delivered another devastating blow to the remaining light infantry and archers.

The heavy infantry continued its advance. When they were fifty paces from Jun's infantry, the black rain stopped. The imperial infantry sprang forward from their resting place to meet the enemy charge. Unlike Shalanum's light infantry, the imperial forces were well trained. Even though they lacked the heavy steel and bronze armor, their hardened leather breastplates and greaves did an adequate job of protecting them. The imperial soldiers were also nimbler than their armored foes and were able to dodge and evade more easily.

A rapid succession of horn blasts set the imperial cavalry in motion. Shalanum's heavy cavalry had been isolated and the imperial horsemen charged from the left side. Three light cavalry regiments against a single heavy cavalry had a deadly result.

To Jun's surprise, the enemy's reserve infantry had decided to engage the rear cavalry. They and the remnants of the archers were doing an adequate job of beating down the traitorous horsemen, pulling them from their saddles and assaulting them with spears and daggers.

The sun was just past its zenith when Jun watched the blue and golden lion's banner fall. It was trampled in the mud as horsemen in blue and gold turned to flee. A series of panicked bugle blasts signaled the general retreat. General Sharav ordered the advance, but not the pursuit. Soon, Jun's forces had cut off Port of Giselle from the rest of the Shalanazi army.

Under flag of truce the new enemy commander had asked for an end to hostilities for the day and had proposed reengagement the following morning.

All very civilized. Jun chuckled to himself.

General Sharav graciously agreed and sent the messenger on his way.

Shortly before dusk, General Sharav took Jun on a ride to inspect their forces.

"What were our casualties, General?"

"About a tenth of our forces were killed or wounded. Hospital tents have been set up for the wounded north of here. Many of the wounds are grievous, however, so the butcher's bill may be higher yet."

Jun nodded soberly. Not great news but given how badly they were outnumbered at the outset, better than should have been expected.

"All in all, our numbers increased with the defection of Minister Cray's horsemen." Sharav added.

"And the enemy forces?" Jun asked.

"It's hard to say. Scouting reports are still coming in. Some say as many as a third of the Shalanazi archers and light infantry scattered and deserted. Their casualties were higher, too, thanks in large part to the surprise attacks. Perhaps a quarter of their troops were killed or wounded. My best guess is that they are left with half of what they started the day with."

Jun returned to his tent following the inspection with a light heart and a smile on his face.

*****

The following morning Jun was greeted by a messenger from General Sharav when he exited his tent.

"What happened?" Jun asked Sharav when he arrived at the battlefield.

"They slipped away in the night is what happened," Sharav grunted with a note of disgust.

Sharav held up a slip of paper and read it aloud. "I regret that I will not be able to engage the forces of Emperor Lao Jun Qiu at this time. I do not believe it is in the best interests of Shalanum Province or its leadership to continue battle this day."

Sharav crumpled the paper and tossed it to the ground. "Coward."

Jun covered his mouth with a hand to hide his smile.

"What now, General?"

"If we can convince the idiot in charge of the forces in the city that they have lost and that he should surrender then we can get on with securing the port. He has almost ten thousand troops in there plus whatever citizens refused to evacuate. I can't imagine they have provisions for more than a few weeks. They were expecting a short battle and an overwhelming victory. They weren't prepared for an extended siege. I think he's hoping he can hold out until the fleet arrives."

"Who commands the city forces?"

"Captain Rouen," General Sharav responded.

Jun groaned. After his humiliation at Eridu it was unlikely Rouen would surrender, especially if there was a chance for reinforcements.

"Can we storm the city?" Jun asked.

"Not without siege equipment. The walls are not that tall, but they are stone. It's easier just to wait them out. We can secure the countryside in the meantime and provision our forces. The rest will do them good, especially if we have to march to Kasha Amur."

Jun surveyed the broken farmland that had been host to the previous day's battle. Thousands of bodies littered the ground. The wounded had been evacuated behind their respective lines following the battle but over ten thousand men had lost their lives in the single battle. The flies and the ravens darkened the battlefield in macabre décor.

"We should see to the burial of the dead if we are going to be here a while," Jun suggested.

"I'll see to it, Your Highness," Sharav responded.

*****

After a three-week siege a rail-thin soldier opened the gates to Port of Giselle.

"The captain has been deposed," the soldier explained. "We would like to negotiate the terms of our surrender."

Jun found, upon riding into the city, what the soldier had meant by *deposed*. Captain Rouen and his officers had been hung from city walls by their own men. They had been stripped and beaten bloody. Ravens cawed possessively from their blackened corpses as the imperial contingent rode past.

"Whatever happened to the Shalanazi fleet?" Jun asked as they entered the heart of the city.

General Sharav shrugged and for the first time in weeks Jun saw the hint of a smile break the stone face. "Nobody knows. There are rumors of a battle at sea. Of mutiny and treachery."

Minister Aydin proved his loyalty, as well. Jun smiled.

Chapter Twenty-Eight
The Siege Begins

Micah studied the western gate. Merchants and visitors still poured into the city as if nothing new were happening. Surely the city's leadership had been alerted to the approaching army. General Hamazi's forces were less than a week's march from Kasha Marka and yet these people acted as if everything were right as rain. He grunted in disgust.

"We're really going to try this again?" Moab asked. His farmer's hat shaded his eyes from the afternoon sun.

Moab rode beside Micah and Joral sat aboard the wagon loaded with large sacks of hops and wheat. Ten more of Micah's men were on foot around the wagon.

"Do they look like they'll try to stop us?" Micah waved a hand at the business-as-usual city guard manning the gates.

Moab laughed.

"I do think we should spread out a bit, though. They don't seem to pay any more mind to single travelers than they do traders. Let's separate for now and meet up at the —"

"The Sour Tart," Moab interrupted and then laughed again. "So many ways to interpret that."

"Yeah, and maybe once we're there you can take a bath," Joral said, holding his nose for added effect.

Moab scowled.

Micah rolled his eyes. "Let's meet there and then we'll distribute weapons and gear."

Swords, spears, and other assorted equipment that might be needed for infiltration and sabotage had been packed in the sacks of grain. The city guards didn't appear to be inspecting any trade goods so Micah had little fear that they would be discovered.

After his arrival, Micah ended up canvassing the city for days before he finally spotted his mother with her little waif in tow. The girl followed Cordelia everywhere, but Micah never saw her actually interact with anyone other than his mother. His mother wore a dark green dress with yellow stitching. It matched her eyes and brought out the highlights in her hair. The little girl was dressed in a pale blue dress that made her seem to fade into the background even more.

He followed the pair for half the day. Cordelia shopped in the market, admiring the fine clothes and inspecting some of the odder delicacies from faraway lands. She purchased a bag of sweet rolls and then left the market. She stopped by the temple of Antu, the Sky Father, and pledged a handful of copper pennies to the offering box. Odd that, Micah hadn't remembered his mother ever being religious. From there, she turned toward the center of the city.

Micah followed Cordelia and the little dark-haired girl to the gates of the palace. He leaned against a building across the street and watched as Cordelia conversed with the gate guards. She gave them each a sweet roll from her bag and then ducked through the gate.

Why would she be going to the palace?

He watched the gate for the rest of the day, but neither Cordelia nor anyone else he recognized came out of the palace. He vowed to return the following day and continue to watch.

*****

Ullani leaned against the parapet and watched the flood of tiny black ants in the distance. Rumors had been circulating about the approaching army for weeks. At dawn soldiers had begun pouring through the Torland Gap. Tens of thousands of ants spreading out across the plains to the north and west. The farmers had abandoned their farms days ago and the shepherds had started driving their flocks east about the same time. The last of the traders had been ushered in quickly and the city gates had been shut tight an hour ago.

"That's not a terrifying sight?" Ullani smiled at the sarcastic comment as Darius sidled up next to her along the wall.

"I heard you were leaving," Ullani commented. She watched his startled expression out of the corner of her eye.

"How did you --?" Darius stuttered before she cut him off.

"Haven't you learned by now that I know everything that goes on in this city?" She leaned a shoulder into him jokingly.

Darius smiled. "Anyway, we're leaving tonight. We want to get out of the city before they get it surrounded. I just wanted to say goodbye first and thank you for all the time you spent showing me around the city."

Ullani waved a hand dismissively. "The least I could do for such a handsome outlander." She winked and Darius blushed. "If you're ever back this way again there's a few more things I'd love to show you." she added suggestively.

Darius face grew a deeper shade of red and he coughed. "Maybe Anna and I will come visit sometime after everything settles down."

"Oh, Anna too, huh? Not exactly what I had in mind but if that's the sort of thing that you're into I'm game."

"What? No, that's not —"

"Relax." Ullani put a hand on his arm. "I'm just teasing you. I would love to meet Anna and to see you again. Be safe on the rest of your journey." She gave him a sincere smile.

Darius sigh and visibly relaxed. He smiled back. "Thank you. It really has been a pleasure. I didn't have many friends growing up and you have been a great friend."

It was Ullani's turn to blush.

"Thanks." She punched him in the shoulder. "Now get out of here. I'm sure the Baroness has a lot to discuss with you before you leave."

As soon as Darius disappeared around the corner Ullani wiped the back of her hand across her eyes.

"You'll miss him," Saria spoke from behind her.

Ullani jumped. She hadn't heard the woman approach, but then again, she never did. "Who? Darius? Whatever. He was a fun distraction, I guess."

"Some distraction. You've spent nearly every day with him for the past three months," Saria said dubiously. "Just a means to an ends though, right?"

"Yeah, of course."

Saria changed the subject. "Quite a sight, isn't it?" She pointed with her chin to the throngs spreading across the valley.

"Yes," Ullani admitted. "An impressive army."

"Bedria's scouts estimated the army at over a hundred thousand strong. The camp followers will probably double that number."

Ullani let out a long, low whistle.

"They'll have the city surrounded by tomorrow. After that we won't be able to get in or out of the city without great effort."

"Surely you aren't worried that they can breach the walls?" Ullani asked, incredulous.

"No, of course not. That's not their goal. The city will be under siege. It will be a long one."

"We have the supplies to last, though, right?" Ullani asked.

"We should be okay. The city is built to withstand a long siege." Saria shrugged. "But that's not why I'm here."

"Oh?" Ullani's curiosity piqued. "What then?"

"Bedria and I have discussed it and we have a mission for you."

"Me?"

"Yes, we've both noticed how well you used Darius's arrival as an opportunity to infiltrate the inner court."

"Really?" Ullani was shocked. She had been so focused on Darius she hadn't considered that she was being observed by others. She hadn't even spoken to Baroness Magora despite all her efforts.

"Even if you did fall for him a little bit in the process." Saria winked.

Ullani started to protest but Saria held up a hand.

"In any case, there's no one else I trust more than you." Saria placed a hand on Ullani's shoulder. "You will be perfect for the job."

Ullani felt a swell of emotion and she fought back a tear. She was proud at the compliment, but also worried now.

This is my big chance. I cannot fail.

"Come on," Saria said as she guided Ullani in the direction of the nearest tower. "We need to prepare. You'll leave tonight."

*****

Abdul Hamazi studied the map laid out on the table before him. It showed a broad open area depicting the valley below. The city of Kasha Marka was sketched on the map, extending more than a league in either direction. He scanned the latest scout report and adjusted the position of the wooden soldiers.

The flap of the tent opened. The sun, low on the horizon, briefly caused the figurines to cast long shadows across the board. Abdul shielded his eyes against the bright light of the late afternoon glare. The figure in the doorway was a shadow. The tent flap closed and Hamazi could make out the man more clearly.

The man was old, older than any man Abdul could recall seeing in recent years. Despite his age the man's bearing was one of command. An ancient scar ran the length of the man's left cheek, disappearing into the perfectly pointed beard at his chin. Hamazi wasn't surprised that the man entered the command tent unannounced. He had been expecting the visitor. Messengers from Eridu had warned of his pending arrival three days earlier.

"Master Guo," Abdul said respectfully and bowed his head. "It is my pleasure to welcome you to our camp."

Guo Wen grunted as he moved immediately to survey the map. "We are behind schedule, it would seem."

"There was some trouble crossing the fens north of the city," Abdul explained. "We'll make up the ground. I have no doubt the city will be encircled by midday tomorrow."

"The gates are all closed?" Guo Wen asked.

"All but the Spice Gate. Caravans continue to arrive at the city from that direction. Bedria will no doubt keep the gates open until the last possible moment in order to increase her stockpile."

"You have men inside the city?"

"The Night Birds infiltrated the city a week ago under the command of --" Abdul rifled through his notes on the table. "--Lieutenant Kabir."

Guo Wen nodded approvingly. "I know the boy. He was instrumental in the liberation of Eridu. He is smart, and loyal. Baroness Kess should not be so confident regarding the disposition of her stores with Kabir and his men under foot."

The praise caused Abdul to reconsider his prior evaluation of the young lieutenant. He hadn't met the officer personally, but Captain Zima had not been as complimentary in his report, calling Kabir arrogant to the point of insubordination. When pressed, however, Zima had refused to pursue any disciplinary action following the events in Isan. At the time Abdul had shrugged off the report, figuring Captain Zima had the right to discipline his men as he saw fit. He was a good commander with years of loyal service. Now Abdul wondered if he had the whole story.

"The emperor has nicknamed the young man *Mustar Atmu*," Guo Wen added.

Abdul laughed despite the company. "Pretentious little bird. That, at least, is consistent with the assessment I have received from his superiors."

"May I review your reports from the field?" Guo Wen asked.

Despite the polite nature of the request, Abdul knew that Master Guo wasn't really *asking*.

"Of course." Abdul gestured at the stack of reports and stepped back from the table. "Everything I have is yours."

"Thank you." Without further ceremony, the emperor's uncle and most trusted advisor began reading.

The light outside faded to black and Abdul lit several more oil lamps to maintain good reading light. He jotted down notes without argument whenever Guo Wen would make a comment or suggestion. Guo Wen would snatch up new reports as they came in, reading them first before passing them to Abdul.

Well past midnight, they received their first surprise. Abdul's secretary, who had been seated outside the tent documenting reports as they came in, escorted a lean scout dressed in nondescript farmer's clothes inside to deliver his report directly.

"An armed caravan left the Spice Gate headed east about an hour ago. By all appearances it's a spice merchant returning to Merkar. There were several wagons loaded for bear accompanied by at least twenty guards. The gates were closed immediately after their departure. The city is now secured."

"Is this the first caravan to flee the city?" Guo Wen asked before Abdul had the chance to respond.

"No, sir," the scout answered. "There was a regular stream in and out yesterday. Most left with empty wagons, though, and no guards. This was the first I've seen so heavily provisioned."

"What do you think?" Abdul asked of Guo Wen. "It could be a Merkari prince. Bedria would not risk her relationship with Merkar if one of the desert princes insisted, and she would allow someone of such rank to leave with supplies."

"Possibly," Guo Wen considered. "She could also be using the caravan as cover to smuggle out her own spies. There is also the matter of some property belonging to Emperor Lao that was rumored to have made its way to Kasha Marka. Lieutenant Kabir had been tasked with its recovery."

"Really?" Abdul answered. "I hadn't heard that." This news cast further doubt on the completeness of Captain Zima's report.

"Send a detachment of riders to catch up to the caravan," Guo Wen ordered. "Search the people and the contents of the caravan thoroughly. I will provide you the details of what you are looking for."

"Of course." Abdul signaled to his secretary to record Guo Wen's notes.

Once the orders were dispatched and they were alone again, Abdul asked, "What is it that the emperor is hoping to retrieve?"

"The reliquary of Chung Oku Mai."

"Really?" Abdul could not hide the fascination in his tone.

Chapter Twenty-Nine
Fly by Night

"Tell me the plan one more time?" Bedria glanced at Darius across table. A wide selection of sweet breads and fruit was arranged between them.

Darius nodded, trying to finish chewing the bite of cinnamon bread. He swallowed awkwardly. "We take the road south to Kantibar where we will meet with your brother, Eshe, who is the governor of the region. We will tell him that your orders are to assemble the southern brigades and march north to lend aid to the defense of Kasha Marka."

Bedria nodded. "We have more than enough provisions to withstand a prolonged siege but that doesn't mean he should dally."

"We will replenish our provisions in Kantibar and continue south to Basara where we will book passage on one of Captain Girma's frigates bound for Ito." Darius patted the left breast of his coat. "The letter you gave me will guarantee us transport without question. Are you sure they will allow Antu on board?"

"If you can get the bear onto the ship and keep him calm during the journey then the captain will follow my orders," Bedria assured him. "After Ito where do you go?"

"There is a monastery in the mountains of Yapon province. They will be able to keep us and the box safe." Darius concluded.

Bedria clapped her hands and a servant emerged carrying the oak box. He handed the box to Darius and bowed.

"Take good care of that," Bedria warned. "The fate of the baronies may depend on it."

"I will," he answered and carefully placed it inside his travelling pack.

She held out her hand across the table. Darius reached for the bronze key that rested in her upturned palm.

"It's a shame we weren't able to replicate the other key," Bedria mused. "I would have loved to see the artifacts. Maybe they will have better luck at the monastery. The metalsmiths there are world renowned."

Darius laced the links of an iron necklace through the bow of the key. He had learned his lesson about leather thongs. He wouldn't risk losing the only remaining key.

"Thank you for your hospitality," Darius said.

Bedria laughed her musical laugh. "The pleasure has been mine, Darius."

They both stood, and Bedria crossed to the other side of the table. She leaned in to give Darius a light hug. "Safe journey, my friend." Bedria planted a kiss on his cheek which made him blush. Then she turned and glided from the room followed by an entourage of attendants and guards.

*****

The tunnels got darker the further they travelled from the city's center. Lord Misrak's men held torches to light the way as they navigated the warren of sewer tunnels. Long gone were glazed bricks and torch brackets on the walls. Here the walls were either rough-cut stone or packed earth. Roots could be seen pressing through from above. Gone too were the raised walkways along the side of the tunnel. Darius tried not to think too hard about what was squishing under his feet as they tromped through the ankle-deep water.

"We're past the city walls now," Misrak commented when he saw Darius inspecting the wall. "This branch empties into a stream east of the city."

"Aren't you worried that they might use the tunnels to get into the city?" Darius asked.

"Not particularly," Misrak responded. "But we have people watching all of the egresses. We can collapse the tunnels if need be to forestall invaders."

The torchlight reflected off something up ahead. As they approached Darius could see an iron gate with bars thicker than his thumbs. Heavy hinges mounted the gate onto a stone wall more than a pace wide. Iron beams secured the gate in place and wrist-thick metal chains connected the grating to a series of pulleys ending at a winch on either side of the tunnel.

Lord Misrak directed his men to remove the iron beams. A group of soldiers heaved on the arms of each winch. The groan of metal echoed through the passageway as the rusty hinges protested. A series of loud pops sounded as each hinge gave up its battle and the gates swung slowly open.

Darius approached the edge of the stone wall. The murky water tumbled over the edge falling the into the bubbling stream below. Darius could have easily dangled from the edge of the wall and dropped into the water, but he had no desire to get down in the muck to try. He freed a length of rope from his travelling pack and attached it to the gate. He held tightly to the rope as he backed to the edge. His foot almost slipped as he placed it on the outside wall and rappelled the short distance.

"Be careful, it's slick near the edge," Darius shouted up once his feet were securely planted on the streambed. He surveyed the sky. Dark clouds roiled overhead making the night an inky black. The flickering torchlight from above was all that lit the area.

Ander came next, followed by Kal. Each rinsed their boots and pants in the fresh water before taking up guard positions on the opposite bank. Darius helped his mother and Lianna descend. Nicolai and Gunnar came next followed by guardsman Klein of Patel's Rest. Their party complete, Darius waved up to Lord Misrak.

"Thank you for your help," Darius said.

"You're welcome. Good luck. I hope to see you again. You have given me better workouts than anyone has in years. Keep practicing your forms."

"I will. Thanks," Darius replied.

Lord Misrak tossed the rope down to Darius and then disappeared back inside the tunnel and Darius heard the whine of the hinges as the grate swung closed.

The group assembled on the grass beyond the stream. They checked their gear and changed into dry clothes. Darius washed his discarded pants and stockings several times in the stream, but the smell of the sewers permeated the cloth. He considered leaving them on the riverbank, but they were his only spare set. Instead he bound them to the outside of his pack to dry while they travelled.

Guardsman Klein was ready first.

"It's been a pleasure, Master Darius." The soldier extended a hand. "I will let Master Patel know of Baroness Magora's request for aid. We will send what troops we can spare to join with Governor Eshe in Kantibar."

Darius grasped the man's hand. "The pleasure has been mine, Mister Klein. You've been a credit to your uniform. Thank you again for your help. Be careful as you make your way past the enemy lines."

"Oh, don't worry about me, sir. I'll be fine." With a wink, the soldier turned south and disappeared into the darkness.

Cordelia lit some spare torches once her clean dress was adjusted. She handed one to Ander and another to Gunnar. The circle of light only pushed the darkness back a few paces, but it was enough to see what lay around them. Flat, grassy plains surrounded them. Darius tried to get his bearings but without the stars it was difficult. He used the hulking shape of the city walls in the distance to serve as his guide instead. He picked a direction that he thought was east.

"Are you all ready?"

As he spoke, the silence of the night was broken by the groan of metal behind them. They heard a loud splash as someone landed in the water. Those who held torches extended them in anticipation. The figure that emerged from the darkness was one none of them had suspected.

Cordelia gasped and held a hand to her mouth.

Chapter Thirty
Sibling Rivalry

"Micah?" Darius asked, not trusting his eyes.

"Darius. Mother." Micah stopped at the edge of the torchlight.

"What are you doing here? Did you escape?" Darius felt the briefest glimmer of hope. His brother looked well, better than he had the last time they'd met.

"What?" Micah seemed confused by the question. "No. Darius, there is nothing to escape from. I came looking for you. To bring you back. You don't need to run anymore —"

"Bring me back?" Darius was incredulous. "To the tyrant that kidnapped you and mother and assassinated my friend?"

"Darius, no, you don't understand. Please listen."

"Darius?" Cordelia's voice was a distant whisper past the thundering in Darius's ears.

"No, Micah, *you* don't understand," Darius shouted. "The men you follow are murderers, plain and simple. Your *emperor* wants nothing other than to subjugate the land just like his predecessors."

"Darius?" Cordelia's voice was louder this time.

"Emperor Lao isn't like that, Darius. You will see. Come back with me. He only wants to help improve the lives of those living under the thumb of the barons. Baron Shalanum never did a thing to make our lives better. Emperor Lao wants to create schools and improve trade and —"

"Darius!" Cordelia shouted.

"What!" Darius immediately regretted the shout. "What?" he said more calmly.

"Did you know that Micah was alive? And you never told me?"

Darius could feel the heat rise to his face at the accusation.

"Yes," he answered softly. "He was there the night Arthengal was killed."

"You have known that my son was alive for almost a year and you never told me?" Cordelia shouted. "Darius, how could you?"

"The time just never —"

"A year, Darius. Don't you dare say you never had time." The pain and betrayal was so clear in her voice that Darius could feel it like a knife to his heart.

"Come back with me, Darius. We can be a family again," Micah pleaded.

"No, we're leaving," Darius said stubbornly. "We have something important to do."

"You're taking the box somewhere, aren't you?" Micah asked.

Darius was too stunned to speak for a moment. "What box?" he answered finally. "What are you talking about?"

"I know about the box, Darius. It's one of the things the emperor asked me to bring back. The box and you. Darius. He will make you an officer in the army if you return. I mean, you are *Nasu Rabi's* protégé, for Antu's sake. You could have your pick of assignments. We could even serve together."

Darius shook his head trying to make sense of what Micah was saying. After Petri and Matia, he knew that the emperor knew about the box, but it surprised him that he had sent Micah to betray him, his own brother. Micah had been tricked again with promises of leniency and even reward for Darius.

"No, Micah. I'm sorry. I'm not coming back with you. We are going. Go back to your emperor. Tell him that I will never join him."

Micah fell silent.

"We have Anna." Micah's voice was so quiet that Darius wasn't sure he had heard him right.

"What did you say?" Darius said menacingly.

"Oh, Micah." Cordelia's sad words told Darius that he had heard correctly.

"We have Anna," Micah repeated. "She is safe. Come with me and you can be reunited."

Micah's words were drowned out by the ring of steel and a cry of fury as Darius unsheathed his swords and charged his brother.

Micah barely had time to react. He freed his own blade just in time to block the assault.

Darius charged Micah with Twin Dervishes. Micah's reactions were fast, but the whirling blades left a dozen small gashes on Micah's chest and arms. Micah finally dove and rolled out of the way. He didn't wait for Darius to attack again but instead went on the offensive striking at him from the side.

Darius countered the blows with The Hawk and The Dove and opened another slashing wound on Micah's chest.

Micah got under his guard with Scooping the Moon, but instead of slashing Darius's calf, Micah hit him with the flat of the blade pulling his foot off the ground. Micah followed with a leg sweep while Darius was unbalanced, knocking his other foot from under him. Darius went down with a crash and he lost his grip on his left sword.

Darius rolled and sprang to his feet as Micah's blade struck the ground where Darius had been a second before. Darius searched in the darkness for his missing blade, but he didn't see it and was forced to defend against Micah's next attack.

With the single blade, Darius settled into forms that he was more comfortable with. Micah soon lost the advantage and was backing away. Darius struck in rapid succession. First Striking Adder, then Lion Shakes His Mane, and finally Water Crashes Over Rocks. Micah's weapon flew from his hand and Darius brought the pommel of his sword down on his brother's head just above the left eye.

Micah collapsed to the ground. Darius threw his sword to the side and leapt on Micah before he could recover.

"Darius." The sound of his mother's voice was a whisper on the wind.

He brought his fist down and heard the cheekbone crack.

"Darius." The cries bit like gnats on his ears.

His fist struck again, and blood gushed from a broken nose.

"Darius!" Cordelia's scream broke the spell.

Micah's bloodied face tilted to one side. His body hung limply, unconscious. Darius released the grip on his brother's shirt that he didn't know he held and let Micah fall to the ground.

Darius leapt to his feet and stumbled backward, horrified at what he had done. He was angry with Micah, but he had never meant to do that. He paced back and forth while Cordelia examined her wounded son and tended to his more serious wounds.

When she was done, Darius cut a length of rope from the coil and bound Micah's hands behind his back.

"What are you doing?" Cordelia asked.

"I have to take him back." Darius rummaged in his pack and retrieved the infamous box. He thrust it at his mother. "You take it. Continue on as planned. I will turn Micah over to Baroness Magora. I need to rescue Anna."

"Alone?" Cordelia questioned.

"Saria will help, as will the Baroness. I won't be alone."

Cordelia sighed, clearly torn.

"It's the only way, Mother. Those here are the only ones I trust enough to see this through. I can't leave while I know Anna is held captive. You have to do this."

Cordelia nodded, resigned. "And Micah?"

"I'm sure they will want to question him, but I'll make sure Bedria's surgeons tend to him. They will be better able to care for him than we are," he said. Seeing the reluctance on her face, he added, "I won't let them kill him, but they will probably put him in the cells for the duration of this conflict. He will be safer as a prisoner of war than he will be on the battlefield."

Cordelia watched as the others helped boost Darius and Micah back into the sewer tunnel. Tears welled in her eyes as she heard the gates close for a second time. She returned to their belongings to stow the box in her things. Kal, Ander and Lianna were similarly preparing to leave. Nicolai and Gunnar were talking quietly at the edge of the torchlight, their packs already in place.

Chapter Thirty-One
Betrayal

The group walked in silence throughout the night, each lost in their own thoughts. Nicolai found a place where they could shelter and rest once they were a few leagues away from the city. The eastern sky was turning from black to orange as they settled down to sleep. Cordelia was exhausted both from travel and the stress of the previous night. She fell immediately to sleep, but her dreams were plagued by the nightmare of seeing her two sons fight almost to the death. She awoke in a sweat to see Gunnar standing over her.

"Is something wrong?" Cordelia asked.

"Wrong? No, not exactly." Gunnar stumbled over his words. She was suddenly alert. Something was wrong. It was then that she noticed his knuckles were white where he clutched his quarterstaff.

"It's not that we don't appreciate everything that Darius, and you, have done for us." Nicolai's voice came from her right. Cordelia scrambled from her blankets and sat upright. She looked around for the others and saw that they were all still sleeping.

"What's going on here?" Cordelia asked.

"A thousand marks is just so much money," Gunnar said. "More than we've made together in a lifetime."

"A thousand marks? What are you talking about?"

"The box, Cordelia. That's the bounty to return the box," Nicolai explained.

Cordelia scrambled back further, her hands reaching for the pack that was no longer there. She saw it then, slung over Nicolai's shoulder.

"Money? You're betraying us for money?" Cordelia's voice rose and she saw the others shift in their blankets. "I can pay you if that's all you want. Not that much, but enough. Leave us. Leave the box."

"Pay us?" Nicolai's tone took on a more insidious tone. "You mean with the coin you keep in here?" He patted the pack with his free hand.

Cordelia pleaded. "You know what it would mean if it fell into the emperor's hands. The superstition surrounding the contents of that box will allow him to increase his power tenfold. Legions would rally to his cause if he secures that prize."

Gunnar waved a dismissive hand. "We've talked about it. Emperor, barons, none of that really matters to us. Either way, we're simple men. A thousand marks in addition to what you have will be more than enough for us to set up a comfortable life someplace nice. We can find a couple wives and settle down. Who cares who is in charge?"

"What's going on?" Kal said sleepily.

Both men turned toward Kal. Cordelia used the distraction to scramble to her feet and free her belt knife. She held it behind her back hoping they wouldn't notice.

"Nothing you need to worry about, Kal. Go back to sleep," Gunnar said dismissively.

Kal glanced back and forth among the three of them. Finally, seeing Cordelia's pack on Nicolai's shoulder, he pointed and shouted, "Thieves!"

The shout woke Ander and Lianna and in an instant they were both on their feet.

Nicolai sighed. "I wish you hadn't done that."

"Look, we don't want to hurt anyone," Gunnar said. "We just want to go."

Kal fumbled at the ground and brought up the sword Darius had bought him.

"Drop Cordelia's pack and be on your way, then," Kal shouted, holding the sword out in front of him with both hands.

"Put that thing away, boy. You're not Darius. You'll just get someone hurt." Nicolai's tone sounded more dangerous than before.

Ander raised his own quarterstaff and moved to stand by Kal.

"Drop the bag and move away," Cordelia demanded, brandishing her knife. "Nobody has to get hurt."

Kal charged at Nicolai with his sword raised. Nicolai was surprised by the attack, but still had time to drop the pack and swing the staff up to block the blade. The quarterstaff spun in his hands and he quickly beat back Kal's novice attacks.

Cordelia used the distraction and lunged at Gunnar. Her knife glanced off his ribs and he jumped back holding a hand to his side.

"Damn you, woman." With fire in his eyes Gunnar raised his own staff and advanced. Ander stepped in front of Cordelia and blocked the attack.

Cordelia heard Kal cry out. She glanced over and saw him on the ground. His sword was an arm's length away and Kal was clutching his wrist. The arm hung at an awkward angle, clearly broken.

Nicolai stepped to his brother and together they beat back Ander's advance. Once Nicolai had the battle in hand, Gunnar stepped around him and turned again to Cordelia. She jabbed again with her blade, but it wasn't nearly long enough to get inside his guard. She glanced around, frantic, looking for anything to help. She ran in the direction of Kal's blade.

"No, you don't," Gunnar shouted, seeing her objective.

He tangled the staff in her legs, tripping her, then swung the staff around. She glanced up just as the weapon came down and caught her in the temple. She heard the crack of bone and her vision fogged.

Cordelia heard a scream like a banshee in the night. She managed to turn her head. Through a sea of fog and tears she saw Lianna. The girl had leapt onto Gunnar's back. She was stabbing him repeatedly in the chest and shoulders while she clung to his back. Gunnar reached back and tried to dislodge her, but the girl had gone berserk. Like a hammer, the belt knife fell again and again. Gunnar stumbled and dropped to the ground.

Nicolai turned from his fight and ran, grabbing the pack as he swept by.

Cordelia couldn't keep her eyes open anymore. She heard voices drifting through the night.

"Ander, come back." *Was that Darius? No, Kal.* "Something is wrong with Cordelia. I think she's hurt real bad."

"Cordelia, can you hear me?" *Ander?*

Her world began to shake.

"Cordelia, open your eyes."

Darkness closed around her and the voices became echoes in her mind and then there was silence.

Chapter Thirty-Two
Prisoner Exchange

"She'll be held in my tent. I don't know where the Night Birds will be camped. I entered the city before the army arrived," Micah mumbled past puffy lips. The bruise on Micah's cheek had already turned a dark, sickly purple. The swelling extended up the left side of Micah's face. His left eye was all but swollen shut. Darius couldn't tell if he had broken his brother's jaw, but he was sure he had loosened a few teeth.

Darius grasped the bars of the cell and leaned closer to his brother, resting on the cell floor. Micah's wounds had fresh bandages and, overall, he looked well-tended, except for his swollen face.

"If any harm has come to her," Darius growled.

"Darius." Sadness was in Micah's voice. "Anna is to be my sister. I would never allow harm to come to her. I have guarded her with my life. My men know that they would face certain death if anyone was allowed to touch her."

Micah seemed sincere and a weight felt like it had been lifted from Darius's chest. He stepped back away from the bars and looked at the baroness's men.

"He's all yours."

Darius heard the clank of metal as he walked down the dark hallway toward the stairs.

*****

"I will go alone if I have to," Darius shouted.

A dangerous look crossed the eyes of Bedria Kess. She was not used to being spoken to in this manner.

"Darius, calm down," Saria urged. "Of course we will help you. But an operation like this takes planning. Anna is in a tent somewhere in an army a hundred thousand strong spread across the Dalaman plains for leagues surrounding the city. It will take time to determine where exactly she is held.

"Let me send out scouts to survey the camp and locate Anna. When we do decide to act, we want the execution to be surgical, in and out. The longer we are in the enemy camp the more risk it presents to the mission."

Saria's tone, more than her words, calmed Darius. It was the same calm, confident tone that Arthengal had frequently used when Darius would get upset. Her voice conveyed understanding but also command.

He took a deep breath. "Fine. Where do we start?"

Saria's tone did not change. "My scouts will report anything that they find to the baroness and me. If any of their intelligence indicates signs of the Night Birds or Anna, I will let you know. Until then you should relax in your rooms, or train with Lord Misrak. Anything you need to do to distract yourself and regain control."

Darius sighed and nodded.

"Take a bath." Saria winked, her tone becoming playful. "That's what Arthengal would do."

Despite himself, Darius smiled.

*****

Days turned into a week before Saria announced that they had a pretty good idea where the rest of the Night Birds were camped and where Anna was being held. She organized a squad of five of her best, men and women who she claimed could walk from one side of the market square to the other at midday without being seen.

They waited for a night that was overcast and scaled down the side of the wall at midnight. Saria and her men moved like shadows. Darius did his best to keep up. It took every trick that Arthengal had taught him about stalking prey and he still felt like he was standing in an open field at noon compared to how well Saria's men were able to stay hidden.

At the first picket line, one of the guards walked within an arm's length of one of Saria's men and had no idea he was there.

Their goal was Micah's command tent half a league to the north of the wall. They would have to pass through two lines of patrols. Once they found Anna they would continue north and meet up in the woods north of the city.

Once they were in the camp, it was easier. Most of the men were asleep and the guards that were patrolling were easy to spot or hear.

They drifted through the darkness until they spotted a tent much larger than the rest. The pennant of a black bird clutching the moon flapped in the gentle breeze overhead. Two guards manned the front of the tent. Saria led them around the back and carefully cut the stitches to one of the seams.

Saria and Darius snuck inside while the others stood guard. They sat still for a moment once inside to let their eyes adjust to the inner darkness of the tent. Darius could make out the dark shape of a table and two cots on opposite sides of the tent. The closer cot was empty, so they crawled across the floor to the second, feeling with their hands along the way so as not to accidentally knock anything over.

Darius knelt beside the cot and looked at Anna's peaceful face. He put his mouth as close to her ear as he could and then, as he clamped a hand over her mouth, he whispered.

"Anna, don't scream. It's Darius."

She struggled briefly and started to shout before the words sunk in. Then she was still.

"We're here to rescue you. You have to be very quiet, there are men outside."

She nodded and he took his hand away.

Step by step they made their way back to the opening and into the night.

They snuck quietly behind the tents, sticking to the shadows. They inched their way through the camp at an agonizingly slow pace. The dark shapes of the forest to the north never seemed to get any closer.

Saria motioned them down and they all crouched. A pair of soldiers passed between two tents in front of them. Darius heard the snap of a twig behind him and a soldier rounded the tent beside him.

"Run," he commanded. "I'll catch up."

Darius's blades were out in an instant. The twin lunge of Antelope Charging pierced the soldier's chest before he could cry out. The sound of the body dropping drew the attention of the two guards who had just passed, and they circled back at a trot.

Darius jumped out in front of them. The Hawk and the Dove silenced the first, but the second cried out before Sun and Moon silenced him.

Darius started running, trying to orient himself to where the others had gone. He dodged around an officer's tent and bowled into a group of five soldiers. Three of the five were sent sprawling to the ground.

The rapid-fire movements of Twin Dervishes dispatched the two that were left standing and Sawing Grass left the men on the ground dead, but not before the alarm had been sounded. The camp began to come alive around him. He sheathed his blades and ran for all that he was worth.

Darius sprinted past the tents, hurdling extended ropes and piled supplies. He spied a squad of swordsmen approaching from the south and darted left. He collided with a soldier clad in black. The two men tumbled across the ground. Darius rolled and then sprang to his feet continuing his escape.

More soldiers emerged from the darkness to his left and right. He could see the tree line beyond the camp. He was close. He ran faster.

A wall of men suddenly stepped in front of him, spears extended. Darius skidded to a stop. He turned to run the other way but saw soldiers encroaching from every direction. Spear points were inches away from his chest.

"Surrender or die," the leader of the spearmen commanded.

Darius looked beyond the commander and saw a familiar dark muzzle emerging from the underbrush. He quickly counted. He was surrounded by more than twenty men. Too many to have hope.

"It's too late, run!" Darius called past the men.

The confused soldiers looked at each other. The commander glanced over his shoulder but Antu had already faded into the darkness.

"I surrender," Darius said.

Using only the tips of his fingers, he slowly drew his swords free from their sheaths and dropped them to the ground. He raised his arms, and someone grabbed him roughly from behind, forcing him to the ground.

*****

There was a thump in the darkness followed by the grating of steel on stone. Micah raised his head and strained to see. A flickering torch approached. The figure holding it was shrouded in shadows. Micah steeled himself for the torture he was sure would soon follow.

The dark-clad figure approached the bars. The man leaned forward, and Micah could finally see his face. Hard, black eyes stared back at him. A greasy mop of dark hair that hadn't seen a bath in weeks capped a swarthy face with pudgy cheeks. A tell-tale scar ran under the man's chin. Thin lips broke into a sarcastic smile.

"I know that bar maids dig scars, but that doesn't mean you have to go out of your way to get your ass kicked."

Micah smiled.

Chapter Thirty-Three
Sands of Saridon

General Hamazi studied the box turning it over in his hands. He had never actually seen the reliquary before, so he wasn't sure if what he held was the real thing. The peasant, Nicolai Something, who had brought it, had been adamant. He glanced up at the man in question. He was completely nondescript. Dark hair, medium height, shabby clothing. He looked like any other farmer from a hundred towns across the continent. And prostrated as he was now, he looked like one of thousands of slaves who had grown their food and mined their ore for the past decade.

"Tell me again how you came by this?" Abdul asked.

"I stole it from the man who was carrying it to Kasha Libbu. I brought it here as fast as I could to return it to the emperor," the peasant replied.

"And where did you say this man procured it?"

"He got it from Arthengal Alamay. You know, Nasu Rabi." The man raised his head and was rewarded by the butt of a spear from one of the soldiers guarding him.

"I know who Arthengal Alamay is," Abdul snapped.

"Of course, of course you do. I'm sorry." He cringed and lowered his head to the floor.

"Well, we shall soon find out if you are lying. Master Guo will be able to verify its authenticity."

As if on cue, the ancient chancellor entered the tent.

"Let me see what you have," Guo Wen said without ceremony.

Abdul handed him the box.

Guo Wen inspected it as Abdul had.

"Hmm, it looks authentic. Where are the keys?"

There was silence in the tent.

Abdul nudged the farmer with the toe of his boot. "Master Guo asked you a question."

"I'm sorry, sir. I never saw any keys. I only ever saw the box."

"Hmph," Guo huffed.

Guo Wen lay the box on its side on the table, locks face up.

"General, if you wouldn't mind, hit it right here with the pommel of your sword." He pointed to a spot on the box between the two locks.

"I thought you said it was authentic. Shouldn't we—"

"I said it *looked* authentic. If it is, then a single strike shouldn't harm the box or its contents."

General Hamazi drew his blade. Holding it upright he thrust the pommel down striking the box where Guo Wen had indicated. A crack formed in the dark wood and a small trickle of sand spilled onto the table.

"Hit it again." Guo Wen ordered.

Abdul did as he was asked. The box split in two with the second strike and sand poured onto the table. Angry at having been duped, Abdul spun on his heels, twisted the sword in his hands, and drove it down through the back of the peasant man. The man gave a sharp cry. Abdul twisted the blade and with a final gurgle, the man collapsed to the floor. Abdul pulled his sword free and wiped it clean on the man's shirt.

"I guess we won't be questioning him anymore," Guo Wen said wryly.

Abdul's face, already red from anger, turned a deeper shade. He shouted at the soldiers. "Get this filth out of my tent and send someone in to clean up the mess."

*****

From her perch in the mesquite tree, Ullani watched the scene in the distance. Soldiers had ridden up behind the caravan and surrounded it. Prince El' Nasir exited his carriage, irate. She could not hear what he said, but by the way he waved his arms, it must not have been good.

The soldiers ignored his protests and proceeded to pull everything out of the wagons. They searched the contents of the supplies thoroughly, spreading the wares across the grassy plain. Then they turned to the travelers. The soldiers inspected all the guards and passengers in the caravan. They even made El' Nasir's wives expose their faces for inspection adding further insult to injury.

Once they had completed their inspections, Ullani saw several of the soldiers move to the side in conference. That conversation was almost as animated as the first and Ullani couldn't help but smile. The commander of the battalion scanned the surrounding countryside. Ullani ducked behind the branches where she hid when his gaze turned in her direction.

She looked up again when she heard the thunder of hooves a few minutes later. The cloud of dust faded into the distance. Prince El' Nasir looked to be beside himself. Shamed and personally assaulted, he took his rage out on his servants, whipping them as they loaded the supplies back in the wagons. Ullani felt bad for them. Baroness Magora had bullied him into taking her along, and now he had paid a price for it.

Ullani hopped down from the tree and returned to her horse. The fingers of her left hand fiddled with the two keys that hung inside her blouse while she retrieved the water skin that dangled from her saddle and popped the cap with her thumb. The tepid water soothed her dry throat, but her mind was elsewhere as she considered opening the box. She had resisted so far, but curiosity was beginning to win out. With a longing sigh she released the keys and climbed into the saddle. It would be a long ride to Kasha Haaki and there would be time enough for her curiosity. With a flip of the reins Ullani turned the mare southeast.

Epilogue

Spring 35 A.E.

Darius peered through the bars at the passing landscape. The wagon rocked from side to side steadily as it rolled down the north road. The cage in the back of the wagon provided him enough room to lie down, if he stretched from corner to corner, but wasn't tall enough to stand up in. Most days he sat, like today, with his back against one side of the cage and his feet propped against the bars on the opposite side watching the rolling hills of northern Shalanum. He gazed at the mountains to the far north nostalgically, longing for simpler days when he and Arthengal farmed hemp and hunted elk.

He remembered long, quiet mornings practicing beside the lake. He hadn't seen his swords since he was captured. He knew they were in the caravan somewhere; the guards had confirmed that. Nasu Rabi's blades would be another prize for the emperor.

Some days he would catch a flash of brown darting between trees in the distance and he knew that Antu still tracked him. He hadn't seen the bear today, but he knew that he was out there. Not that it mattered. General Hamazi had taken great care with the emperor's prize and had ordered an entire company of light cavalry to escort the caravan. There were more than a hundred soldiers in the camp, far too many for the bear to handle alone even if he was a god made flesh.

Summer 35 A.E.

Cordelia's eyes fluttered open. She felt pressure on her hand and wiggled her fingers. In an instant, Anna's face was above hers.

"You're awake. Thank the gods. We were so worried." Anna squeezed her hand. "Saria!"

"Water," Cordelia croaked.

Anna poured a cup of water and held it to her lips, letting Cordelia sip.

"Saria!" the girl called again. "She's awake."

Cordelia turned her head. She was back in the palace. She remembered her rooms from before. But they had left, or had they? She remembered the sewers and something...a fight. Darius and Micah. Her heart ached as the memory flooded back. Watching her two boys try to kill each other had been the most painful experience of her life. More painful even than the years of captivity.

But how did she end up back here?

"What happened? Darius? Micah?" Cordelia's voice came out a whisper.

Anna squeezed her hand again and then glanced nervously toward the door.

"Saria!" She shouted this time.

Anna, sweet Anna. But wait, what was she doing here. Micah said... what? What had Micah said? Captured? He said *they* had

Anna. Darius must have rescued her. That's what he had promised to do, wasn't it? Cordelia's head pounded.

"Darius?" She asked again. He must be here. If Anna was here, he must be too. Were those tears in Anna's eyes? Why was she crying?

"Saria!" The scream was frantic this time.

Cordelia was distracted when the door to the room opened. The statuesque Saria entered the room. She painted on a smile when she saw that Cordelia was awake, but the smile didn't reach her eyes. She looked thinner. She was still a commanding presence, to be sure, but she looked as if she had lost a stone or more since Cordelia had last seen her, which was odd since that had just been the day before. Hadn't it?

"Darius?" Cordelia asked again. Her voice felt a little stronger.

Saria strode to the bed and sat on the edge. She grabbed Cordelia's other hand in her own.

"Darius and I snuck into the enemy camp with a small group of soldiers. We found Anna and were able to free her. We were fleeing the camp, and he was right behind us when we stumbled upon a patrol. Bad luck. He distracted them so we could get away but the camp had been roused, and we didn't have time to wait until we reached the rendezvous. We kept expecting him to come out and meet us. We waited for as long as we could, but he never showed. We don't know what happened to him."

Cordelia tried to speak, but the words stuck in her throat. She finally forced them out in a whisper. "Is he dead?"

"We don't know," Saria answered sadly.

"I'm so sorry, it's my fault." Anna collapsed across Cordelia's chest hugging her.

"Don't be ridiculous," Saria snapped. "None of this is your fault."

"If I hadn't been a captive —"

"You cannot blame yourself," Saria said calmly. "It's *their* fault, not yours. If you want to blame anyone, blame *them*."

Cordelia patted Anna's back absently. Another thought occurred to her.

"Micah?"

Saria's eyes darkened.

"He was being held in the cells below the city. We had him for maybe a week before his men broke him out. Since then, they've been wreaking havoc all over the city. We have armed patrols looking for them everywhere. We've caught two or three of them, but they always manage to turn up dead before we have the chance to question them to any degree."

"A week?" That wasn't right. Had she really lost a week. "How did I get here? How long?"

Both women looked at each other.

"You don't remember?" Saria asked, concern in her voice.

Cordelia shook her head.

"Darius had sent you on to Kasha Ekur with the box. The first night you were attacked by your own men, Gunnar and Nicolai I think their names were. You were struck in the head during the attack. You've been unconscious for two months. There was bleeding in your head. Bedria's physician had to drill a hole in your skull to drain the blood." Saria touched the side of Cordelia's head gently. "Your wounds healed, but you still didn't wake up. We had almost given up hope."

"The box?"

"Nicolai took it," Anna cut in.

"Don't worry though, it was a fake," Saria added. "The real box is on its way to Kasha Nisir and then on to Ito. It will be safe at the monastery there. The monks at Ito are no friends of the empire. Their order endured centuries of persecution under Emperor Lao's predecessors."

"The siege?"

"It's not going well for us," Saria admitted. "We had supplies enough for a year, but in two months your son and his Night Birds have managed to cut that in half."

Cordelia scrunched her eyes closed trying to hold back the tears that were already flowing freely.

I've lost everything. Again. I had them both back, if only for an instant, and now they're both gone. The box is gone. The city is falling. Why have the gods forsaken me so?

A long wailing sob escaped her lips.

Anna was there in an instant, holding her tightly. Together they mourned, together they cried.

*****

The tent had been erected on the plains outside of Kasha Amur. When Jun entered the tent, the ministers of Shalanum were already seated at a long table that stretched the length of the shelter.

"Emperor Lao Jun Qiu." The steward announced his presence as he entered. He stepped forward and took his place in the lone seat on his side of the table. General Sharav took position behind Jun's right shoulder.

Jun assessed the men assembled opposite him. Some looked angry. He guessed they had that right. Some looked broken and miserable. Most looked resigned. If there was any chance for them to leave with their positions, let alone their heads, they knew this negotiation had to go well.

"Gentlemen, my terms are simple," Jun began. "The unconditional surrender of Shalanum province to the Chungoku Empire and an oath of fealty to the Lao dynasty. If you can agree to that, then we have a place to start. If not, well…" He let the last word linger.

"We will never surrender," one of the angry men spoke and spat on the floor of the tent. He was balding and in his mid-sixties. His opulent coat and his abundant jowls shook as he spoke.

"Minister Orin does not speak for the rest of us." The oldest of the ministers, seated at the center of the table, spoke.

"That is good to hear, Minister Aydin." Jun spoke calmly. "You have terms to add, I assume."

"Yes, you will return all prisoners of war and allow the soldiers to return to their families," Aydin demanded.

"Of course. Those that do not wish to join the imperial army, anyway. I can't imagine what the professional soldiers would do, but if they, or any others, wish to take up other trades they will be free to choose. Provided that they make *some* contribution to the greater good, that is. For those that can't provide for themselves or their families we will welcome them with open arms and a fair stipend into our infantry ranks."

"No harm will come to the citizens of Kasha Amur or Shalanum province?" Minister Cray spoke next.

Jun feigned horror at the suggestion of harm. "The people of this land are my children. I have nothing but the best intentions for all citizens of the empire once they are liberated."

"You will not re-implement the caste system," Minister Cray added.

Jun waved a hand. "An antiquated system that didn't allow individuals to contribute to society based on their aptitude. I will go one farther, we will use state funds to finance apprenticeships and open trade schools focused on the greatest areas of societal need. It will further the needs of the state and open opportunities that people may otherwise not have had."

Several of the ministers nodded surprised approval at the suggestion.

"All generals and ministers serving at the pleasure of Baron Shalanum shall be granted pardons for acts committed during the war," Minister Barden demanded.

"See, that will be difficult." Jun drummed his fingers on the table. "Since there is no Baron Shalanum. The former baron has been dead for more than a year and, to my knowledge, the ministry was never able to select a successor. So, either the generals were acting under orders from the ministry, or they went rogue and were acting on their own. In either case, an inquiry will be commissioned, and responsible parties will be tried accordingly. Anyone who was truly only *following orders* will, of course, be granted pardon."

Several of the ministers coughed at this pronouncement and Minister Orin's red face lost all color. Several of the ministers began studying the surface of the table.

"Anything else?" Jun asked.

"We will be allowed to keep our lands and our titles," Minister Tartif said weakly.

Jun smiled.

"Minister Tartif," Jun spoke with delicate grace. "Your estates are granted as part of your commission as ministers. They belong to the state. They are not your personal property. As such, the empire reclaims all state lands and titles. Following the outcome of the inquiry, we will appoint governors to the various districts in the province to help rebuild and fairly see to the care of all citizens. If any in the current role of minister prove to be loyal to the empire it is, of course, possible that they may obtain such a commission, but that decision will have to wait."

More eyes fell to the table.

"Now, if that is all, gentlemen, I will have my secretary draw up the conditions of surrender for your signature." Jun stood. "I encourage you all to sign it." He added just a hint of menace in the last statement.

As Jun left the tent General Sharav took up position near his right shoulder. He was much closer than usual, almost uncomfortably close.

"You have a question, General?" Jun asked in a low tone that only the two of them could hear.

"Those were your father's words," Sharav said simply. His tone almost sounded disapproving which, for Sharav, meant he was very conflicted, indeed.

"You mean the schools?" Jun asked.

"And the abandonment of conscription," Sharav added.

"Yes, I find that some of my father's ideas have a certain appeal to the ministers here."

"So, it was deceit? You don't mean to implement those policies?"

"No, I do," Jun corrected. "For a time, at least. Let's see how it plays out. I know my father was a dreamer, but some of his plans may have merit. In any case, our goal at this time is to win approval and to solidify our support. We must first liberate the nation before we can reshape it."

"As you say, Majesty."

*****

The wagon rattled to a stop in front of the magistrate's hall. Darius looked up. It was still early evening. The soldiers began to disperse to gather supplies and get their orders. They left a dozen men to guard him and the rest drifted in different directions. Darius tried to go back to sleep. It seemed like that was all he did these days, weeks, months, on the road to Eridu.

A noise woke him. It was dark now. He expected to see torchlight from the men that were guarding him, but there was only darkness.

"Darius," the whisper came. "Are you awake?"

Darius lifted his head. His eyes focused on a middle-aged man wearing a dark wool coat. His face looked familiar. It looked like Gabriella Portor's husband. Darius's mind drifted to happier days when he and Arthengal would visit Sew Elegant, Gabriella's shop to buy new clothes every spring.

"Darius," the whisper came in a hiss.

"Arnon?" Darius's voice was weak. He hadn't spoken in…how long? Weeks at least.

"Good, you remember. Are you okay?"

Darius groaned.

"Hold tight. We're working on the lock."

There was a click and the gate to the cage swung open.

"Can you get out on your own?" Arnon asked.

Darius tried to move but his legs didn't want to work right.

"I don't think so," he answered.

Strong hands grabbed him and dragged him from the cage. He tried to stand, but his legs buckled. Two men flanked him and supported him between them.

Darius glanced around. The bodies of the guards lay in the dirt around the wagon.

Arnon returned to the cage and placed something on the straw inside.

"What was that?" Darius asked.

Arnon handed him a wooden disc.

"Come on," Arnon instructed the others. "We've got to get him to the boat before a patrol wanders by or this lot's replacements come. He has to be out of the harbor before the alarm is raised or we're all sunk."

Darius half stumbled and half allowed himself to be dragged toward the pier. His eyes focused on the wooden disc in the dim moonlight. He turned it in his fingers. On one side was a painted golden crown and on the other side was a winged lion. Darius glanced at Arnon, confusion on his face.

"It's the mark of the Shadow Crown," Arnon explained. "We want them to know who took you."

Made in the USA
Middletown, DE
09 August 2021